"Plakcy keeps the waves of suspense crashing!"
—*In LA Magazine*

"Hits all the right notes as a mystery."
—*Mystery Book News*

"Kimo brings needed diversity to the genre,
and the author handles the island setting well."
—*Honolulu Star-Bulletin*

"Spotless pace, intriguing plots twists, and an earnest depiction of the
real challenges faced by people transitioning out of the closet."
—*Honolulu Advertiser*

"A real page-turner and a good mystery. . . . A unique blend
of mystery, surfing, and sexual orientation."
—*Armchair Interviews*

"A steamy mystery, and a healthy dose of Hawaii.
Kimo Kanapa'aka is hot, and deep enough to make him interesting.
A nice, easy beach read that will keep you entertained."
—*Edge Boston*

"Kimo is a smart and appealing protag who instantly
wins your sympathy."
—Josh Lanyon, author of *The Hell You Say*

"In the action-packed *Mahu Surfer,* Kimo's out of the closet and making
up for lost time. Neil Plakcy's characterization is sensitive and real, and
Kimo is one of the sexiest cops to set about nailing his man."
—Hope McIntyre, author of *How to Seduce a Ghost*

"A compelling and complex story. Hawaii has never
looked better or been more interesting."
—Les Standiford, author of *Havana Run*

MAHU
FIRE

A Hawai'ian Mystery

NEIL S. PLAKCY

alyson books
NEW YORK

Manufactured in the United States of America

Published by Alyson Books
245 West 17th Street, New York, NY 10011

Distribution in the United Kingdom by Turnaround Publisher Services Ltd.
Unit 3, Olympia Trading Estate, Coburg Road, Wood Green
London N22 6TZ England

FIRST EDITION: APRIL 2008

08 09 10 11 12 13 14 15 16 17 a 10 9 8 7 6 5 4 3 2 1

ISBN: 1-59350-079-3
ISBN-13: 978-1-59350-079-5

Library of Congress Cataloging-in-Publication data are on file.

Cover design by Victor Mingovits
Interior design by Jane Raese

To Marc—

I've had the time of my life, and I owe it all to you.

Chapter 1

A FEW JUDO MOVES

IT HAD BEEN a tourist office day on O'ahu, with sunny skies, temperatures in the eighties, and a light trade wind sweeping down over the beaches and chasing the few wispy clouds out to sea. We'd had a parched winter, and as April began, and with it our dry season, there were already reports of wildfires in dry spots on the Ko'olau Mountains.

I stepped out the door of my apartment building on Waikīkī as dusk was falling, and the smell of distant smoke rolled over me. There had also been a couple of arsons at gay-owned businesses in the past couple of weeks, and I wondered what was burning—a few acres of mountain scrub, or the property and dreams of a gay man or lesbian.

Hawai'i had been one of the first states to consider legalizing gay marriage, and though Massachusetts, New Jersey, and a few other states had moved ahead of us, the movement in the islands was still strong, and in fact, the media had tied a rise in violence against gays and lesbians to the renewed visibility of the campaign, led by the Hawai'i Marriage Project.

I walked the few blocks to the Gay Teen Center, housed in the annex of a church on Kalākaua Avenue. At that hour of the day, Waikīkī was crowded with tourists heading back to their hotels from the beach, older people out for early dinners, and skateboarding teens getting in everybody's way. I passed up a half dozen chances to pick up discount meal coupons, skirted an elderly Japanese bag lady haranguing the Wizard Stones at Kuhio Beach Park, and stopped for a minute to watch a sailboat setting out for a sunset cruise.

I'd been volunteering at the Gay Teen Center for a couple of months, counseling kids and leading a self-defense workshop in a big open room. My favorite student was Jimmy Ah Wong, a thin Chinese boy with a bright yellow coxcomb that stood straight up and then, at the very top, drooped over. He looked like a bit actor in a British art film of the 1980s, but he was smart and infinitely kind to the younger kids.

Sixteen of them were waiting for me, Jimmy among them, when I walked into the room. We talked for a few minutes, and then I led them in a couple of warm-up exercises.

We did some yoga, to get them in touch with their bodies, and then a couple of simple judo moves I'd picked up somewhere. When we'd finished the judo, we sat in a circle on the hard wooden floor and talked. I always had to kick things off; they were all shy, and sometimes in order to get into difficult subjects I had to reveal more about myself than made me comfortable. "I had a date on Saturday night," I said.

A couple of the kids broke into spontaneous applause. I smiled and bowed. "Yes, I know it's been a while. I wish I could say it was a more positive experience."

I waited, but no one said anything, so I continued. "I met the guy online. And of course, he wasn't anything like he'd said."

"I know that drill," a chunky boy said. His name was Frankie, and he had some island heritage in him, and sleek black hair pulled into a ponytail. "Nobody on the Internet is who they say they are."

We got into a little discussion about that, and about how

they could be safe with people they met. "We agreed to meet at the Rod and Reel Club," I said. "Remember, always meet people you don't know in public places, so you can get away easily if things don't work out."

"Yes, officer," Jimmy said, with attitude.

"That's yes, detective," I said, and the group laughed. "We had a couple of beers together," I continued. "We seemed to be hitting it off, and we started making out on the outdoor patio."

"Is there video?" Frankie asked, and everyone laughed again.

"You wish," Jimmy said, and Frankie sent daggers his way. I gave them both a sharp look.

"So one thing led to another, and he invited me back to his place," I said.

"Always use a condom," Jimmy said.

"Have I told this story before?" I asked, pretending to be annoyed. But I was glad that the lessons I'd been trying to teach were sinking in.

"Does it end with you getting your ass fucked and your heart broken?" a boy I only knew as Lolo asked. He was the toughest of the kids, and I had yet to break through the barricades he had set up around himself. "Because if it does, yeah, we've heard it before."

"I save ass fucking for the second date," I said dryly. "You all should, too."

"Let him finish the story," a skinny girl named Pua said. She looked Filipina, but her name in Hawai'ian meant "flower," which was totally inappropriate in her case.

"The sex was lousy," I said. "Alcohol does that. The guy'd been all hard in the bar, but when we got naked, he couldn't perform. Of course, I worried it was me. That somehow I'd disappointed him." I smiled. "He took care of me, and then as we were cleaning up, I realized he'd come in his shorts at the bar." I batted my eyelashes. "So I guess I wasn't that disappointing after all."

"He couldn't get it up again?" Frankie asked.

I shrugged. "He wanted to do some coke, and I said I didn't, and he said that I might as well go, then. So I did. Not exactly a heartbreaker, but not much fun, either."

"You need a boyfriend," Pua said.

We talked for a while about some experiences they'd had, and a few of them opened up. I tried not to judge, though in some cases I was horrified by the sexual abuse, drug use, and petty violence they talked about. I was pretty sure that Frankie hung out near the men's room at Ala Moana Beach Park after dusk, giving blow jobs to johns, and there was at least one other kid I thought was a prostitute as well.

I knew that some of the others snuck back into suburban homes where no one knew their secrets, and I wanted to take every one of them and say, "Someone loves you. Someone will love you in the future. You are all good people." But there's only so much you can do.

Jimmy hung around for a few minutes after the class, and I asked him how things were going. He had given me some important information on the big case that cracked open my sexuality, and I still felt responsible for any fallout from it.

"My dad and I have a meeting with that lady from the DA's office next week," he said. "It's called a deppa, deppa-something."

"Deposition. She asks you a bunch of questions, and you answer, and they have somebody write it all down. It's not a big deal."

"It will be when my father finds out." He looked at the polished hardwood floor. "He doesn't know a lot of it yet."

A couple of bad guys had coaxed Jimmy into helping them with a smuggling operation through sexual favors, and though his father knew the bare outline of the case, I figured he didn't know about the sex. "I think it'll be OK," I said, putting my arm around Jimmy. "Your father loves you."

"I hope so."

On my way out, I dropped in on the woman in charge of the center, a tiny, half-Japanese lesbian named Cathy Selkirk. Cathy was a poet whose love for kids ran deep in her soul. I often found her working long hours, filling out endless grant applications, talking to the kids, or interceding on their behalf with parents, teachers, or the police. Though she was only in her early thirties, like I was, the dark circles beneath her eyes and the lines around her mouth made her look older.

She smiled when I walked into her office. "Kimo, I'm glad you're here. I was going to come look for you. Didn't you once tell me you knew one of the Clarks, from the department store?"

"Sure, Terri Clark is one of my best friends. Terri Gonsalves, she is now. She's a widow, that is, but she still uses her husband's name."

"I'm working on this application for a grant from the Sandwich Islands Trust, the Clark family foundation. Do you think she has any influence on their decisions? I want to expand our outreach to gay teens on other parts of O'ahu, maybe open a satellite center on the North Shore."

I shook my head. "From what I know, Terri's great-aunt runs that foundation, and she's very conservative. I don't think gay teens are going to be on the top of her list, but I'll talk to Terri and let you know what she says."

I sat in the overstuffed armchair across from Cathy's desk. I could see kids getting comfortable enough in it to talk to her about their problems. "Sandra's been trying to find out about one of these horrible organizations that demonstrates against gay marriage," Cathy said. "Do you know anything about the Church of Adam and Eve?"

Sandra was Cathy's life partner, a prominent attorney with a downtown firm and the most politically connected lesbian in the islands. "This mainland minister and his wife relocated to Honolulu about three months ago, to save us from the plague of homosexuals." She smiled wryly. "They're very well financed, and they advertise their prayer meetings all over the place. Sandra hasn't been able to find any dirt on them—yet."

"But she thinks there's something wrong."

"There has to be, don't you think, Kimo?" Cathy looked at me. "How else can they pretend to be loving Christian people when they have this terrible anti-gay agenda?" She sighed. "They're having one of their revival meetings tonight. Maybe it's just the smoke everywhere, and these arsons at gay-owned businesses, but I have a bad feeling."

Chapter 2

SUCH FRIENDLY PEOPLE

AS I WALKED BACK HOME, the smoke still hung over Waikīkī, and I had the same bad feeling as Cathy. So I decided to check out the Church of Adam and Eve for myself. After a quick dinner of grilled pineapple chicken with sticky rice, I put on the only suit I own—a conservative navy blue—and slicked my short dark hair back with gel. Since my time in the spotlight, people occasionally recognized me on the street, so I put on a pair of horn-rimmed glasses with clear lenses and hoped no one would connect this conservative young businessman with that gay detective in his aloha shirts and Topsiders.

I drove up into the hills of central O'ahu, to a place called the Pupukea Plantation. The atmosphere in the parking lot was festive, like I remembered when I was young and my parents used to drive us out into the country to watch fireworks displays on July fourth. Everybody was so friendly, smiling and shaking hands. Boys and girls played in the grassy aisles and "Onward, Christian Soldiers" poured out of big speakers.

Hundreds of folding chairs had been lined up under a tent, but even so, by the time I got there it was standing room only. It was warm, with a buzz of conversation going on around me and the high giddy laughter of little kids. Everybody got a paper flyer with a list of the hymns and the topic of the preacher's sermon, and an address where you could send donations. An elderly Filipina moved through the aisles, handing out paper fans imprinted with the logo of one of the big car dealers.

The crowd was a cross section of Hawai'i. Young people courteously gave up seats to their elders, and islanders, Asians, and *haoles,* or Caucasians, smiled at each other and talked about politics and business. Maybe Cathy and Sandra were wrong; the people around me seemed so nice. How could they advocate violence?

The minister and his wife appeared from the sidelines, to rapturous applause. They were both in their early thirties, neatly groomed, and overly cheerful, as such religious people often are. He was a little on the pudgy side, but his fleshy face just seemed to hold a smile that much better. She was slim, without much of a figure, obviously the more serious of the two.

The minister led us in the opening prayer, through a couple of hymns, and then into his sermon. He began slowly, talking a lot about morality and family values, about the need for a return to spirituality. It all made sense, even to a confirmed non-churchgoer like me. My family was a real polyglot of religions, and we'd gone to a couple of different churches as kids, never settling on any one. Our parents seemed to feel that as long as we grew up as moral, ethical people it didn't matter where we worshipped.

Then the minister's wife stepped up to the podium. She began by speaking about their family, extending an invitation to all of us present to join in the love that they shared. "But there are some people who aren't deserving of our love," she said, and there was general nodding and agreement among the people around me.

"You know who I'm talking about. Homosexuals. They

call themselves gay, to cover up their depravity, but we won't let them get away with that. There are other names for them, nasty names, but we won't use those either. We'll just call them like we see them—homosexuals. Keep the sex right up front there, because that's what they're all about, after all. Sex. That's all they care about. Everything else is just window dressing."

I started to feel the heat under the tent, regretting having worn my suit. As I pulled at my collar, I glanced around, to see if anyone was looking at me as if they knew who I was. She had that knack of making you think she was speaking directly to you, and I felt more like an impostor with every word.

I wondered what would happen if someone recognized me. I'd seen crowd mentality at work first hand, when I was a patrolman. All it took was a trigger, and ordinary people would turn into a mob, capable of looting, rioting, and other violence that seemed to lurk unsuspected beneath all of our solid exteriors. I had no doubt this crowd would turn on me, hurt me if they could.

I started to make my way out of the tent, slowly, politely squeezing between people. The sweat dripping down my back got worse as I tried to fold myself up as narrowly as possible. Behind me, I heard the minister's wife continue. "We need to take action, friends. It's up to all of us to make this the right kind of world for our families, for our children and grandchildren. It starts with each of us, when we make a commitment in our hearts to accept Jesus, to practice what he preached."

Then I was spotted. Our eyes met for a moment, and he looked away. My heart did a double backflip, but I knew that my own brother could not be the catalyst who could turn a crowd against me. Or at least I hoped so.

Lui, my eldest brother, stood with his hands on his wife's shoulders. She hadn't seen me; her attention was focused on the woman at the podium. It was clear Lui wasn't going to look at me again, so I continued to the exit, wondering. It was surprising to see him there, but even more so was the way he looked. He wore an aloha shirt, shorts, and sandals, and had sunglasses on a chain around his neck.

You have to understand, my brother wears a suit and tie to family luaus. I hadn't seen him in an aloha shirt since high school, and I wasn't sure I'd seen his bare legs since he reached puberty. He had always been more precise than our other brother Haoa or I, the most formal, and his business degree and high-paying job seemed to suit his personality.

He was in disguise, I realized, as I made it outside without further incident. Just like me, he didn't want to be recognized. Lui was the station manager of KVOL—"Your Volcano Alert Station, Erupting News all the Time"—the scrabbling non-network station in Honolulu. KVOL concentrated on the most inflammatory stories, the ones on the dark side of the news. I wondered if he knew something about the Church of Adam and Eve, if he was there for professional reasons.

Or maybe he just believed what they preached.

Chapter 3

THE DEATH OF HIROSHI MURA

KVOL WAS HEADQUARTERED in one of the gleaming high-rises downtown, and Lui's position as station manager gave him access to the private club on the top floor, a white-linen place with stunning views of the airport and Honolulu Harbor. About a month after I saw him at the Church of Adam and Eve, he asked me and Haoa to meet him for breakfast on a Monday morning, reason undisclosed. I'll always be their little brother, younger than Lui by eight years and Haoa by six, so I agreed without question.

Haoa and I met in the parking garage and rode up in the elevator together. We were greeted, as the doors opened, by a vista of sunshine and sparkling water. From the window we could see a flat barge making its way past the end of Sand Island, surrounded by a couple of fishing boats heading out to deep water. All around us, waiters in white jackets hurried from table to table. My eldest brother, whose sad-looking features were often enough to turn any day gloomy, waited for us at a round table near the window.

My family was a polyglot mix of Hawai'ian, Japanese, and *haole,* and though my brothers and I shared the same genes we all seemed to have taken a different dip in the pool. Lui was the shortest, at just under six feet, and the most Japanese, both in features and bearing. Haoa was the most Hawai'ian, tall and bulky, and his spirit lay deep in the island soil. He had never left the islands, except for brief vacations.

I had the most pronounced *haole* features, though my skin was always tan and my eyes were just a little elongated. I was six-one and my build was slim but muscular. If Lui belonged in a glassy high-rise and Haoa out working the land, then I belonged in the water. Line the three of us up and you could see we were brothers, but just barely.

We ordered quickly and then Lui said, "Look, I know you guys don't have much time, so I'll get to the point. Mom says Dad is sick and he refuses to see a doctor. She wants us to lean on him."

"Dad's sick?" I saw my parents every couple of weeks, and they never seemed to change. We'd had dinner in Waikīkī about a week and a half before. My father had been uncomfortable, I remembered, but had passed it off as something bad he'd eaten.

Lui nodded. "He's been feeling down for a while, upset stomach, general blah feeling, Mom says. But he's grouchy and all he wants to do is complain."

"Like that's a change," Haoa said.

"Did you ever know him not to do what she says, though?" Lui asked. "That's the scary part."

My dad had a strong personality, and he was always the one to enforce discipline among us boys. But my mother was the one who made our family go, the one who pushed me and my brothers through school and college. She managed the money, decided on major purchases, and bullied us all when we needed it.

"Tatiana's dad had prostate cancer two years ago," Haoa said. "They got it early but still, she was freaked."

"Don't even say the word." Lui sat back as the waiter delivered his eggs. "Dad's always been as healthy as a horse. That's why I think he's scared."

Lui's news was enough to put all of us off our appetites. I picked at my macadamia nut–pancakes and drank some orange juice, but by the time we were done there was a lot of food left on our plates. If our mother had seen that, she'd have wondered if we were the three boys she'd raised. When I was growing up, there was never any such thing as leftovers.

"I think if we all gang up on him, we can force him to see the doctor," Lui said. "Let's make some time Wednesday night, at the party."

"If that doesn't work, maybe we can get Kimo to arrest him and take him to the doctor in handcuffs," Haoa said. For once Lui and I were united against him; we both gave him the same dirty look.

"I thought Liliha didn't want to go to the party," I said. It was a fund-raiser for the Hawai'i Marriage Project, and my friend Harry had bought a bunch of tickets because his girl-friend's cousin worked there. He'd invited me, my parents, and my brothers and their wives. I was surprised that Lui and his wife would consider going, after having seen them at the Church of Adam and Eve.

He wouldn't meet my eyes. "We have to go to a lot of social occasions for my job, and I wasn't going to force Liliha to go to something that wasn't a command performance. But if we're all together, it gives us a chance to gang up on Dad. I put my foot down, told Liliha she didn't have a choice."

"Wonders never cease," I whispered to Haoa, and we both smirked. It was no secret that Lui had married a woman just like our mother, and that it was rare enough for him to stand up to her. He just glared at us, and then a cell phone rang at our table.

We all started fumbling. The phone bleated again, and I said, "It's mine." I answered, listened for a minute, and said, "I'm on my way. I'm downtown, so I can be there in about fifteen minutes."

I snapped the phone shut. "Sorry, murderers always have bad timing."

"You know you're getting old when your little brother is busier than you are," Lui said.

I had hoped to get to my desk at eight-thirty and catch up on paperwork. I'd been stationed in District 1, at the Honolulu Police Department headquarters on South Beretania Street, for about six months by then, after two years at the substation in Waikīkī and a brief stint undercover on the North Shore. It seemed that there was a lot more paper moving around downtown than there had been in Waikīkī, but maybe that's because I had had a partner there to share it. I'd been promised a partner downtown, but there hadn't been anyone available so I was still working solo. I didn't know if it was because no one wanted to work with the new guy—or with the gay cop.

Along with the arsons, there'd been a rash of murders lately, all over the city. Another thing to chalk up to El Niño, maybe, like the hot, dry weather. The hills were turning brown and catching fire. Even the hibiscus hedge outside the station was looking a little limp.

The media was calling it a "hot wave," playing up the combination of the weather and the crime. The department was under a lot of pressure to clear cases quickly, and to increase the local police presence so that the rush of homicides might slow down. So far, nothing much was working. I had half a dozen unsolved cases on my desk, the kind that started out with no clues and never developed any.

It wasn't like you see on TV, where somebody gets killed before the first commercial break, and by the time the credits roll the detective has tracked down the murderer and seen him safely behind bars. And now, instead of pursuing those old cases in the hopes of clearing one, I was on my way to a new homicide, with its own already accumulating file of paperwork.

On the way to the crime scene in Makiki, a residential neighborhood outside downtown, I phoned the department secretary and told her I was responding to a report, that I'd have my cell phone on. It was still early enough that most of the traffic was heading into downtown, and the drive outbound was relatively easy.

The address I'd been given was a small frame house on a corner a few blocks *mauka* (or toward the mountains, as we say in Hawai'i) of the H1 freeway. I saw, across the street, a beat cop I knew named Lidia Portuondo standing guard next to a little shack of cardboard and palm fronds. I didn't have to look much further to see the body at her feet.

I'd worked with Lidia in Waikīkī, where she'd dated another beat cop named Alvy Greenberg. I'd asked Lidia to sit in on the taking of a witness statement, and she had figured out from the questions I asked that I was gay. She'd told Alvy, who'd told the rest of the squad. I got a temporary suspension and Alvy got promoted to detective.

The lieutenant found out about Lidia and Alvy and decided they needed to be split apart. She'd spent a couple of months in Pearl City, but when the papers played up the shortage of female cops downtown, she'd ended up driving a patrol car through the outlying neighborhoods, sometimes on foot patrol around the capitol building.

I didn't bear Lidia any grudge—as a matter of fact, our past association had made us a little closer. It had been hard for both of us, adjusting to our new posts. I considered it a mark of my fellow officers' comfort level with me when they were able to return to treating me as just another cop, when people stopped whispering and pointing and spreading rumors about me and my position in the department.

People had pointed and whispered about Lidia, too, after her transfer from Waikīkī. She was a good-looking woman, about twenty-six, with long brown hair that she kept pulled up into a bun when she was on the job. In uniform, as she was that morning, she looked tough and competent. Nobody was going to mess with that body while she was on duty.

"What've you got?" I asked, walking across the street to her.

"Japanese male, approximately mid-fifties, one bullet hole to the head," she said. "Looks like a street person. I think this is his place." She nodded to the hut behind her. "Since there's some powder and tattooing around the wound, it looks like somebody held the gun right up to his head, almost execution style."

I nodded. "Good. Got any suspects yet?"

She smiled. "Thought I'd leave that part for you."

"Gee, thanks. Medical examiner on the way?"

"Should be here any minute. Crime scene tech, too."

I leaned down to look at the corpse, who was as Lidia had described. He was slumped against the base of a mahogany tree, its long thin branches creating a shelter for his little shack. At the base of the tree a baby gecko poked his head out, looked at me, and then skittered away.

I stood up again. "There wouldn't happen to be any witnesses, would there?"

She pointed over toward the house where I'd parked. "Neighbor over there called it in. Heard the shot, but didn't think anything of it until she looked out the window a little later and saw the guy slumped over."

"I'll talk to her. You'll wait for the M.E.?"

"All things come to she who waits."

"I'll keep that in mind." I wished I'd stopped for a cup of coffee on the way over. I was starting to regret my lack of appetite at breakfast, more so as I approached the front door of the house and smelled bacon frying.

My knock was answered by a plump, elderly *haole* woman with thinning white hair. Lidia had told me her name was Rosalie Garces and she lived alone. I showed her my ID and asked if we could talk.

"Certainly, detective. Come on in. Have you had breakfast?"

"Well . . ."

"Sit down. You like your eggs scrambled?"

"Scrambled would be fine."

While she cooked, Rosalie Garces told me that sometime around six that morning she'd heard a loud noise outside. "I guess it was probably a gunshot, but you never know. Some of the people in this neighborhood, they drive cars that aren't that great. You hear a lot of backfires and noisy mufflers. After a while I just take those sounds for granted."

She poured some runny scrambled eggs onto my plate and passed me a platter of fresh bacon draining on paper towels, then sat next to me to eat. "How'd you know I like my eggs just like this?" I asked.

She smiled. "I raised a houseful of kids, detective. I know a few things." She'd gone out around seven-thirty to the store, but hadn't noticed anything unusual then. "No, I don't often go out that early, but I'd been feeling a little poorly yesterday and I never got to do my shopping. I didn't have what to make for breakfast." She paused to eat for a minute. "When I go out, I back out and go the other way. I wouldn't have noticed Mr. Mura anyway, what with my back to him."

"That was his name? Mura?"

She nodded. "Hiroshi Mura. He used to live in a house there, where his shack is. Him and his wife and his daughter. His wife, she got cancer when the girl was still little, and she died. The girl grew up kind of wild. You know, I don't know that Mr. Mura was all there even back then, when things seemed to be going all right." She took another mouthful. "She was just sixteen, I think, when it happened. She was hitchhiking, meeting boys, doing drugs. They found her body out by Diamond Head one day."

"I'm sorry."

She nodded. "It hit him hard. He let the house go, and the neighbors started to complain and then they had to have it condemned. He picked up a few things and built that little shack. He always thought Patty was going to come back, his daughter. He was waiting for her."

"You know anybody who'd have a reason to kill him?"

She looked surprised. "Who'd want to kill him? I mean, he was a little crazy, but he was harmless. Sometimes he'd go through people's garbage, and I know there's some in the neighborhood who didn't like that, but that's no reason to kill someone, is it?"

She looked so worried I had to say, "No, no, that's no reason at all," though I knew from experience that people had been killed for a lot less.

When I got back outside, the medical examiner, Doc Takayama, was already there, looking at the body. He pointed a gloved finger at the bullet hole in the man's temple. "Single shot, fired from close range, as your officer here has already pointed out." He smiled a little.

I sensed something going on between him and Lidia Portuondo. Doc looked barely old enough to be out of medical school, but he had to be my age, at least. That would make him just the right age for Lidia. And after the messy breakup of her affair with Alvy Greenberg, it might be time for her to start dating again.

"Any idea as to caliber?"

"Looks like a .38. Won't know for sure until I pull the bullet out."

"Anything else you can tell me?"

Doc shook his head. "Not much to say. From the blood it seems pretty clear he was shot right here. Death would have been fairly instantaneous."

I looked up. One of the techs, Larry Solas, was already going over the ground very carefully. "Guess that means I start canvassing the neighbors."

"You're in luck," Lidia said. "Here comes one right now."

A man had emerged from the house across from Mrs. Garces's, caddie-cornered to the site of the old man's shack. As the neighbor got closer, I saw he was Chinese, somewhere around middle age, and very agitated.

"You here for shooting, no?" he asked Lidia.

"This is Detective Kanapa'aka," she said, pointing to me. "He's the investigating officer."

"You know anything about this, sir?"

"'Nother shooting, same morning," the man said. "You come see. Somebody shoot my cock."

I looked at the man's crotch. There didn't seem to be anything out of the ordinary. I stole a glance at Lidia and immediately had to look away. She and Doc were looking at each other, and both of them seemed on the verge of laughter.

"You come, must see." The man, who wore faded jeans and an aloha shirt with a tattered collar, plucked at my shirt sleeve.

"I'll be back, officer," I said, and I could see Lidia was already laughing. I turned and followed the man back to his house. "What's your name, sir?"

"Chin Lam," he said. "Chin my last name. C-h-i-n. Like this chin." He put his hand to the bottom of his face.

"I get it. Tell me more. Who got shot?"

"My cock," he said, impatiently. He led me around the side of his house to a small low shack. A couple of chickens pecked at the ground around it.

"You allowed to have livestock in this area? Isn't there an ordinance against it?"

"My chickens not the trouble." He led me to the far side of the shack, to a pile of feathers and flesh that was already starting to stink in the hot sun. From the coxcomb, still intact though a few feet away, I figured out somebody had killed his rooster.

He kneeled down to the ground, and motioned me to follow. "See, somebody shoot." He pointed, without touching, at the fleshy part of the chicken's breast. A piece of bullet was lodged there.

"When did this happen?"

"This morning, early. Maybe just dawn. My cock, he always crow then. Better than alarm clock. I hear him crow, wake up. Then I hear shot. First I think, car noise. But I know gunshot. I turn on light, look out window. Don't see anything. We get up, my wife go work, I go collect eggs. Find this."

"You have any idea what time that was, first light?" I did some calculating in my head. Though I hadn't been out surfing for a few days, I knew roughly when the sun came up. "Say, five-thirty?"

"Five-thirty sound right. It maybe seven-thirty when I go collect eggs."

"You see or hear anything else this morning?" I asked. "A second gunshot?"

He shook his head. "We have four *keiki*. House very busy, very noisy all morning, 'til they leave to school." He looked at his watch. "Damn! Now I late to work. You call me, you find out who shot my cock?"

I took down his name again, his address, and phone number. He hurried into the house and I went back to my truck for an evidence bag.

Chapter 4

A DIRTY BUSINESS

I GOT MY DIGITAL CAMERA from the truck and took a few pictures of the crime scene before Doc Takayama's techs loaded Hiroshi Mura's body onto the gurney. I tried to get Doc to take the rooster, too, but he wasn't having any of it. Parts of the dead chicken were in six different evidence bags, and Doc insisted they could go directly to ballistics without passing through his office. "People yes, chickens no," he said. "I gotta have some standards, Kimo."

Lidia thought this was all very funny, and I was having trouble keeping from laughing myself. "And I get to tell Lieutenant Sampson about this," I said. "Lieutenant, we've got a serious situation out there in Makiki. Double homicide. Man and *moa*." I used the Hawai'ian word for chicken—just because it sounded right.

"Isn't that chickencide?" Lidia asked.

"Poultrycide," Doc said.

"Get a new lifecide."

Once the body had been removed and Doc and his team had left, Lidia and I scoured every inch of the area looking for evidence. There wasn't any.

"Can you run the chicken downtown for me?" I asked her. "I want to do a quick canvass of the neighborhood and I don't want to leave it in my truck."

Just then her radio crackled to life. There was a traffic alter-
cation on McCully Street, a few blocks away. All available
units were called to the area. "Sorry, Kimo, got to go." She
jumped into her black-and-white and burned rubber.

I put the dead chicken in the bed of the truck and hoped
it'd be safe from marauding cats, then I started knocking on
doors.

It was a working-class neighborhood, and by ten o'clock in
the morning most people were doing just that—working
somewhere else. I went down the block, ringing doorbells at
small, often run-down houses from the 1950s, and leaving my
card in the jamb with a note at each place. There was little attempt at landscaping there: the occasional hibiscus blooming
forlornly in a corner of the yard, a couple of stunted wiliwili
trees, a few cabbage palms. One house had a little shrine in
the center of the yard, a chipped statue of St. Joseph with
slanted eyes, surrounded by a burst of morning glories. Who-
ever lived there had trouble cutting the lawn, because the
grass grew around the base of the statue in long spikes, and
hadn't been trimmed in a long time.

Then I came to a small green bungalow with white shut-
ters, much better kept than the neighboring houses. You
could tell a lot of loving care had gone into the placement of
the rocks, the neatly weeded beds, the precise arrangement of
the miniature trees.

There was also a rainbow flag hanging above the garage,
and a Suzuki Samurai in the driveway. That was a good sign.
The man who came to the door was *haole,* in his late forties. I
showed my badge and introduced myself.

"Come on in, detective," he said, stepping back. He said
his name was Jerry Bosk, and he showed me into the living
room. When I was sitting on the chintz sofa, falling backward

into a mass of plush cushions, he took a good look at me. "You're the gay cop, aren't you?"

My stomach felt queasy. "I don't like to think of myself that way, but, yes, I'm gay."

"I'm sorry, I didn't mean it as an accusation." He sat forward in a gnarled wooden rocking chair, one hand on his thigh. "You've been an inspiration to us, you know. I mean, to me and the people I know. You've been showing the world that all gay men don't have to be nelly queers who like to dress up in women's clothes and wear makeup. I admire you."

"Thanks. I'm here about a murder that happened down the street. Did you see or hear anything unusual this morning?"

"A murder? Who was killed?"

"A homeless man named Hiroshi Mura. Did you know him?"

Bosk sat back and rocked a little in his chair, thinking. He was a handsome guy, sandy hair and a strong face, with a smudge of sawdust on his cheek. "The old man who lived in the shack down the block? I didn't know his name. I wish I could help you, but I didn't hear anything. I'm a carpenter, a cabinetmaker, and I've often got equipment going. When I'm not working, we've always got music in the house—it helps to drown out the neighborhood racket." Indeed, I could hear some kind of baroque concerto coming out of the stereo speakers, very low, just enough to wash out background noise.

"You didn't see anyone unusual, hear any strange sounds?"

He shook his head.

"You said 'we,' Mr. Bosk. Someone else lives here with you?"

"My lover, Victor Ramos," he said. "He's at work now."

I stood up and handed him a card. "Well, thank you. If you or Mr. Ramos think of anything, will you give me a call?"

"Have you talked to our neighbors?" he asked, as he walked me toward the door. He nodded with his head to indicate the house to the left, the one with the statue of St. Joseph. "She jogs early in the morning. She might have seen something."

"No one was home. I'll be sure to check back with them, though. Thanks."

"They're a funny couple," he said, as we stood at the front door. "They don't fit in with the rest of the neighborhood." He laughed. "I mean, not that Vic and I really fit in either, but we try. We talk to people, we have a mango tree in the backyard and we always give people fruit." He laughed again. "Funny, fruits from the fruits. But them, well, there's just something strange about them. I can't say any more than that."

"I'll keep that in mind."

As I walked down the path to the street, he called out behind me, "Keep up the good fight, detective."

I wasn't sure which kind of fight he meant.

≈

I MADE IT BACK to headquarters just before noon, and took the dead rooster down to ballistics on the first basement level of the building. A couple of hours in the hot Hawai'ian sun hadn't done much for the carcass, and as I walked down the hall carrying the evidence bags people stopped, stared, and sniffed.

"Homicide's a dirty business, isn't it, detective?" said a secretary from the photo lab.

"Jesus, Kimo, get some air freshener," a detective from narcotics said, waving his hand in front of his face. I smiled at everybody, nodding politely, like I wasn't carrying something that stank to high heaven in my outstretched hand.

Special Investigations, which encompassed ballistics, wasn't excited to see me. "Ew, what is that?" said Gloria, the secretary at the front desk. There was an incredibly handsome guy standing next to her—tall, dark-haired, and Eurasian—wearing a khaki shirt with a fire department emblem on it.

"The remains of a murder victim. Where do you want it?"

"Don't remains go to the coroner?"

"Only human remains," I said.

The handsome fireman looked my way and made a big show of squeezing shut his nostrils for Gloria. "Seems like fowl play," he said, and she laughed.

I saw Billy Kim, one of the techs I knew, in the back area and called out to him. "Hey, Billy, your chicken lunch is here."

I walked past Gloria's desk to show him what I had. "What the hell?"

"I got a murder out in Makiki this morning. Neighbor's rooster got shot at the same time. I need a ballistics match between this bullet"—I held up the evidence bags—"and the one from my stiff."

He took the bags from me, his nose crinkled up. "This is above and beyond the call of duty."

"Many are called, but only the really dumb ones answer," I said. "I don't think the owner wants the carcass back when you're done with it."

"I'll keep that in mind."

When I came out, the handsome fireman was gone. I stopped at the men's room before getting into the elevator, but no matter how much I washed my hands, there was still a faint aroma of dead chicken around me.

People looked at me funny in the elevator, but I ignored

them. I hoped the scent would dissipate during the day, but I wasn't holding my breath. Only the people around me were.

I stuck my head into Lieutenant Sampson's office. He was a big, burly guy, wiry beard going gray, fond of polo shirts. He had them in every color ever made in extra large. He once told me he hated wearing suits because you had to wear a tie with a suit, and his neck was larger than it should have been so he never could get dress shirts that closed properly.

Today his polo shirt was emerald green. He was on the phone, but motioned me to a seat in front of his desk. My eye was caught, as always, by the photos he kept there. One was an old clipping from a newspaper, an AP wire photo of a half-dozen people in their early twenties, a mixture of men and women, dancing naked in the mud at Woodstock. The tall man in the middle, with the wiry hair, was Lieutenant Sampson, at a younger and more foolish time in his life. He said he kept it there as a reminder of who he was. I wasn't sure what that meant, but I kind of liked it—working for a guy who'd once danced naked in the mud at a rock concert and who was comfortable enough about it to keep the picture on his desk.

The other was a photo of his daughter, Kitty. I picked it up to look more closely at it. She was quite a beautiful young woman, in her late teens or early twenties. She looked like a young Catherine Deneuve, that same icy blondness, yet with a simmering sensuality underneath. I didn't envy him being her father.

He put the phone down and I said, "Your daughter's very pretty."

"Stepdaughter," he said. "Kitty's my second wife's daughter from her first marriage."

I took a minute to process that. I knew Sampson had been married and divorced three times. "Kitty's mother and I got married when Kitty was six," he said, nodding toward the picture. "We were only married for three years, but Kitty got attached to me. No matter who her mom was married to, she thought of me as her dad." He smiled. "Her mom moved back to the mainland when Kitty was thirteen. I think that was husband number four, though maybe it was number five."

"I thought Kitty lived with you?"

"She does. When my ex left she asked if I'd take Kitty, and I said I would, but only if I could adopt her. So I did. Kitty goes to visit her mom during the summer, wherever she happens to be living. It's good for her—gets her off this rock. I see too many of these island kids whose world is bounded by the Pacific Ocean. Kitty'll never feel that way." He stopped and sniffed the air. "What do I smell?"

"Chicken."

"Don't eat at that place again."

"I didn't eat there. You know that homicide in Makiki?"

"Yeah. What do you know about it?"

"Doesn't look like an easy one. Homeless man, nobody in the neighborhood saw anything or heard anything. No clues at the scene, either."

He shook his head. "I don't like these statistics. Unsolved homicides are piling up here like empty dishes at dim sum."

"I do have one lead, though. Neighbor's rooster was shot around the same time. I've got ballistics doing a match on the bullets."

"The dead chicken," he said, nodding. "You think that's a homicide, too?"

"Don't even start," I said, holding up my hand. "I've heard the jokes already. I'll keep you posted."

"From a distance," he said, waving me out. He turned on a little fan on the credenza behind him. "I always knew homi-

cide was a dirty business. Try not to make it a stinky one, too."
He paused. "That's a residential neighborhood out there,
isn't it? Working class?"

I nodded. "Tried to canvass this morning, but most people
had already left for work."

"Why don't you sign out for a couple of hours. Go home,
take a shower. Then hit Makiki after some of the neighbors get
home."

"You just want to keep me from stinking up your squad
room, don't you?"

He laughed. "Close a couple of cases for me, will you, detective?" he asked. "This one would be a good start. I don't
need PETA picketing downstairs over cruelty to chickens."

"I'll get right on it, boss," I said.

Chapter 5

MR. AND MRS. WHACK JOB

I STOPPED AT MY DESK on my way out, and Steve Hart, a night-shift detective who'd come in early to work some cases, pointedly got up and moved away. At least I was getting shunned for being smelly, rather than being gay. That was a start.

I ran Hiroshi Mura through the computer, but didn't get anything more than I already knew. So I gave up and went home. I took a nice, luxurious shower, then dropped my stinky chicken clothes in the washer on the ground floor of the building. While they ran through rinse and spin, I researched my latest case, using my spiffy wireless laptop.

The network didn't have far to reach; I live in a studio, with a galley kitchen, a small bathroom, and a picture window with a view of a narrow slice of Waikīkī Beach. I sat at the kitchen table and pulled up the property appraiser's Web site, where I saw that Hiroshi Mura was no longer the owner of the property where he'd been shot; it had been transferred a few months earlier to a corporation.

I made a list of all the homeowners on the streets around where Mura had been killed, and typed up the notes on my interviews with Rosalie Garces and Jerry Bosk. By then it was time to switch the clothes to the dryer. After that, I checked department records for all shootings of homeless men and women over the past year, hoping that there would be a match in some way to my crime.

No luck. But at least I felt I was earning my pay, even as I sat around in my boxers nibbling on a microwave pizza. Around five, I drove back to Makiki and started canvassing the neighborhood again. I interrupted a few dinners and got no response from a few houses, and I was starting to give the whole enterprise up when I came to the house with the rainbow flag.

I remembered speaking with the cabinetmaker that morning, and checked my notes. Jerry Bosk, and his lover, Vic Ramos. Ramos had already left for work by the time I arrived. But now there was a second car in the driveway, which I thought might be his.

Bosk answered the door. "Hey, detective, come in," he said. "Vic just got home from work. I haven't had a chance to ask him about this morning, but you can."

A handsome olive-skinned Filipino man in his mid-forties, dark hair cut short, stepped out of the kitchen and Bosk introduced us. "There was a homicide down the street this morning," I said. "Hiroshi Mura, the homeless man. I wondered if you saw or heard anything out of the ordinary."

"Poor guy," he said. "We tried to talk to him a couple of times but he always ran away. If you want weird, though, how about the creepy woman next door in a lead-lined apron and plastic goggles? Out of the ordinary enough for you?"

We sat in the living room. This time I avoided the plush cushions on the chintz sofa, taking the hand-carved rocker instead. I pulled out my notebook. "When did this happen?"

"Saturday," Ramos said. "I sing with the Honolulu Men's Chorus, and we had a rehearsal on Saturday afternoon. I got home around six, and I saw Mrs. Whack Job from next door looking like some kind of mad scientist. I tried to tell Jerry that there's something strange going on out in their back shed, but Jerry likes to think the best of people."

"What's her last name?" I asked, not understanding what he'd called her.

"We don't know," Jerry said. "Vic has decided she and her husband are crazy, so he calls them the Whack Jobs. Mr. Pender died a couple of months ago, and his daughter is renting the house out. I tried to introduce myself to them but neither of them would even answer me." He smiled. "Guess they're not accustomed to living at the end of the rainbow."

The neighbors Jerry was describing were next on my list to canvass, so I made a note to keep an eye out for anything strange. Unfortunately, Ramos hadn't seen or heard anything that morning, so, declining offers of a drink or staying for dinner, I said my good-byes.

There was a breeze blowing down from the Ko'olaus, bringing smoke and tiny particles of soot with it. I'd been smelling all too much smoke lately, and I knew the fire department was under the same pressure we were to solve the rash of arsons.

A couple of the fires had been simple accidents—a cigarette extinguished in dry brush, an air conditioner short-circuiting. But others were clearly arson—a failing restaurant in Chinatown, a trash fire outside a gay bar in Salt Lake, a duplex in Kaka'ako where a married woman had moved in with her new boyfriend, an amateur Molotov cocktail through the window of an X-rated video store on Kuhio Avenue, a warehouse fire just off the Pali Highway where a particularly greasy brand of potato chips had been used as an accelerant.

About half the arsons had some connection to gay people or businesses serving them, which was enough to get the local bar rags in an uproar about official indifference to the gay and lesbian community. I'd been called for an opinion by one of them, but I'd said I had no comment.

It seemed that all over the island, gay and straight people were living in an uneasy balance. When we'd been quiet enough in our closets, our businesses had been allowed to run, with darkened windows and little advertising. Now that we were pressing our claims to live freely, and marry like everyone else, things were getting more difficult.

It couldn't have been easy for an openly gay couple like Jerry Bosk and Victor Ramos to live next door to a religious family, the kind who kept a statue of St. Joseph on the front lawn.

The house itself was nondescript, maybe a little more run-down than the average home on the street. It was a single-story ranch, painted a faded green, with brown grass in the front yard and a small outbuilding at the back. The slant-eyed St. Joseph said nothing as I walked up to the door and rang the bell.

A trim, dark-haired young woman answered. I showed her my badge and introduced myself. Though I knew she was a tenant, and not the owner, I asked, "Are you Mrs. Pender?"

"Mrs. White," she said. "We're renting from the Penders." She didn't invite me inside.

"I understand you're a runner," I said.

"Sometimes."

"A man was shot about a block away from here, early this morning," I said. "Did you hear or see anything out of the ordinary?"

She shook her head. "I'm not surprised. All kinds of things go on in this neighborhood." It seemed to me that her glance darted next door. "But I wouldn't have heard anything. I wear headphones when I run. I get into a zone, and I block everything else out."

"I know what you mean," I said. "I'm a surfer, and I focus the same way." I paused for a minute. "Did you ever notice the homeless man living on the empty lot?"

She grimaced. "Creepy guy," she said. "The city shouldn't let people like that live on the street."

"Did he ever threaten you?"

I thought I saw something flicker in her eyes, but she said, "No. I never had anything to do with him."

"Well, thanks anyway." I checked her left hand for a wedding ring before I said, "Your husband. Can I speak with him?"

Again, there was something strange about her eyes, the way alarm seemed to register in them. "He sleeps late," she said. "He snores. He wouldn't have heard anything."

"If it's OK, I'd still like to talk to him," I said. I looked over her shoulder. A man I assumed was her husband stood in the background. "Mr. White?"

Grudgingly, the woman stepped aside, and her husband came forward. He was dark-haired, a bit pudgy. There was something familiar about him, but I couldn't place him. I repeated what I'd told his wife. "Did you see anything this morning?"

When I'd first come out, my friend Gunter gave me some interesting advice. "Straight men won't look you in the eyes," he said. "Gay men will. That's a big part of gaydar. It's not about whether a guy has a limp wrist or says Mary every five minutes. It's about whether he'll look you in the eyes or not."

I'd put that to the test a couple of times, with interesting results. Because an awful lot of gay people on O'ahu knew who I was—because I was the gay cop—I'd gotten some surprising readings. It was equally surprising that this guy, Mr. White, looked me in the eyes with something that looked a lot like hunger.

No wonder his wife hadn't wanted me to talk to him.

Unfortunately, Mr. White really had been asleep that morning, and hadn't heard a thing. Probably to interrupt any additional flirtation, his wife put her hand on the door. "I'm sorry, detective, but we're very busy right now. You know how it is, you get home and there's so much to do."

"Thank you very much, Mr. and Mrs. White. You have a good evening, now."

She shut the door firmly without wishing me the same. I could see why Vic Ramos called her Mrs. Whack Job. Not the friendliest person to have for a neighbor. But rudeness still wasn't a crime under the Hawai'i Penal Code, though if my mother had her way it would be.

I still had a couple more houses to canvass, but didn't learn anything more about either shooting—man or chicken. Sometimes it goes like that. I didn't like to think that this murder would add to my string of unsolved cases, but without a break it probably would.

The next morning, I was adding notes on the evening's canvass to those I'd already written when Sampson appeared at my desk. "Seen the paper this morning?" he asked, dropping the local section in front of me. It was opened to an article headlined "Makiki Tragedy Continues."

"Twenty years ago this month, Patricia Mura was brutally slain, her body dumped on the slopes of Diamond Head. Her killer is still at large. Yesterday morning, her father, Hiroshi Mura, was just as brutally murdered, a single bullet fired into his brain at close range."

"How'd the press get that information?" I asked Sampson. "I haven't released anything."

"Read on," Sampson said.

The article went on to imply that the murders of Mura and his daughter, twenty years apart, were somehow connected. The heart-wrenching story detailed his tragic fall into mental illness, beginning with the death of his wife, continuing with Patty's drug use and arrests for prostitution.

To make things worse, though, the article's author, a reporter who was generally critical of the HPD, brought up the rash of unsolved homicides, ending with a generalized indictment of the department for decades of ineptitude.

It was the kind of article that made me angry. Honolulu police officers risked their lives every day to protect and serve, as our logo promised, and there was a wall right downstairs with dozens of names of officers who had died in the line of duty. I believed that the press should be able to criticize us, especially if we weren't doing our jobs well—but reporters like that were simply out to grab headlines rather than engage in a debate over police procedures.

"The chief's already been on to me," Sampson said. "He wants to see some progress in this case. Have you looked up the information on the daughter's murder?"

I looked at Sampson. "You think it's connected?"

"I don't think anything," he said. "I want you to do that."

"I'll get the file," I said. He retreated to his office, and I finished my notes on Mura's murder, then printed them up and stuck them in the case file. I spent most of the rest of the day digging up what little information there was on Patricia Mura's arrests, her time in juvenile hall, the times she had run away, and her murder.

The crime scene guys had pulled fingerprints off the belt that had been used to bind her hands, though there had been no match at the time. I took the card and went downstairs to the Special Investigations Section and found Thanh Nguyen, a fingerprint tech I knew who worked downstairs in the Records and Identification Division. His division was responsible for serving warrants, firearms registration and permits, handling of evidence, and fingerprinting and identification. He was a Vietnamese guy in his early sixties, and word around the building was that he'd been in the South Vietnamese army, getting out just as Saigon fell.

"Can you run these through the system for me?" I asked.

He looked at the tenprint card I handed him. "You on a cold case?"

I shrugged. "You see the paper today? This girl was the daughter of the homeless man shot yesterday in Makiki. The *Advertiser* dug it up, so I figured I'd rule out any connection."

Thanh nodded. "Come on. I'll see what I can do. We must have over two hundred thousand sets of prints in the system by now. Maybe you'll get lucky." He was a short, skinny guy, and I was struck by his general resemblance to Hiroshi Mura. Maybe he could help me bring some measure of peace to Mura's restless spirit.

The card was old and a little faded, but Thanh sat at the AFIS console and scanned it in. While I watched, the computer marked the minutiae points– the things that differentiate one print from another—and assigned each a weight. Then it went through its database looking for matches.

"What do you know," he said finally. He motioned me to look at the console. "See that? You've got a match."

The system brought up a mug shot and arrest record for Edward Kapili Foster. He had been convicted of similar crimes around the same time as Patricia Mura's murder, and had died at the Halawa Correctional Facility, a medium-security prison, a few years before.

Case cleared. I took the information in to Sampson, and he called it in to a source he knew at the paper. "This doesn't get you off the hook for Mura's murder, though," he said.

"I'm on it." Back at my desk, the phone rang. It was Rory Yang, the sergeant in charge of the holding cells in the basement of the headquarters building. He asked, "Hey, Kimo, you know about that sweep last night in Waikīkī?"

"Another one?" I knew that Vice had been cracking down on prostitutes and drug peddlers in anticipation of a big Shriners' convention in a few days. The bad thing was that once all the prostitutes and pushers were moved out of Waikīkī, they just moved into District 1.

"One of 'em says he knows you."

"Who?"

"Kid we picked up on solicitation. Name of James Wong."

"James Wong." I thought for a minute. "Jimmy Ah Wong?"

"Chinese kid about sixteen, blond hair in one of those funny stand-up cuts?"

"That's him. I'll come right down."

My mind was racing ahead. The last time I'd seen Jimmy he was reasonably happy, going to the Gay Teen Center in Waikīkī and gradually getting accustomed to being gay. But then I realized I hadn't seen him at the teen center for the last few weeks.

Downstairs, Rory Yang showed me Jimmy's arrest record. He had no priors, and a preliminary drug screen had come up clean. Then Rory buzzed me through to the cell block, where I found Jimmy in a tight T-shirt and a pair of torn cutoffs, sitting on a bunk. His back was against the rough concrete wall, and his head was down between his knees. His effusive coxcomb of yellow hair, however, was a dead giveaway.

"Hey, Jimmy."

His head came up. "They told me I could call someone, but I didn't know who." He looked anxious. "I hope it was OK. I'm not gonna get you in trouble, am I?"

"No. What happened?"

He looked away. "They picked me up on Kalākaua Avenue."

"What were you doing there?"

"What do you think?"

"Does your father know?"

"He doesn't give a shit."

I leaned against the cell bars. "You want me to give him a call?"

"He won't care. He kicked me out."

"He did? When? Why?"

"About a month ago. I told that DA lady everything, all that stuff I told you, about having sex with Wayne and forging my dad's name. He hit the roof and threw me out."

"Where have you been living?"

"Around. I stayed with friends for a while, but then my dad stopped paying my tuition at Honolulu Christian, and since I wasn't going to school nobody's parents would let me stay there."

It was a pattern I'd seen before. Gay teens get tossed out of their homes after they come out, and they end up on the street. "Are you clean?"

"I don't do drugs, OK? I just do stuff to get some money to eat and all."

"You want me to get you out of here?"

For the first time I saw something like a smile cross his face. "Can you?"

"I can try. You hang in there. I'll come back when I know where you stand."

Jimmy wasn't the only teenager they'd picked up in the sweep, though he was the only boy. A caseworker from Social Services was already on the ground floor, talking to one of the girls. While I waited, I called Melvin Ah Wong at the pack-and-ship company he ran.

I didn't exactly get the reception I wanted. "Why are you calling me?"

"You're his father."

"Not any more. I don't want anything to do with him."

"It doesn't exactly work like that, Melvin. He's a minor. You're his father. You can't just abandon him."

"He's a *māhū*," he said, and I could hear the venom in that one little word, Hawai'ian for homosexual. I'd been called it myself more than a few times. "He's no longer any son of mine." And then he hung up.

The social worker was a pleasant, heavyset woman named Wilma Chow. I'd met her once or twice before but didn't know her. After the teenage girl was escorted back to her cell, I walked into the little conference room Wilma was using as an office.

"Sorry, I haven't gotten to his case yet," she said, when I told her I wanted to talk about Jimmy Ah Wong. "Let me take a look at the file."

She read for a moment, and then looked up. "You know him?" I explained about Jimmy's evidence, and that I felt responsible for him because I was the one who convinced him to talk. "What about the father?"

"He's pissed off. Says he doesn't want anything more to do with Jimmy."

"I could get him out of here on his father's say-so, since he's clean and he doesn't have any priors. But he's only sixteen, so if the father doesn't want him he becomes a ward of the state. I have to find him placement somewhere, most likely in a group home. The prospects aren't very good. He'll have to stay here for a few more days, and then the group home won't be much better. He'll probably run away again as soon as he can."

"There must be something else we can do." I paused. "How about if I sign him out myself?"

"You can't do that, detective. You don't have any authority here."

"How can I get myself appointed his guardian?"

She sat back. "I know you're trying to help, but this isn't the right way. No judge is going to release a gay teen to a gay man he hardly knows." She held up her hand. "We have to pay attention to the way things look." She checked the file again. "His hearing is this afternoon, four p.m. I can't find him placement by then."

"How about if I get somebody else to vouch for him. My parents, for instance."

"It would be better if it was somebody not related to you. Somebody who can give him a home, put him back in school. You find me somebody like that, and I can work."

I knew who I could call.

Chapter 6

HELPING A BOY

UNCLE CHIN is not my uncle, but my father's best friend. Because of that long-time relationship, I never spoke with Uncle Chin about what I knew were his impressive if quiet connections to the tongs, the Chinese criminal gangs that flourished in the islands, and tried to avoid the topic with my father as well.

Uncle Chin had cancer now, and we feared that every hospital trip would be his last. He'd just come home from one stint, and I hoped he and Aunt Mei-Mei would be up to the favor I was about to ask of them.

I signed out on the Vice case and drove up to St. Louis Heights, the residential neighborhood above Honolulu where I grew up, and where Uncle Chin and Aunt Mei-Mei lived in a simple split-level house that did little to demonstrate how wealthy they actually were. Aunt Mei-Mei answered the door. "How is Uncle Chin doing?" I asked.

"*Ai ya,* not good, Kimo. They send him home but he still very sick. Not just body sick, but heart sick too. He miss Derek."

Derek, Uncle Chin's grandson, had gone to jail a few weeks before, and as soon as he went away, Uncle Chin's health declined.

She sighed. "He lonely old man, Kimo. Derek gone, he feel he done here, go on next world, see Robert and Tommy."

Robert and Tommy were Uncle Chin's sons. Robert over-dosed, and Tommy, who had become a drug pusher, had been murdered.

She led me to the bedroom, where I found Uncle Chin propped up in an elaborate black lacquered bed, his reading glasses on the night stand and his eyes closed. "He very tired," whispered Aunt Mei-Mei behind me.

Uncle Chin opened his eyes, and smiled. "*Ni háo ma?*" I asked, using the traditional Chinese greeting he had taught me when I was barely old enough to speak.

"Good to see you, Kimo." He tried to sit up and failed, sinking back against the pillows. Seeing how frail he was, I re-gretted the idea that had brought me to his bedside, but I felt I had no choice but to see it through.

"I have come to ask you a favor, Uncle." I sat gently on the edge of his bed, while Aunt Mei-Mei hovered in the doorway. "There's a boy who needs your help."

"Derek?"

I shook my head. "Not Derek, but a boy like him. Chinese boy, sixteen years old. His father found out about him and threw him out of the house. He was arrested last night for prostitution. His father won't take him back, so he'll have to stay in juvenile hall, and then go to a home." I paused. "You know those are bad places."

"He should come here," Aunt Mei-Mei said behind me. I turned to face her. "We have much room. He could be com-pany for Uncle Chin."

I looked back to Uncle Chin. "I'll find him someplace per-manent. I just need a place to put him for a few days. I can't take him myself—it wouldn't look right."

"If I know Derek earlier, maybe I help him more," Uncle Chin said. "This boy, maybe help him instead."

I opened my briefcase on the edge of the bed. "You have to sign these papers. Then I can get him out and bring him up here."

As I handed the papers to Aunt Mei-Mei to sign, I caught a glimpse of my watch. It was almost three, so I had an hour to drive back downtown for the four o'clock hearing, where I hoped the judge would agree to release Jimmy.

I took the papers back from Aunt Mei-Mei, and leaned down to kiss Uncle Chin's forehead. "I'll be back soon, Uncle. Thank you."

He was already dozing again as Aunt Mei-Mei walked me to the front door. "You're sure this is all right?"

"Doctor say he need something care about. Maybe this boy give him."

I kissed Aunt Mei-Mei on the cheek and hurried out to my truck. Back downtown, I showed the signed paperwork to Wilma Chow and she added her own signature. "This is a little irregular, you know," she said. "I ought to meet with these people before I authorize him to be released. I'm trusting you here."

"And I appreciate it. I just want to get Jimmy out of jail. Then we can work out a long-term plan for him."

We hurried to the courtroom where Jimmy was being arraigned, and waited through a half dozen other cases before his came up. Judge Yamanaka heard Wilma's recommendation, and waived bail in light of Jimmy's youth, his lack of a record, and his past cooperation with the police.

When the Judge slammed his gavel and called for the next case, Jimmy looked confused, even younger than I knew he was, and tired and scared. It was like he didn't want to believe that anything good was happening, because then he'd just get put down again. "This is only temporary," I said as we walked through the garage to my truck. "You have to hold up your end of the bargain, and I have to find a long-term place for you. You think you can stay out of trouble for a while?"

He had his jaw set and wasn't answering me. I stopped and grabbed him by the shoulder, pushing him up against a white panel van we used for stakeouts. "Listen to me, Jimmy. These people are like family to me. And this man, he's sick. But they're putting themselves out to be nice to you. To get you out of that cell back there. So you better not give them any trouble."

"Why?"

"Why?" I felt anger bubbling up inside me and tried to tamp it down. "Because they're being nice to you, that's why."

"No, why are they being nice to me? I mean, what's in it for them?"

"They're doing me a favor." I paused. I figured I might as well give him the whole story. "It's Derek's grandfather. You remember Derek. They feel bad that he's in jail. I guess they hope they can help you."

He nodded. Somehow that seemed to reassure him. On the way back up into the hills, I asked him if he was hungry. "I guess."

"I'm sure Aunt Mei-Mei will feed you. You like Chinese food?"

"I guess."

"You want me to stop and get you a burger? Tide you over until dinner?"

He finally smiled a little. "Yeah, that would be OK."

We drove through a McDonald's, and he wolfed down his burger and fries as if he hadn't eaten in weeks. I thought maybe he hadn't, and then I remembered that when I was a kid I ate like that all the time, and my mother was always worried people would think she didn't feed me.

We got stuck in traffic on Wai'alae Avenue and I drummed my fingers against the steering wheel in exasperation. I'd done nothing all afternoon on the murder of Hiroshi Mura, and Lieutenant Sampson wasn't going to like that. But I didn't think there was anything left to do, other than wait for a neighbor who saw my card to call, or the results of the ballistics test, or some tip that would break the case open.

Clouds were gathering above the mountains, and I hoped that meant we might get a little rain, but the air around us was so dry I doubted it. We were going so slowly that I could follow the progress of two boys in parochial school uniforms, flipping pogs on the sidewalk in front of a Chinese restaurant with a fake pagoda front rising above its plate-glass window. Inside the restaurant I saw an old woman sitting at a table, pouring grains of rice into salt shakers. Usually Honolulu is so humid you need the rice to absorb the excess moisture in the air and keep the salt from sticking, but I didn't think it was necessary now.

A guy in an aloha shirt sat in an open Sebring convertible next to me, talking on his cell phone. He had a laptop computer in a black leather bag on the seat next to him, and a foam boogie board on the backseat. I wanted to get out in the surf myself, to put the murder of Hiroshi Mura, Uncle Chin's illness, and Jimmy's situation aside for at least a few minutes.

The Toyota ahead of me had a UH decal on the back windshield and a bumper sticker that read, NOTHING IS LOST IN THE KINGDOM OF GOD. I was thinking about that when Jimmy asked, "How old were you when you first had sex?"

"What brought that on?"

"Just asking."

"Man or woman?"

"You slept with girls?" He looked interested.

"Mostly," I said. "Until pretty recently. I had a lot of problems with being gay." *That was an understatement,* I thought.

"So how old?"

I had to think for a minute, do the math. "With a girl, I was
about your age. With a guy, nineteen. I was in college. I suppose I could have when I was in high school—looking back
now, I had opportunities that I was too scared to take."

"Scared how?"

"Jeez, you don't mind asking hard questions, do you?"

He slumped against the side of the door. "You don't have
to tell me."

I inched the truck forward then sat on the brake. "I had all
these confusing feelings. I knew I was supposed to like girls,
that there was stuff I was supposed to do, to want to do. And I
liked girls, I had lots of friends who were girls, but they didn't,
I don't know, get me excited. Then there were these feelings I
had, like in gym class, and these kind of romantic daydreams
of guys touching me, and I knew those were wrong. So it was
all a big mess."

"Did you like doing it with girls?"

"Jimmy," I said, whining in spite of myself. Traffic moved
forward a little more, and I looked at my watch again. "I guess
so. I mean, it's nice to have that physical contact with someone, even if it's not, I don't know, exciting. I ended up having
sex with a lot of women, and it was usually nice, but not
great."

"And with men it's great?"

"It can be. I don't have a lot of experience with guys,
Jimmy. I can't give you much advice." I gave him a sidelong

glance. He was staring out the window, trying to be nonchalant. "Have you been on the streets long?"

"A couple weeks."

"When'd you start hooking?"

"And you complain about me asking questions!"

"Turnabout's fair play. I answered yours."

"When I had to drop out of school and leave my friend's house, I ended up in Ala Moana Park, sleeping on the beach. I met this guy there, late one night. He told me I could make some money. That was maybe, two weeks ago."

"You use protection?"

"I just suck, Kimo. I won't let anybody do anything else."

"It's still dangerous. With people you don't know, you should get the guy to wear a condom."

He laughed. "Like that's going to happen."

"You gotta promise to stop hooking, at least for a while," I said. "While you stay with these people."

"What am I gonna do for money?"

I opened up my wallet. I had about fifty dollars in it. I gave it all to Jimmy. "Take this. I'll get you some more. And you won't have to pay for anything there, like food or anything."

He took the money and stuffed it into his pocket. "Why are you being so nice to me?"

The lane next to me moved a little and I swerved into it. We made almost a block's worth of progress. I could see Uncle Chin's turn just ahead, tantalizingly close. "I think you're a good kid. If you hadn't come forward with the information you did, you might still be living with your dad. So I feel bad about that."

"I think you're really nice." He reached over and put his hand on my thigh. "Really cute, too."

I picked up his hand and put it back on his own leg. "Don't

get any ideas. Sometimes people care about you without ex-pecting anything back."

"Yeah, right."

I looked over at him. "Get this one thing straight, Jimmy. I like you, and I care about you, but I do not, repeat do not, want to have sex with you. And it has nothing do with you. If you were ten years older, then, well, maybe. But you're not. I don't think it's right for adults to have sex with kids, whether they pay or just do it to be nice. I don't think it's right and I won't do it."

"All right, don't get excited."

We finally moved forward enough to make the turn up into the Heights, and I felt like I could let go of a long breath I'd been holding.

Chapter 7

LIVING IN DIFFERENT WORLDS

IT APPEARED THAT Aunt Mei-Mei had been cooking nonstop since I left, and she had set up TV trays in the master bedroom so she, Uncle Chin, and Jimmy could all sit and eat together. I sat with them for a while, eating some of Aunt Mei-Mei's special Hunan chicken, and then I left them in that room decorated with embroidered prints and black lacquer, sitting at their tables, eating and watching the news on TV. They weren't talking much but it didn't seem like a strained silence.

On my way home, I called my parents and told them what I'd done. My father thought it was a good idea, like Aunt Mei-Mei, that taking care of Jimmy would give Uncle Chin something to live for. My mother was worried, though.

"You know this boy?" she asked. "Does he come from a good family?"

"His father runs a pack-and-ship place in Chinatown," I said.

"Are you sure you can trust him?" my mother asked. "Uncle Chin and Aunt Mei-Mei are old, and Uncle Chin is sick. What if this boy causes trouble?"

"Enough, Lokelani," my father said. "If Kimo says this is a good boy who needs help, then we all help him if we can."

We ended the conversation by saying that we were all looking forward to seeing each other the next evening at the party for the Hawai'i Marriage Project. My mother and her two daughters-in-law had apparently been burning up the phone lines discussing what to wear, and my father complained about having to wear a suit. Business as usual in the Kanapa'aka household.

I spent most of the next day working all my old cases, reviewing my notes, tapping away at the Internet trying to find information, reviewing autopsy reports, and generally working hard and getting nothing accomplished.

Just as my shift was ending, Sandra Guarino called me. Cathy Selkirk's partner, she was the director of the Hawai'i Marriage Project, and she was so upset she could hardly speak. "What's up?" I asked.

"Bastards," she said. "Somebody tried to trash our office this afternoon."

I calmed her down a bit, then looked at the clock. I blew a deep breath out. If I hurried, I could stop at the Marriage Project office on my way home to get dressed for the party. "That would be terrific, Kimo," Sandra said. "I'm sure Robert would feel a lot better."

Robert, I thought, as I drove the couple of blocks from headquarters over to the Marriage Project. Harry had fixed us up; Robert was a first or second cousin of Harry's girlfriend Arleen, and they'd been anticipating double dates, because Robert and Arleen were so close.

Robert had skinny bird legs and two front teeth that he always felt were too prominent. He'd told me that someday he wanted to get braces to rein them in. And someday, too, he might motivate himself to get to the gym and fill out his muscles. But in the meantime, he was accustomed to making do with what he had. "A little eyeliner and a little blush could go along way toward making a boy look better," he'd said, the one time we went out to dinner together.

He was a nice guy, but I wasn't his type, and he wasn't mine. Harry and Arleen were more upset than either of us were; that's the way it goes with dating.

I pulled up in front of the two-story stucco building that housed the Marriage Project to see a very butch lesbian nailing a piece of plywood over what had been a front window.

"If you need something done, ask a lesbian," Robert said, after we'd exchanged greetings.

We went inside, and I asked, "Want to tell me what happened?"

"I was on the phone with Haley's Helium Heaven asking why the rainbow arc of multicolored balloons wasn't here yet, when there was this noise and the window just exploded."

He pointed to the square pane in the front window, now securely covered with plywood. "The floor in front of my desk was just strewn with shards of glass. I was so startled I actually just hung up the phone and stared."

He shrugged at me. "I mean, I was a pretty girly teenager, bad at sports and in love with Broadway show tunes—your typical fag-in-training—so I got teased a lot, got pushed around in the halls a few times and called a couple of names that I'm glad to admit to now, like cocksucker and butt pirate. But I was never gay-bashed, and I just couldn't believe it."

I smiled reassuringly, and as I did, I wrinkled my nose with the recognition of a bad smell. At first I worried that maybe the aroma of dead chicken was still lingering around my truck, attaching itself to me, but there was a different note to this stink.

"You smell it," Robert said, noticing my reaction. "The rock that came through the window was just part one. The guys yelled, 'Take that, faggots!' And then I smelled shit. I looked through the window at the pavement outside the building. A half-dozen paper bags were split open, and there was brown, mucky goo spilling out of them."

He handed me a piece of brown paper bag, with writing on it. "There was a note, too."

I read FAGGOTS DESERVE TO DIE scrawled with a pencil in crude block letters, then slipped the note in my pocket.

I took notes on everything Robert said and promised to file a report. All the time he was talking, I kept looking at my watch, worrying that I wouldn't have enough time to get home, get showered and changed, and pick up my date.

Harry had encouraged me to invite someone to the Marriage Project party, and I'd deferred until a week before, when I'd been having drinks with my friend Gunter at the Rod and Reel Club, a gay bar in Waikīkī not far from my apartment. I'd mentioned the party to Gunter, complained about having to get into the tuxedo I owned but tried never to wear.

"I've got a tux," Gunter said. "But you can bet I jump at any chance to wear it. I think men look more handsome in tuxedos than in any other clothes." Then he smiled at me. "Even better than in no clothes at all."

Gunter was what I'd come to call a "friend with benefits." We had sex every now and then, when no one else was available, but mostly we were friends. "Come with me, then," I said. "Be my date."

"Serious?"

"Serious as a hot dick on a cold night," I said, repeating back to him one of his favorite expressions.

Since then we'd talked a couple of times about the party. Gunter was about as far from marriage minded as a guy can get, but the party meant free food and booze and a chance to look his best, and there was nothing wrong with that. I was pleased I'd been able to make him so happy.

By the time I got home, he'd already left a message on my answering machine, saying he was ready, so I jumped through the shower and started pulling on my tuxedo. When we went to my cousin Mark's wedding, which was black tie, my parents had bought it for me, over my complaints. "I'm never going to wear this thing again," I'd said, while my mother supervised the fitting.

"Every man should have a tuxedo," she said. "Just in case."

I sometimes think she and I live in different worlds. In hers, people go to black tie dinners and dance until dawn, drinking champagne cocktails and flirting like they're in some old movie. In my world, people commit murder, they force teenage kids into prostitution, and they shoot chickens, which start to stink in the hot sun. The two worlds don't seem to go together that well.

I clipped the black satin bow tie on just as I was ready to leave, then stopped to look at myself in the mirror.

I considered myself lucky to have gotten the best genes from my varied ancestors: black hair and skin that tanned easily from the Hawai'ians; a slight epicanthic fold over the eyes from my Japanese grandfather, just enough to make me look exotic and dashing; and solid lines in my face, good cheekbones, and a strong chin from my *haole* grandmother. I was normally not vain about my looks, figuring it was all genetics, but that night I had to admit I looked handsome.

Gunter shared a small house with a roommate, just outside Waikīkī proper, behind Diamond Head Elementary. I pulled up in his driveway and walked up the front sidewalk. The orange and yellow hibiscus blossoms on the bushes by his mailbox were already closing up, and the evening sky was shading from pastel blue to lavender above the mountains. The pervasive smell of smoke still lingered, and I hoped we'd get that rain sometime soon. Somewhere in the distance I heard someone pounding an *ipu* gourd and chanting rhythmically in Hawai'ian.

Gunter came out the door. "You look gorgeous!" he said, stopping to admire me. "Who knew you dressed up so well?" He put one finger on my chin and turned my head from side to side. "Darling, you need somebody to take you in hand and bring out your potential!"

"Come on," I said. Gunter looked better than usual himself. He's about six-three, lean and gawky, with a buzz-shaved head. The first time I met him, at a gay bar in Waikīkī, I thought he looked like a giraffe. But the tuxedo had worked its wonders on him as well. All gawkiness had disappeared, and he seemed suave and debonair. His short hair made him look European, but a little exotic as well.

"What's this?" he asked, fingering my tie. "A clip-on bow tie? I can't be seen with a man wearing a clip-on. Fortunately I have an extra one inside. Come on." He tugged on my hand.

"Gunter, we're running late already."

"Then we'll just be a little later."

His house was spare, almost Oriental. No clutter, no books or magazines or sports equipment strewn around, like you find at my place. He led me back into his bedroom, and I started wondering if we had enough time for some quick fun before the party. The answer, of course, was no, but that didn't stop me thinking. I'd been going through a sexual dry spell, too busy to troll for dates in bars or online, and Gunter had been busy himself with a series of Filipino gardeners at the condo where he worked as a security guard.

"Take that thing off," he said, rummaging in one of his bureau drawers. I took off the tie and put it in my pocket. "And take your jacket off, too, and put your collar up."

He turned back to me with a long strip of black fabric in his hand. "Here we go." He stepped up close to me, his face almost at mine, and started fiddling with the tie. "It's harder to do this on somebody else," he said. "Let me get behind you."

"Get thee behind me, Satan," I said.

"Oh, you tease."

I felt his body close to me, and sensed a familiar stiffening in my groin, a sensation I resolved to ignore. Then I realized he was feeling the same thing. What a damn shame that we were on a schedule. "We have a dinner to go to, Gunter," I said. "No time for fun."

He finished the tie with a flourish. "There you go," he said, turning me around so I faced the mirror. "Doesn't that look better?"

≈

GUNTER AND I met my high-school friend, Terri Gonsalves, as we walked from the parking garage toward the party, and I was able to ask her about Cathy's application to her great-aunt's foundation. She promised she'd look into it. I told her I thought she looked lovely. I knew it was the first time she'd been out to a big party since her husband had died, and I was sure she was feeling melancholy.

"Since I don't have a man of my own, you'll both have to be my escorts," she said. She hooked her arms around Gunter and me and we strolled down the street.

The evening was clear and dry, despite the smell of smoke, and beyond the lights of downtown I could make out a few dim stars above. We walked through a neighborhood of one-

and two-story offices and stores, a travel agency with vertical columns of Chinese-language ads next door to a place selling medical uniforms. The sounds of a jazz piano floated toward us as we approached the offices of the Hawai'i Marriage Project, glowing with light. The two-story stucco building had a big open office on the first floor, where Robert worked. There was a bathroom at the rear and a door that led out to an open lanai. Up on the second floor there were two offices, one looking to the street and the other to the back. The front room was used for meetings and storage, and Sandra Guarino used the back office.

When we walked in, Harry and Arleen were standing around Robert's desk talking with him. Arleen was holding her young son Brandon, who had already fallen asleep. "I'm going to take this big boy upstairs," she said. "Sandra said I could leave him in her office."

"You're sure he'll be all right?" Harry asked.

"I'll leave the window open. If he wakes up and starts to cry, you can bet we'll hear it."

I asked Robert what he was saying to guests about the broken panel in the front window. He pulled me aside. "I don't want anybody to know," he whispered. He explained he was telling people that one of the caterers had accidentally knocked into the window.

"There is a problem, though," he said, keeping his voice low. "I've heard a rumor that we might get some protesters tonight."

"Really? How'd you hear that?"

"I have a friend who works at Homeless Solutions," he said. I knew of it; it offered temporary and transitional housing services. It was a place that might have helped Hiroshi Mura, had he been willing to leave the shack in Makiki. "He told me that somebody was going around today, recruiting for a demonstration tonight. They were paying twenty bucks just to show up here and be part of a crowd."

I shook my head. "What's up with that?" I asked. "Who cares enough about us to go to so much trouble?"

"The same people who broke the window?" Robert asked. "Or the ones who threw the shit on the sidewalk?"

Just then, Cathy and Sandra came down from the office above, and Robert and I stopped talking. The four of us walked out to the lanai together.

It was surprisingly large, paved with flat stones, with several big kukui trees shading it. A large frangipani tree with its exotic purple blossoms bloomed directly in the center, above a bar set up on folding tables. The waiters and waitresses all wore plumeria leis and aloha shirts, and they were offering a choice of mai tais or champagne cocktails. I noticed several of the women guests were wearing long, formal muumuus in colorful patterns.

Sandra steered Gunter and me toward a short, chubby man in an immaculate tuxedo, with a lavender cummerbund and matching bow tie. "I want you to meet one of our biggest benefactors, Charlie Stahl."

"I knew I should have gone on a diet before coming to this party," he said. Everybody laughed, and Sandra introduced us. "So, detective," he said to me, holding my hand for just a little too long to be comfortable. "You're even more handsome in person than you are on television."

Gunter snaked his hand around my waist and said, "Yes, I always tell him that. Especially when he's . . . out of uniform."

Charlie Stahl gave him an appraising glance, said, "I'll bet," and went on to meet some other guests.

Gunter and I were momentarily alone. "If I didn't know you better I'd say you were jealous, Gunter."

"You don't want to get mixed up with that old leather queen."

"He's also the heir to a huge pineapple fortune." While Dole made sure that every pineapple off their plantation came with a red-and-yellow sticker on the side, the Stahl pineapples were primarily canned under store names, pressed into juice, and used in flavorings. But that didn't make them any less successful than Dole.

"Well, who would you rather be with?" Gunter struck a pose, one hand on his hip, the other behind his ear. "The heir to a huge fortune, or *moi?*"

I pretended to look around behind him. "Did you see which way he went?"

My parents arrived a few minutes later with Lui and Liliha, followed almost immediately by Haoa and Tatiana. All three women wore modern versions of the *holoku,* floor-length formal dresses in floral patterns. My father and brothers were handsome in their tuxes, though I could tell Haoa would rather have worn an aloha shirt and flip-flops no matter the occasion. For a few minutes I forgot about the unsolved murders on my desk, about the rumors Robert had heard, and the vandalism earlier in the day.

This is what my life could be, I thought. Surrounded by family and friends, a handsome man on my arm. Maybe all the torment that had accompanied my coming out of the closet was over, and I was ready to move on with my life. It had been six months, after all. I'd dated a couple of guys casually, had some good sex and some bad sex, and gotten more comfortable being recognized.

Right after I'd returned to the force, I'd spent a month undercover on the North Shore, working on a big case, and that
chance to get away had been good for me. I'd met some gay
friends, I'd surfed, I'd caught a killer. Then I'd returned to
Honolulu and begun a fresh start.

I introduced Gunter to my family, and we all made small
talk for a few minutes. Then, expertly, Lui cut my father from
the crowd and led him away, with a nod to me and Haoa to
follow.

"Well, isn't this nice," my father said. "All my boys together."

"So what's up with you, Dad?" Haoa asked. "You won't go
to the doctor?"

I saw Lui groaning at Haoa's lack of tact. "I thought you
were going to let me handle this."

"Handle what?" Dad asked.

"Mom says you don't feel well and you won't see Dr. Yu."

"I feel fine."

"No you don't," I said. "We can all see it. Your stomach
hurts, you're tired."

"Why are you being stubborn?" Haoa asked.

"Why are you doing this?" Dad asked. "It takes three of
you big boys to gang up on one old man like me?"

"We love you, Dad," Lui said. His eyes flashed at the both
of us. "We want you to be well, to live a long time to spoil your
grandchildren. You remember you and Mom used to drag us
to the doctor every time one of us sniffled? Well, it's the same
thing. We just want you to take care of yourself."

"I'm fine," he said. He squared his shoulders and stepped
away from Lui. "Now if you'll excuse me, I'm going to see if
your mother would like a drink."

Chapter 8

PREACHING TO THE CHOIR

I FOUND GUNTER in the office.

"Time to eat," I said. "Let's find our table."

We were walking past the bathroom when the door opened and a guy in a tux, sweating heavily, stepped out. "Sorry," he mumbled, as he pushed past us.

"Hope he didn't eat something bad," Gunter said.

I looked after him. There was something familiar about him, but I didn't know what. Had I met him in a bar somewhere? I didn't think I'd slept with him; there hadn't been that many guys since I'd come out, and I could still remember all their names and faces.

We sat down, and as the waiters began delivering our salads, a man I recognized as Vic Ramos stepped up to the microphone at the front of the room and cleared his throat. "Hi, my name is Vic, and I'm HIV positive."

The audience was silent. "I guess we don't have many veterans of twelve-step programs here," he continued. "You're supposed to all say, 'Hi, Vic.'"

There were scattered calls of "Hi, Vic" from around the room. Gunter's voice was among them.

"Well, that's a little better," Vic said. "You see, I know about twelve-step programs, because I'm also an alcoholic. I've used intravenous drugs. Oh, and I'm also a homosexual, and I'm in love with a guy in the audience named Jerry and I want to marry him."

He smiled at us. "Guess that gives me a lot to talk about, doesn't it?" The audience laughed a little. "But I'm not going to get into most of that. Let me just tell you that when I was a teenager, growing up in a little town about an hour outside Manila, I started to realize that I was sexually attracted to other guys."

He started to walk around. "Can you hear me without the microphone? Good. I'm a salesman, you know, and salesmen love to walk around while they make their pitches. Now, I don't know about where all of you grew up, and what it was like there, but I can tell you that in a small town in the Philippines in the 1960s, we didn't have gay porn. We didn't have magazines like the *Advocate* or TV shows like *Will & Grace* to tell us that it was all right to feel the way we did." He stopped under the multicolored arc of balloons. "No rainbow coalition, gay pride, pink triangles, or tea dances."

He put one hand in front of his stomach and the other up in the air and did a little Latin dance step. Somebody in the audience called out, "Olé!"

Vic gave us a quick bow. "There was one guy in our town I was pretty sure was gay. He cut all the ladies' hair and gossiped with them, and he wore these gauzy shirts and bell-bottom pants. Once a month he went in to Manila and got a permanent in his hair. One day, he saw me hanging around his little shop when he was about to close. I guess I was about fifteen then. He must have recognized the look in my eyes, because he invited me inside."

I looked around for the sweaty guy, still trying to figure out where I'd seen him before. Also, I worried that he had gotten sick from the appetizers; I'd eaten a bunch of them myself, and I'd seen most of my family eating them, too.

Back at the front of the room, Vic smiled again. "You probably all know what happened next." There was some laughter in the audience. "What you don't know is that my father found out almost immediately. He kicked me out of the house, and the hairdresser said he couldn't take me in because he'd get thrown out of town, lose his house and his business. He gave me the name of a guy in Manila and he lent me money for the bus fare.

"You know what a fifteen-year-old boy does in Manila when he doesn't have a family or any money, not even a high school diploma? He goes to work in a pleasure house. That's where my hairdresser friend sent me; it's where he went once a month, before he got his hair done. It was the height of the Vietnam War and Manila was full of GIs, on their way to the war, or on their way home, or taking some R&R. There were plenty of them who were happy to have sex with a cute little Filipino boy with a nice ass."

The sweaty guy seemed vaguely familiar; perhaps I'd met him in a bar somewhere. I generally have a good memory for faces, which comes in handy as a homicide detective. That made it particularly frustrating when I met someone I just couldn't place.

Vic looked rueful. "My ass was pretty nice then," he said, nodding. Gunter gave him a wolf whistle, and he smiled. "You can see me after the party," he said, and everybody laughed. "Me and Jerry, that is. I don't want you to forget about Jerry. He's the most important person in my life, but I'm gonna get to him in a couple of minutes."

He looked out at the crowd. "Now, where was I? Oh, yeah,

I was a fifteen-year-old prostitute, and I was pretty miserable. I missed my mama and my family and my friends, and a lot of the guys were pretty rough with me. They called me names, ugly names, and sometimes they had to hurt me in order to make themselves feel good. A couple of the other guys and I used to get hold of this terrible cheap beer and drink. The madam who ran the brothel started smelling our breath, though, so we couldn't drink as much, and we started using heroin."

He held his arms out to us. "I haven't shot up in years, so my tracks have faded, but you can still see them. Eventually, this one older gentleman, a Frenchman living in Manila, took a liking to me, and he bought me away from the pleasure house. I lived with him for four years as his houseboy, until he died. Then I made my way, doing this and that, and eventually I landed here in Hawai'i."

I looked around for the sweaty guy again. Had he gone back inside to the bathroom? I worried that if he was throwing up, there could be a big mess.

"Things are a lot better for me now than they were when I was fifteen, even though the HIV is making a mess of my body," Vic continued. "I've got a good job—district sales manager for the Pacific Rim—for a big farm-equipment manufacturer. I'm in love with a great guy, and we own our own little house. You all should come over and see us sometime."

He pointed at Gunter. "Especially you," he said, and Gunter blushed. "The point of all this, though, is how easily that can get taken away from me. From us, from me and Jerry." He started walking again. "I'm the primary breadwinner in our household. Jerry builds some of the most beautiful hand-carved furniture you'll ever see, but he's still developing his business. You know how expensive it is to get health insurance as a small businessman? I'll bet some of you know."

Across the table from me, I saw my father frowning, moving around uncomfortably on his chair. Was this another example of his ongoing illness? Or had he eaten what the sweaty guy had?

Vic continued, "My company doesn't offer domestic partner benefits, and they probably never will. So I can't put Jerry on my health insurance. I can't pass on my pension to him, or my Social Security when I die. If I get sick, the hospital may not even let Jerry in to see me, or let him make decisions for me. I've got this goddamned Bible-thumping bitch of a sister who lives here in Honolulu now, and if she gets wind of me being sick she's going to take that opportunity to come on in and take over my life, no matter what kind of papers Jerry and I fill out."

I twisted around in my seat to look for the sweaty guy. I just couldn't let go of it—I knew I recognized him from somewhere. But I couldn't find him in the crowd.

Vic was standing at the podium. "You see, without a marriage license the government presumes your blood family knows what's best for you," he said. "Until gay men can legally marry each other, until lesbians can legally marry each other, teenaged kids are still going to keep thinking there's something wrong with them when they find they're attracted to their same sex. Until the government treats us like every other citizen— with the right to serve in the military, to receive the legal benefits of marriage, to be protected from discrimination in our homes and on our jobs—we are not going to be able to enjoy the benefits of full citizenship in the United States."

He gripped the edges of the podium and stared out at us.

"Now I don't know about you, but I've worked too damn hard to become a citizen here to give up any of the things I'm entitled to. You all feel the same way?"

The audience applauded. "You going to fight to get us the benefits we deserve?" More cheering and applause. He walked over to Jerry, took him by the hand, and stood him up. "This is Jerry, folks. I said I'd show him off to you."

"Hi, everybody," Jerry said.

I shot another glance at my father. There was sweat beading on his forehead, and he wiped it with a napkin.

Vic held Jerry's hand up, clasped in his. "I want everybody here to see this. I love this guy and I want to marry him. That's why he and I are joining the lawsuit tomorrow. And we're both pledging to do whatever we can to make sure that gay kids can grow up to feel proud of who they are, because they have the legal right to be, and love, whoever they want."

The applause was loud and long.

Chapter 9

BLOW UP

I PUSHED MY CHAIR back from the table. "I ate too much. The food was great." I thought I'd get up and walk around the room a bit, walk off some of the food and look for the sweaty guy again. I wanted to know if he was all right, or if there was something in the food we should all worry about.

"Better watch out," Gunter said. "Too many rich foods build up down there in the stomach." He reached over to pat mine.

I flexed my abs. You couldn't tell in the tuxedo, but they were still strong and flat. "Build that up," I said, pointing down.

"I'd like to." His smile had a little bit of a leer to it, and I had to smile myself. That's when we heard the first chant. "No more ho-mos, no more ho-mos." It wasn't too loud, but there could have been twenty or thirty voices. They sounded like they were right outside. I headed straight through the courtyard toward the door to the street, and met Sandra just before I got there.

I looked around and saw that Gunter and Harry were right behind me. I figured chasing the sweaty guy would have to wait for another time. "Sandra and I will take care of this," I said.

"We're just the backup," Harry said. Behind them I saw my brothers as well.

Sandra and I walked out front while the four of them remained just behind us. A group of about twenty men and women stood in front of the building carrying signs that read things like HOMOSEXUALITY IS THE WORK OF THE DEVIL and YOU'RE NOT CONVERTING OUR CHILDREN.

"Great," I muttered. I assumed that many of those in the crowd were people who'd been recruited at the homeless shelter earlier that day. For some reason that bothered me more than anything. I believed in democracy. People who had a problem with something were entitled to stand up and voice their opinions. But paying somebody to support your cause was just lame.

A man stepped forward from the group and I recognized him as Wilson Shira, the vice mayor of Honolulu. He was a short, angry Nisei, or first-generation Japanese-American, and his political capital was built on ethnic strife. I guessed he was taking the "vice" in his title seriously.

"I assume you have a permit for this demonstration, sir," I said.

"Absolutely." He pulled a piece of paper from his jacket pocket and showed it to me. The city of Honolulu had granted him a permit for a peaceful demonstration at our address, for nine p.m. that evening. It was just a few minutes past nine then.

"I'm Sandra Guarino. I'm the executive director of the Hawai'i Marriage Project. We're having a private fund-raising event here this evening, and I'd like to ask you to reschedule your protest."

"We know about your fund-raiser," Shira said. "That's why we're here. We want to know who supports you and we want them to know we know who they are."

"Our membership roster is open to the public," Sandra said. "We're a not-for-profit corporation. I'll be happy to show you our membership list."

Shira looked at his crew. They all nodded encouragingly. "Good."

"In exchange, you agree to leave us alone this evening," Sandra said.

Again Shira looked at the crowd to read their sentiment. Besides the homeless, the people behind Shira looked like regular working folks, with families and jobs. I knew they didn't want to be out too late on a Wednesday night. There seemed to be grudging approval of the plan, so Shira followed Sandra back into the building. Gunter stepped up next to me, Harry and my brothers right behind me. "We'll stay here with you until they leave," Gunter said.

Partly because I wanted to, and partly just to spite the crowd, I took Gunter's hand and squeezed. We stood there in front of them, holding hands. Gunter's was warm in mine and it felt good. I don't know how long we stayed like that, but it probably wasn't more than ten or fifteen minutes, nobody saying much. Then, suddenly, the crowd in front of us was lit with a great light.

A second later a huge boom rocked the building behind us, knocking me to my knees. Everything seemed to move in slow motion. A blast of hot air burst out from behind us. Gunter fell to the ground, my brothers and Harry tumbling too. I remember looking at the palm of my hand, seeing where a piece of gravel in the street had scratched it. I reached into my jacket pocket and pulled out my cell phone.

I looked behind me. Haoa looked the least dazed. "Call 911." I threw him the phone and followed it with my wallet, with the badge flapped open on the end. "Tell them there's already a detective on the scene. Give them my number."

Then I ran toward the entrance of the building.

I looked around behind me. Gunter and Harry were getting up. Lui already had his own cell phone out, probably calling his station with the exclusive. I pushed open the front door, going after Sandra and Wilson Shira. The front wall of the bathroom was gone, leaving shreds of drywall and twisted metal studs, and tongues of flame licked the surrounding area. There was gritty smoke in the air, like a dozen guys had been puffing on stinky cigars. Water was pooled on the floor in the corner and seemed to be spreading.

I met Robert coming in from the lanai. "All our data!" he said. "I have to get our files out!"

"Get out of here!"

He pushed past me and hurried to his desk. I shook my head and ran for the stairs. Sandra and Shira had to be up there. Fortunately the staircase was on the opposite side of the building from the bathroom, so all I had to contend with was some smoke rising around me.

As I climbed I heard Brandon crying. "God, let Brandon be all right," I said to myself. Arleen had left him in a bassinet on Sandra's desk, but when I rounded the corner from the staircase the room was totally unrecognizable. There was a huge hole in the floor and I could look down directly into a pit of flames that I thought was the bathroom.

Brandon was lying on the floor in a nest of papers and files. Sandra was unconscious, lying half on her desk, her legs hanging dangerously close to the fiery abyss. I couldn't see Wilson Shira anywhere in the room.

Harry was right behind me, rushing toward Brandon. "Be careful!" I shouted, above the noise of the flames. It was much hotter in there, even though I could look up through the roof to the sky. The heat rose up from the first floor in waves, and the wallpaper was starting to blister. The back window was gone, just shards of glass stuck in the frame.

As Harry ran to get the baby, I picked my way over to Sandra. I had to go very slowly because I wasn't sure how strong the floor was, and I didn't want to get too close to any of the furniture in case it was hot. By the time I reached her, Harry had picked up Brandon and gone back down the stairs.

Sandra still had a pulse. I took off my jacket and wrapped it around her, and then I undid the bow tie Gunter had so carefully tied for me, leaving its ends hanging around my neck, and ripped open my shirt collar. It was so hot up there I was sweating like crazy, and I was worried my hands would be too slick to hold on to Sandra.

I heard a distant siren but knew I couldn't stay in that building a minute longer than I had to. I managed to get Sandra over my shoulder in the fireman's carry and struggled back across the room, picking my way carefully again. By the time I made it to the top of the stairs, though, the fire had spread considerably.

Flames crackled around the narrow staircase as I slowly moved down, trying to balance Sandra's weight over my shoulder, praying that the fire would come no closer, that it wouldn't collapse the treads and risers under me. It was hard to breathe without getting a lung full of smoke, and the air burned on its way down my throat.

By the time I made it to the first floor, I was ready to collapse with exhaustion. The air was a little fresher down there as the updraft forced the fire and smoke out through the roof. I paused at the foot of the stairs, leaning back against a wall, and saw Gunter dragging Robert out the back door. Flames rose around them, and I couldn't tell if they were both on fire, or if it was the kind of illusion you saw in the movies.

The staircase began to collapse behind me, and I knew I had to get out. I took big, heaving, running steps toward the street, chased by a wall of flames rushing toward my back. The last thing I remember is getting to the front door where Haoa waited for me, feeling that utter sense of relief that I imagine only little brothers feel, when you know a big brother is there to take over for you.

Chapter 10
COLORED PINWHEELS

I WOKE UP flat on my back on the street, an oxygen mask on my face and an EMT leaning over me taking my blood pressure. Somebody was pounding a jackhammer inside my head, while the shrimp I'd so gleefully dipped in cocktail sauce and swallowed only a short while earlier seemed to be rising in revolt inside my stomach. I pulled the mask off and immediately started a coughing jag that seemed to loosen everything inside my lungs and throat.

"Don't worry," the EMT said, as he tried to put the oxygen mask back on me. "You swallowed a lot of smoke in there, but we're going to get you to the hospital and by tomorrow you'll be just fine."

I struggled to sit up and pinwheels of colored light went off behind my eyelids. My legs and arms felt so heavy I thought they might be pinned to the pavement. "My family," I finally croaked out. "What happened to my parents and my brothers?"

"Hey, big fella, you just lie down there." He tried to ease me back down flat, but I wouldn't let him. "Tell me your name."

I told him, and he pulled out his radio and made a call. "They've got an Al Kanapa'aka at Queens. Smoke inhalation. They're admitting him for observation. Any other names?"

We went through the list. I kept coughing every time I tried to get a name out, but the EMT was remarkably patient. My brothers and their wives hadn't been hurt. Sandra Guarino was the worst, with a concussion, burns, maybe some internal injuries. Robert and Gunter had both been admitted for observation, with burns and smoke inhalation. I couldn't think of anyone else to ask about and it frustrated me.

Sitting up, I could see what was going on around me. The streetscape was bright with high-intensity lamps, headlights, and the last glowing embers of the fire. At least four fire trucks, dozens of firemen, and a phalanx of cops were present. Off to one side I saw TV cameras from KVOL, my brother's station. It reminded me of the carnivals at the Hawai'i State Fair.

"Feel better now?" the EMT asked. "You want to cooperate? You ought to go to the hospital, let them check you out. Just to be safe." He was a skinny, red-haired *haole* with a stethoscope hanging sideways around his neck. He had a bunch of different patches sewn onto his white tunic but I didn't bother to read them.

"I'm a cop," I said. "I've got to find out what's going on." I stood up and swayed on my feet, jackhammer pounding, stomach churning, pinwheels dancing. I took a deep breath and for the first time smelled something other than smoke: a deep underlayer of saltwater and seaweed on an ocean breeze that was coated with car exhaust, smoke, and urban grime. I felt like the coughing was getting a little better.

"I can't be responsible for you if you won't listen to my advice," the EMT said.

"So don't be." I patted myself down, just to make sure everything was there, and discovered that Haoa had returned my badge and cell phone to me while I was knocked out. I felt a cool breeze against my back and realized that my shirt must have been torn or charred at some point. But my jacket, which I'd wrapped around Sandra Guarino, was on the ground next to me, and I slipped it on. I flipped the phone open and scrolled down to Haoa's cell number. He picked up on the first ring.

"Hey, brah." I started coughing again.

"Kimo? Hey, brah, where are you?"

"I'm still back here. What's up with Dad?"

"They want to keep him overnight, run some tests. Everybody else is OK—Lui is still over by you somewhere, running his coverage, but Mom and Tatiana and Liliha are all here. Mom has been shaking down half the hospital trying to find out what happened to you."

"I've gotta stay here for a while. You guys be OK?"

"We'll hold it together. Liliha says if you see Lui, send him home."

"Like he'll do anything I say," I said, laughing and coughing at the same time. I heard Haoa laughing too. "Hey, brah."

"Yeah?"

I didn't know where to start. How do you thank your brother for being there for you? It was just what brothers did. It's what we expected of each other, what made the love between us so fierce, and also what made us want to rip each other's hair out from time to time. "Thanks," I said. "Just thanks."

"I hear you, brah. Aloha."

I said good night and then scanned the crowd, looking for any face I recognized. Unexpectedly, I saw Lieutenant Sampson, incongruously wearing a suit and tie. Next to him was a tall, blonde young woman I recognized from the photograph on his desk. I started walking toward him, happy to see that my legs had begun to respond again. By taking deep breaths I was able to control the churning in my stomach, and the colored pinwheels seemed to be dying away. The jackhammer I figured I'd have to live with for a while.

"I thought it would be you, Kanapa'aka," Lieutenant Sampson said. "I was driving Kitty home and I heard the report of this blast on the scanner. I couldn't figure out at first how one of my detectives was already on the scene even before the fire department. I had to come by and see for myself."

He introduced his daughter. "Kitty just made the dean's list at UH. Tonight was our celebration. She got to pick the place, so of course she chose a restaurant that made me wear a coat and tie."

"That explains it," I said.

"I give the guy ties every time there's a holiday and he never wears them," Kitty said with a smile. "I just want to know that what I do is appreciated."

He grinned and then turned back to me. "So tell me what happened here."

"We had some trouble with protesters, and I was outside with them." I gave him a quick rundown of the evening. "I gave my cell phone and my badge to my brother and told him to call it in and then I went inside."

"So I understand," Sampson said. "You were lucky, Kanapa'aka. You were able to get inside and get that woman, and get out in time. They could just as easily be pulling your body out of there now, as well as the vice mayor's."

"Shira? I looked around for him when I was inside but I didn't see him."

"Looks like he was the only fatality, so far. Which makes this a homicide case as well as a fire department investigation."

I wanted to work the case myself. I wanted to find the bastards who blew up my friends and my family, who didn't care if any of us lived or died. I'd do it on my own time, work nights or weekends. I wanted to make sure the people responsible got what they deserved. I realized I had already assumed I'd be investigating, and I'd started thinking about how to do it.

"I've got some ideas about this," I told Sampson. "I want to check out all the groups that have opposed this legislation. See if any of their members have criminal records. Find out where their money comes from, what their motives are."

Sampson held up his hand. "You're assuming you're investigating this case. You're not on duty tonight. You aren't even on this shift."

I stopped short. "I've got to work this case, lieutenant. You've got to give it to me. If you don't, I'll . . . I'll . . ."

"You won't do anything without my authorization," Sampson said. He stood there menacingly, taller and bigger than I was, my boss, the man who had saved me when it didn't look like there would be a job left for me on the force. I stared right back at him, forgetting about everything else. He blinked first. "But I've got enough troubles without trying to hold you back when you want to investigate. Steve Hart pulled this case, but I'm sure he'd turn it over to you, considering how many open cases he's got."

I remembered I had a few open cases of my own, starting with Hiroshi Mura.

"You tell Hart I said it's all right," Sampson said. He turned to his stepdaughter. "Wait for me in the car, will you?" She looked like she was going to give him an argument, but then she caved.

"Good night, detective," she said. "Good luck."

He waited until she was out of earshot and said, "You know what kind of a case this is going to be, don't you? High profile."

"I understand."

"I want to make sure you do. We've got a prominent victim, so City Hall is going to be all over this investigation. It's got a news hook—this gay marriage thing." He looked at me. "And then there's you. You're not exactly low profile yourself."

"There hasn't been any coverage of me since I got back from the North Shore. I've been keeping my nose clean, concentrating on my job."

"But the media is going to come after you again, you've got to realize that. You're the gay cop, investigating a gay crime. You prepared for that?"

"I'll have to be."

"All right, then." He nodded his head toward where the medical examiner's truck was parked. "Looks like your victim's on his way out. You'd better take a look."

"Thanks, lieutenant." I reached out to shake his hand and realized mine was grimy with smoke and pavement dust, but he took it anyway, and shook it.

"Be careful," he said.

Chapter 11
THE FIRE INVESTIGATOR

I STARTED TOWARD Doc Takayama, but on the way I saw Steve Hart and detoured over to talk to him. He was a tall, skinny Anglo with slightly shaggy blond hair, recently promoted from patrolman to detective. He worked District 1 with me, though he was on the night shift so we hardly knew each other.

"Well, well, it's the big hero," he said. "Come to give me your side of the story?"

"Actually, I want to tell you I'm taking over the investigation."

"What the fuck? You think I can't handle this? 'Cause I just got my shield? Let me tell you, I've been working the streets for long enough, I know how to run an investigation."

"I talked to Sampson . . ."

"So he doesn't think I can handle this? Jesus Christ, they don't even give you a chance here. I mean, I know I've got a lot of open investigations, but shit, everybody's got them." He looked at me. "I see your name up on the board a lot. You're not short of work." Then he closed his jaw tight and nodded. "I get it. This is some kind of gay thing, isn't it? You think because I like girls I can't relate to this."

"Whoa!" I held up my hand. "Don't get bent out of shape. This doesn't have anything to do with you. Shit, I don't know what kind of detective you are. I hardly fucking know you." I held my thumb up, pointing back at the burned-out building. "But you know who was in there? My parents. My brothers. My best friends. I asked a friend to go with me to this thing, and he's in the hospital now. Two other people I know are at Queen's too, along with my dad. You know how crazy that makes me?"

"I can work this case," he said. "I want you to know that. I know I'm green, but I'm a good detective."

"I don't care. You can be the best fucking detective on this force, but I'm not going to let this case go." I pulled out my cell phone. "You want me to call Sampson, have him tell you himself?"

"You're his pet, aren't you? I know the deal—the department wanted to can your ass and Sampson pulled you in. Reach out to the gay community and all that shit."

"Goddamn motherfucker!" I reached over and grabbed a piece of Hart's shirt, startling the shit out of him. "This is not about who I choose to have sex with, you asshole. These people messed with my family and I'm gonna get them. And anybody who stands in my way gets run the fuck over. You understand?"

I finally got through to him. "All right," he said, backing away a little as I let go of his shirt front. "You want the case, it's yours." He pointed over to a recessed storefront across from the Marriage Project offices. In the sheltered area a couple of uniforms were sitting at folding tables, taking statements from people in evening clothes. "You got some guys collecting over there. I got the street blocked off. I'll leave all my paperwork on your desk. OK? Just don't go crazy on me."

I thought I heard him mutter the word "faggot" under his breath but I wasn't sure. I said, "Yeah, right. Whatever," and stalked over to Doc Takayama, who stood in consultation with a guy in a yellow fireproof jumpsuit. It was unzipped halfway down his chest, so I could see a white T-shirt and dark chest hair. Something about the hyper-masculinity of his fireman's outfit gave me a little jolt. But I focused on Doc.

He looked at me with interest. "Didn't expect to see you investigating, Kimo. I thought you were on the other side of this one."

"Well, you could say I've got an inside perspective. This our illustrious vice mayor?"

Doc nodded and looked down. Wilson Shira's head and shoulders were smudged with smoke but relatively undamaged, though there was a place on the side of his head where the hair and skin had burned away, leaving an ugly piece of skull clearly visible. The rest of him, however, had not fared so well. His arms and torso were still recognizable, though blackened in places, while from the waist down he was a mere skeleton, just a few charred bones. It was obvious that extreme care had been taken to remove him from the fire.

Doc looked back up at me. "Kimo, you know Mike Riccardi from the fire department?"

The fireman stuck his hand out to me and I finally got a good look at him.

He was the handsome guy I'd seen the day before, in ballistics.

We shook hands as Doc completed our introductions. "The detective's reputation precedes him," Riccardi said with a smile. "I got a whiff of some of his work Monday."

He was a mixed-breed like me, a lot of Anglo and probably some Japanese or Korean in him, but he was movie-star handsome. He had a thick black mustache and wavy black hair that I was sure danced just short of any fire department regulations on length. I could not tell what color his eyes were, but there was a smudge of soot on his left cheek. I had a crazy impulse to wet my finger and reach over and clean him up, but fortunately I restrained myself. At that point, though, I couldn't tell if the hammering in my heart and head were aftereffects of smoke inhalation, or if they came from looking at him.

"So tell me what you think about the fire, Mike," Doc said.

"Let me ask a few questions of the detective here," he said, and there seemed to be a kind of condescension in his voice. It might have been that I was still dressed in a grimy tuxedo and a pleated white shirt that was now torn and sooty, the ends of Gunter's bow tie still dangling from my neck. I didn't exactly look like the cream of the Honolulu police department.

Then again, he'd said my reputation preceded me. It was possible that he, like most of the rest of metropolitan Honolulu, knew I was the gay cop. If he wanted a pissing contest, though, he'd learn soon enough that I didn't have to sit down to enter. "What can I tell you that a trained fire investigator couldn't figure out for himself?" I asked.

He raised an eyebrow. "Eyewitness accounts are part of any investigation," he said mildly. "Surely you know that, detective?"

"I'd like to get this guy back to the morgue sometime in this century," Doc said. "If you two dogs could stop growling at each other long enough to get your business with my friend here out of the way."

"Sorry, Doc," I said. "It's been a long day." I turned to Riccardi. I gave him the same quick rundown I'd given Lieutenant Sampson, ending with me and Gunter standing outside the building, facing down the crowd. I left out the part about us holding hands.

"You heard one explosion?" he asked. I nodded. "Did the fall knock you out at all? Could there have been any other blasts you might not have heard?"

"I was stunned but I wasn't knocked out. There was only one explosion."

"That was my guess based on the fire pattern. Now tell me exactly what it was like when you ran back into the building. Where was the fire? Was it all around you, or contained in one area?"

I took a moment to remember, and in that time I was surprised to see how many levels my mind was working on. Riccardi was talking just like a detective, asking the kind of clear, analytical questions I would have if I hadn't been a witness. It was a little strange to be on the other side of an investigation, even if only for a few minutes. Another level of my brain was collecting memories of what it had been like when I burst into the first floor of the building. And the third level couldn't help noticing how sexy Mike Riccardi was when he was serious.

"The door wasn't hot when I opened it, and I could see clear to the back. Robert—he's the administrative assistant—he was coming in that way and I remember telling him to get out. He was determined to save some files, though. We kind of knocked past each other as I was heading for the stairs."

"So the stairway was clear then?"

"Absolutely. The only fire was in the back corner, where the bathroom was." I closed my eyes and tried to picture it. "I don't think there were any walls left there. I just had the impression of flames." When I opened my eyes again I saw he was taking notes on a secretary's steno pad.

Suddenly I remembered the sweaty guy who came out of the bathroom as Gunter and I passed him. "If the bomb was in the bathroom, I might have seen the guy who planted it."

Riccardi's eyebrows rose. "Yes?"

"Just an idea. I don't know for sure. But this guy was sweating, looking like he was going to be sick. Could just have been nerves."

"Anyone you knew?"

"He looked like somebody I've seen before somewhere, but I couldn't put a name or a place to him. I'll get with an artist as soon as I can and see if I can get a picture of him."

"Good. So go on. You ran in the door of the building?"

"I ran up the stairs. There were two rooms up there, a big meeting room that faced the street and an office that overlooked the back lanai. I didn't go into the front room; I went straight ahead, into the office. I remember I stopped short, almost fell over, because I saw a big chunk of the floor was missing."

He wrote furiously. "Go on."

"My friend Harry came up right behind me. His girlfriend's baby was in there, on one of the desks, but the blast had knocked the kid to the ground. He was crying, and he definitely looked alive. Harry went around to the left, toward the baby, and I went to the right. Sandra Guarino—she's the executive director—she was slumped over a desk at the back of the room. I had to work my way around carefully because there was this big hole in the floor, and there were sparks jumping up out of the flames, crackling and catching on things, and it was very bright, from the fire, but also kind of dark, because of the smoke." I looked over at the Doc, who was listening intently. "It was like a picture in a Sunday school textbook of what hell was like." I started to shiver a little.

"It's all right, Kimo," Riccardi said, and he put a hand on my shoulder. "We're almost done."

I took a deep breath. "I made it around to Sandra and I felt for a pulse. She had one, but it was weak. I put her over my shoulder—I guess you know what the fireman's carry is—and I headed back for the door. Harry had already gotten the baby and gone out. The footing was harder going out because the floor was hotter, and every time I took a step I thought I was going to slip and go into that pit."

My throat was dry and my lips were parched. Damn, reliving those moments was tough. This must be what victims felt like when I interviewed them.

I licked my lips, took a deep breath, and coughed. Riccardi waited patiently while I got my breath back. "I made it out to the stairway, but by then the walls were broiling hot and I was afraid the stairs were going to collapse under me. I wanted to go fast but I was afraid to put too much stress on the steps and it was hard to move with Sandra over my shoulder. By the time I got downstairs there were flames everywhere. I saw the door ahead of me and I just bulled my way through."

I looked up at him and smiled. "The last thing I remember is bursting through the door, and my brother was right there, and I knew that he'd take care of things from there. Kind of silly, isn't it?" I shrugged.

"I don't think it's silly at all," Riccardi said. He turned to Doc. "OK, that tallies with what I've seen so far. A single blast concentrated in the area of the restroom. Probably some kind of plastic explosive, one with a simple timer. Once we can go through the debris I'll know more. Now, we know Shira was upstairs in the office. If the bomb had blown out the floor directly under him, he would have gone through the roof and he'd be in little bitsy pieces. My guess is that he and the woman were far enough away from the hole that they didn't get blown up right away. He probably got knocked out, though, and then slid or fell downstairs."

He looked over at me. "We recovered the body on the first floor, not on the second."

"That would explain the pattern of the burns," Doc said, "if he fell feet-first into the fire."

"Do you think he burned to death?" I asked.

"I have to examine his lungs—or what's left of them. My guess is that he was knocked out by the blast and then the fire finished him off. I'll get you the results as soon as possible."

"Thanks. You know this is going to be a nasty one."

"The folks at City Hall do tend to look up when one of their own gets killed," Doc said. "So, you guys finished with me now? Can I take the body?"

I looked at Mike. "Fine with me," he said, and I nodded along. "Thanks for your help, Kimo. It looks like things have cooled down a little, so I'm going to take a walk through the ashes. I'll let you know what I find."

"I'd like to come with you."

He smiled. "You aren't exactly dressed for it. I think you might be missing your smoking jacket." There was that condescension again.

"I think this tux is beyond repair. I don't care if it gets a little smokier."

"It's not that. You need special gear to walk around after a fire." He looked at me. "You sure you're up to this?"

"I've got a job to do. I'll be up to it."

He nodded. "All right. I've got an extra fire suit in my truck."

"I heard that the Queen of England was touring Disneyland with Prince Charles when he was a little boy," I said, as we walked together. "And he told his mother that he wanted a Mickey Mouse costume. So she bought him a fire suit."

"Very funny," Mike said, as we stopped in front of a black pickup with red-and-yellow flames in a stripe down the side.

"Guess you want the world to know you're a fireman," I said.

I couldn't be sure because of the darkness, but I think he blushed. "I bought it from another guy. I didn't bother to have it repainted." He had a big locked case that spanned the truck bed, and all around it were piles of junk: scraps of wood and metal, broken-down tools, and what looked like half a surfboard.

"Don't bother to clean too often either."

"Please. I grew up in a house with plastic slipcovers on the sofa and a plastic runner on the hall carpet. My mom used to dust every day. I think I'm in rebellion."

"My mom would have tried that, too," I said, as he opened the chest and rooted around in it. "But she had three sons. By the time I was born she'd pretty much given up hope of keeping the house clean."

He pulled a big yellow suit out and held it up to me. He looked at me appraisingly, checking out my body. I haven't got anything to be embarrassed about there; I keep in good shape, between surfing, rollerblading, and riding my bike. "I think it'll fit you."

Our eyes met, and I knew. Maybe Mike Riccardi didn't know it himself yet; maybe he knew but he just wasn't admitting it. But in that glance, when our eyes locked on each other, I knew. This hunky fireman with the sexy mustache and dancing eyes was just as gay as I was.

Chapter 12

THROUGH THE FIRE

I HELD HIS GLANCE for a minute, smiled, and then said, "So where do you think I can go to put this on?"

We both looked around. It was almost one in the morning by then, and the area had begun to empty out. We were about two blocks away from the offices of the Hawai'i Marriage Project, and the storefronts and office buildings around us were closed and locked. "Just go behind the truck," he said. "I promise I won't look."

"I haven't got anything you haven't already seen." Our eyes met again and he smiled. *This had definite possibilities,* I thought. Then I yawned, and felt an ache in my back, and once again I was conscious of the hammering in my head, which had muted. I remembered I had enough on my plate without wondering how I could get into Mike Riccardi's pants.

I stripped off my jacket and shirt. My back hurt, but I assumed it was because I'd been laying on the pavement. My shirt was a wreck; the back must have caught a stray ember and there was a big hole with brown edges there.

I did allow myself to wonder, as I pulled my pants off and threw them into the cab of the truck, what Mike Riccardi looked like under all that baggy material. My dick started to respond, and I had to turn away. In turning, though, I exposed myself to the glare of a spotlight, and I'm pretty sure he saw a revealing silhouette.

I stepped into the suit and pulled a pair of booties over my good dress shoes—also ruined. I had some trouble getting the suit buttoned up and Mike came over to help me. "You get accustomed to this after a while," he said. "At least it keeps half your clothes from smelling like smoke."

Together we walked back to the fire site, me clomping along in the ungainly booties and bulky fire suit. A series of high-intensity lights were focused on the ashy remains, but even so Mike handed me a small flashlight. All the engine companies but one had left, and most of the firemen were standing around in the street talking while their last few fellows prowled around looking for stray embers. Mike called out some greetings as we walked in through what had once been the front wall, and I remembered Robert telling me about the rocks that had come through the window that afternoon, the manure on the sidewalk. I wondered if there was a connection, and told Mike about them.

"My first guess is that this is an amateur bomb, which fits with that kind of shit," he said. "No pun intended. But let's keep an open mind as we look around."

We started a careful, inch-by-inch search, looking for anything that might have been out of place. I saw the melted remains of Robert's computer, settled in the midst of a hunk of molten steel and plastic that had once been a desk. A couple of the framed posters on the wall were still recognizable, though singed at the edges, and the glass was gone. There wasn't much else left to indicate what this place had been.

"What's this?" I asked, pointing my flashlight at a small white object on the floor. I kneeled down and picked it up. It was a piece of plastic about an inch square, with a few round depressions in it. It didn't look like anything that had been in the office.

"Golf ball." Mike took it from me and examined it. "Say you want to use a plastic explosive, like RDX. But that's pretty stable stuff, so you have to trigger an initial explosion in order to set it off. What you do, see, is you cut a golf ball in half and you fill it with something that will blow up more easily. There's a lot of different stuff you can use—I couldn't speculate yet what might have been in here. But the basic principle is, you put some kind of condensed acid inside some gelatin capsules, and you bury them in the less stable explosive inside the golf ball. After a while, the acid eats through the gelatin, and when it comes in contact with the first explosive, you get a little boom. That sets off the big boom."

He shrugged. "You can read about it all over the Internet. If you're an amateur, you don't know much about using clocks and timing mechanisms, so you go for something simpler, like this."

"You must have been hell as a teenager," I said.

"Hey, did you know everything you know about homicide when you were a kid?" He smiled.

A little later we were joined by a couple of agents from the local office of the Bureau of Alcohol, Tobacco, Firearms and Explosives. They usually were dispatched to investigate any kind of bombing, and these two weren't happy about getting roused out of bed in the early hours of the morning.

Mike and I went through everything we knew with them, and after a while I was yawning and stumbling on my feet. At one point I fell against Mike and he grabbed me. But it didn't even feel sexy; I was just exhausted. The ATF guys left, promising to come back in the morning. "Come on, I think it's time to get you home," Mike said to me.

I yawned again. "My truck's in the garage." I smiled. "I think it's a little neater than yours."

"Let's leave it there overnight. I don't want to see you falling asleep behind the wheel. Where do you live?"

"Waikīkī," I yawned again.

"Almost on my way. Come on, let's go."

I tried to argue but I was just too tired. I remember getting into the truck, and then we were on Kalākaua Avenue and he was gently shaking me awake. "Sorry, bud, but I need a little more direction."

"Left at Lili'uokalani," I yawned. "Geez, we're here already."

"Yeah, you're not the best driving companion." He looked over at me and smiled. I directed him to my building and he pulled up in front. I stumbled as I got out of the truck, but got my balance before he could help me.

"I can make it."

He nodded. "Thing is, you don't want that suit inside your place. You'll be weeks getting the smell of smoke out." He grinned. "The voice of experience."

"OK." It seemed perfectly reasonable to me. I unbuttoned the suit and let it drop from my shoulders. There was a warm breeze off the ocean that tickled the skin on my back as I stepped out of the boots and the legs of the suit.

"Whoa," he said. "I didn't mean you should strip down right here on the street." He moved to stand between me and any passing car, although there weren't any.

"I wear less than this any day on the beach," I said, looking down at my boxers. It was hard to relate all those parts that I saw—legs, arms, and torso—to my body. I felt disconnected from them. I reached into the truck cab and got my shirt, pants, and shoes. I tried to muster up some dignity as I turned, naked but for socks and boxers, to climb the steps to my apartment. But I stumbled again.

"Let me walk you up the stairs." He put an arm around my shoulders, and I shivered from the contact.

"You gonna tuck me in, too?" I asked.

"Maybe another night." We walked up the steps and I fumbled for my keys. He took them from me and opened the door.

I wanted to kiss him good night. I wanted to touch my skin to his and feel what that was like. But instead I said, "Will you call me tomorrow with whatever you find out?"

He smiled. "It's already tomorrow, bud," he said. "I'll call you later. Get some sleep." He gave me a little pat on the butt that moved me a step further inside, and turned away.

≋

I MUST HAVE MADE IT to the bed under my own power, because that's where I was a couple hours later when I woke up. My mouth was dry and my head was pounding, but my bladder was full. It was almost dawn and after I finished in the bathroom I couldn't go back to sleep. I kept remembering the fire, worrying about the people I knew who had been inside, thinking about how much I had to figure out.

Whenever my head is too full, I go surfing. There's something about the serenity of the water, the discipline of the physical activity, that helps me put everything in perspective. So I pulled on my Speedos, tried to smooth down my unruly hair, and grabbed a board. Everything around me smelled like ashes until I walked outside and caught a fresh, sweet breeze full of seawater, frangipani, and the last, lingering scents of yesterday's coconut tanning lotions.

I love to be outside in those moments just before dawn, when the city streets are quiet, the tall palms dozing under a fading quilt of stars. Even before you can see the sun, the sky begins to lighten, the night's blue-black shading into the palest blue imaginable. When I was a little kid working my coloring books, I used to search for a blue just that shade, composed, it seemed to me, of equal parts of yellow and white. I never got just the right mix; maybe that's why my art career never blossomed beyond kindergarten.

The sun was just peeking over the tops of the Ko'olau Mountains as I reached Kuhio Beach Park and launched my surfboard into the water. There were only a few other surfers around, the hardcore who, like me, had a physical need that drew them out on the waves. I lay flat on my stomach and paddled out past the low breakers, feeling my cheek against the cool fiberglass of my board.

Back on land, the high-rise hotels and the little stores on Kalākaua Avenue were just waking up. In the distance I could see the fading green hills, turning brown in the protracted dry spell. I thought if I could just stay out there, waiting for the perfect wave, I could keep the world and its troubles at bay. I knew that almost as soon as I launched my day it would get away from me—too many calls to make, reports to read, details to organize. I was facing a major investigation alone, without any preparation, already physically debilitated.

I felt a good wave building beneath me, and stood to ride it. At the same time, though, the sun jumped quickly above the mountaintops, as it does in the tropics, and the flash of blinding light stabbed at my retinas. I lost my balance, and went tumbling into the cool water. Almost immediately I jumped up, howling in pain.

I learned to swim before I could walk, and the sea had

always been kind to me, even at its most stern. This blinding pain in my back, though, was new and terrible. I dragged myself and my board out to shallow water and stood, trying to look around over my shoulder. What I saw there disturbed me: a big patch of my skin was raw and red, probably from a burn I'd suffered the night before and not noticed. Not until it came into contact with saltwater, that is.

Reluctantly I splashed out of the surf and carried my board home. I had wanted nothing more than an hour or so of uncomplicated surfing, clearing my head for the work before me, but I was not to be so lucky. Instead I showered quickly and awkwardly tried to lather some sunburn cream on my back, without noticeable effect. I pulled on a pair of light cotton pants and a polo shirt and realized I was starving.

It was barely six-thirty, too early to go into the office. The streets were still empty of tourists, only the occasional hotel employee or store clerk hurrying to work as I walked over to my favorite breakfast place, a buffet restaurant in a hotel right on the water. It was called the Beachside Broiler, and you could sit at tables overlooking the sand, eat your fill of pineapple and papaya, ham and eggs and biscuits and whatever else you wanted. I liked to go there after surfing sometimes, when my body was tired and aching but I still needed to be near the water.

Connie, the elderly hostess who favored sarongs and way too much eye makeup, smiled when she saw me walk in. "Kimo! You hero!" She reached down to the pile of morning newspapers next to the register and held one up to me, the front half from the masthead to the fold. There was a huge picture of me coming out of the fire, Sandra over my back. I guess I must have blushed.

"Hey everybody, Kimo big hero!" she said to the restaurant at large. There were about twenty people there, mostly Midwesterners on package tours, and a few of them looked up with mild interest. "He save lady from big fire last night."

There was some slight applause. "Come on, Connie," I said. She wouldn't take money for my breakfast, just handed me a tray and waved me through. I walked all around both steam tables, loading up on bacon, eggs, and sausages. It was going to be a long day and I wasn't sure I'd get any lunch at all, maybe not even dinner.

When I'd finally piled as much food on my tray as possible I walked over to the long counter that faced the water. I laid the paper down face up and put my tray next to it. Just then one of the Midwestern couples, an elderly pair in matching aloha shirts—blue pineapples against a purple backdrop—came up to me. "You did a good thing, son," the man said. He reached out to shake my hand.

"I knew she was inside," I said. "I didn't think about it."

"We'd be proud to have police officers like you back home," his wife said. "You just hold your head up high and don't listen to anything bad anybody says about you, all right?"

I didn't quite understand what she meant, but I nodded anyway. "I will. Thank you."

"Enjoy your breakfast," the man said, and they left. I was puzzling over his wife's comments when I opened the paper and saw the headline, in big twenty-point type, written just below the fold. GAY COP SAVES WOMAN AT GAY MARRIAGE PARTY, it read.

Oh, god. It was starting again.

Chapter 13

THE LOOK ON HIS FACE

I TOOK A CAB to the garage where I'd parked the night before, ransomed my truck, and was at my desk by seven-thirty, staring at a pile of paperwork. Steve Hart had left me a detailed account of everything he'd done, as well as all the witness interviews collected by the uniforms the night before.

I've never been a big paperwork cop. When I worked on Waikīkī, my partner, Akoni, and I used to alternate filling out the endless forms required by the department. I liked to be out on the street, talking to people, gathering information, making my own judgments. But without a partner, there was nobody to push this mound of paper off on.

Regretfully, I moved Hiroshi Mura's murder to my pile of unsolved cases, and buried myself in paperwork regarding the bombing, reading endless variations on how no one saw anything or heard anything. I looked up around nine only to see Lieutenant Sampson coming my way. "Have you seen the circus outside?" he asked.

I shook my head. "I got here pretty early."

"The pressure is already building, Kimo. What have you got so far?"

I looked at him. It was barely 9 o'clock in the morning. What did he expect me to have, the bomber on a silver platter? I told him about walking the fire with Mike Riccardi, the cooperation with ATF, the ideas we had on the bomb and the amateur nature of the crime. I told him there was nothing much in the witness statements but I would continue to go through them.

"One thing, I'm wondering if this is tied to the arsons lately. I'm going to get with the arson guy again, see if he's found any connections. A couple of the places that burned were gay businesses, so they could have been done by the same people."

"Solve this one, Kimo," he said as he walked away. "Solve this one fast, or it's both our asses on the line."

"Yes, sir," I muttered. I called for one of the department sketch artists, and a little later a guy came up to my desk so I could try to recreate the sweaty guy's face. I didn't do a very good job of it; after all, I'd only seen the guy in passing, and it was just because he seemed familiar that I had paid any attention at all.

The morning crawled by. I left a message for Mike Riccardi, asking if he thought the bombing was related to the other gay arsons. I read eyewitness reports in between reviewing the artist's sketch, dodging calls from the press, and searching for past crimes that might be similar. By noon I was antsy to get away from my desk, to feel like I was actually doing something. I decided to walk over to The Queen's Medical Center, check on my dad, and see if anybody there could help me.

At the front desk I found out that Robert and Gunter were sharing a room, down the hall from Sandra Guarino. The clerk gave me a knowing look, and I remembered what it had been like before, when it seemed everybody in Honolulu was looking at me, puzzling over the details of my private life.

Robert was asleep in the bed by the window when I walked into the room, but Gunter was awake. He looked funny against the white sheets, his dark blond hair so short it was barely there. The stubble on his chin was the same color, and almost as long. I remembered that I still had his bow tie, and I told him. "You can keep it for a while," he said. "Though I'll have to teach you how to tie it."

"You'll have to do that." I sat on the side of his bed. "How are you doing?"

He shrugged. "Not too bad. I've got some second-degree burns on my arms and legs." He coughed. "Some smoke inhalation, too, they said. But I'll probably get out of here today."

"You have somebody to stay with you at home?"

He smiled. "Baby, I've always got somebody to stay with me."

"So you know what happened, right? Somebody planted a bomb in the men's room."

"I read the morning paper, Mr. Hero. I notice that even though I carried Robert over there out of the fire, I didn't get my picture on the front page."

"Believe me, I wish it had been you rather than me. Did you see anything suspicious, any time during the party? Anybody who looked like they didn't belong?"

"You mean somebody who might have planted a bomb?" He paused. "Well, there was this one guy I remember." I must have smiled, because he said, "Don't look like that. I remember guys for more than one reason. I mean, one reason the most, but I can think about things besides sex." I grinned even more and he said, "If you don't want to hear this you can just go on back to your police station."

"I want to hear it, Gunter. I'll be serious."

"Yeah, right. Just before the speaker started, I helped Robert carry some plants in from the lanai, and I needed to wash my hands. I went into the restroom, and when I came out, there was a line, a couple of people wanting to get things taken care of before they sat down."

He coughed a little, and I felt like a jackass pressuring him to remember and talk when he was in the hospital. But there was no way around it. Once he'd gotten his breath back, he continued.

"There was this guy at the very end of the line," Gunter said. "He was all sweaty, his hair plastered down over his head, looking like he was going to be sick. But when Charlie Stahl tried to get behind him, the guy insisted that Stahl go first."

He took a little sip of water. "That was when I got a good look at his face. I see it sometimes on guys at the Rod and Reel Club. You, maybe, that first night I saw you. This look that says you want so much to be a part of what's going on but you're dead scared."

"So you're saying this guy was gay."

"I don't know for certain. Curious, absolutely. But you know how these bi guys are. They're on a seesaw; one day it's boys, one day it's girls, up and down, up and down. Never make up their mind."

"Was that the guy we bumped into when we were going out to the lanai? Do you think you'd recognize him if you saw him again?"

He frowned. "That was the guy. But I'm not sure I'd recognize him again. The look, I'd recognize the look again. I could give you a general description of him. I can tell you one thing—I'd bet you a blow job he was wearing a rented tuxedo."

"That's a bet you can't lose, either way. What makes you think so?"

"Darling, I know how clothes are supposed to fit. If he owned that tux then the store that sold it to him ought to be fire-bombed." He suddenly realized what he had said. "Oh, well, that's an expression I'm going to have to retire."

"I'll send over a police artist this afternoon. We'll see if your sketch matches mine."

Gunter sank back against the pillows and feigned great illness. "I suppose I can rise from my sickbed to help the police with their inquiries." Then he sat up and looked at me slyly. "This artist you're going to send. Is he cute?"

"He's fifty years old, with a pot belly," I said, smiling. "I'll let you decide if he's cute or not."

He flopped back against the pillows. "Oh, you."

I was about to move over to speak with Robert when Harry came in. He looked ready to speak, and then he yawned instead. "Sorry," he said, shaking his head. "We didn't get much sleep last night. They wanted to keep Brandon overnight for observation, and Arleen wanted to stay with him. So of course I stayed, too."

I noticed that Gunter had dozed off, so I motioned Harry over to Robert's side of the room and we pulled the two chairs together so we could talk quietly. Robert was still sleeping, too, his breathing steady but raspy. He had bandages around both arms and legs, as well as on his face.

"How's Brandon doing?"

Harry yawned again and settled back against the plastic cushions. "Arleen's mom came down and they took him home a little while ago. I said I'd come up and check on Robert and then head home for some sleep." He looked closely at me. "You look like shit, brah. You get any sleep last night?"

I yawned. "Now you've got me doing it. Yeah, I got a couple of hours. Tried to surf in the morning but I got a burn on my back and it hurt like a bastard."

"Idiot." He started to smile but it stretched into a yawn again. "You know anything about what happened yet?"

"A little." I told him about walking the fire with Mike Riccardi, about the witness statements and press phone calls. "I was hoping Robert would be awake so I could ask him some questions."

"Slow down," Harry said. "Tell me about this fireman again."

I must have blushed because he said, "Aha! I knew it. You dog, you. You've got the hots for the fireman!"

"Har—ree." I shrugged. "So I think he's cute. I don't know if anything's going to happen. I've got to figure out this case."

"Can I do anything to help?" He yawned again. "That is, after I get a little sleep?"

"You could. I need to find out as much as I can about the groups that are opposing the gay marriage suit, and I don't see myself having much time for research. Can you do some of that for me?"

"I'll bet there's a lot of stuff on the Internet," Harry said. "I can narrow down the materials for you."

"That'd be great."

We heard a groan from the bed and turned to Robert. He was just waking up. He tried to talk, but started coughing. Harry jumped up and gave him the oxygen mask and said, "Here, try this."

Robert took a couple of deep breaths and then put the mask down. "Hey, Kimo," he said weakly.

"Hey, Mr. Hero," I said. "I couldn't believe it when I saw you running into that building last night. I was like, hey, isn't he going the wrong way?"

Robert smiled. "I didn't do much, not rescue any babies or women or anything."

Harry said, "He did a hell of a lot. He managed to save all the membership lists, all the legal research on precedents, all the testimonials they had from supporters. Years' worth of work that would have burned up otherwise."

"And then Gunter had to come and pull me out." Robert tried to sit up and look around the curtain but he was too weak. "How's he doing?"

"He looks great," I said. "And his personality came through undamaged."

Robert smiled. "Good. I like his personality."

"I've got a couple questions to ask you, buddy," I said, pulling my chair up close to the bed. "We think somebody planted a bomb in the restroom. Did you see anybody suspicious last night?"

He tried to shake his head, but grimaced. "No. I was too busy making sure everything was organized to pay attention."

"Gunter saw a sweaty, nervous-looking guy waiting for the bathroom, and then he and I saw him come out of there. Did you notice him?"

He frowned. "I don't think so. I just don't remember."

I patted his arm, one of the few places that wasn't wrapped in gauze. "That's OK. Listen, you gotta get yourself better, all right? You know that place can't function without you."

"There isn't a place anymore."

"There will be. You and Sandra are gonna get out of here and start things up again. After all, you saved those records. You gotta do something with them, right?"

"I guess." He smiled, and then dozed off again.

When I looked up, Harry was napping in the easy chair by the window, and Gunter was still asleep, too. I looked back from the doorway at the three of them, the sterile light-green walls, and the array of monitoring equipment. I was going to get the bastards who did this.

Chapter 14

FIGHTING BACK

SANDRA GUARINO WAS IN a private room on the same floor. When I looked inside, the first thing I saw was a big red floral arrangement sent by her law firm. Sandra was lying very still in the bed, IV tubes in her arms and the mask of a respirator over her face. Then I saw Cathy Selkirk sitting by the window, her tiny frame dwarfed by the oversized chair. She had her knees pulled up to her and was staring out at the highway beyond.

"Hey. How's Sandra?"

"Kimo." Cathy got up and came over to me. Her head barely reached my breastbone. I held on to her as she started to cry. I felt my own tears welling up, but I pushed them back down.

I let her cry for a minute or two and then pulled back. "Come on, everything's going to work out." I sat on the window ledge. "Tell me about Sandra."

"She hasn't recovered consciousness yet." She pulled a linen handkerchief from the pocket of her dress and I realized she was still wearing what she had worn to the party. She dried her eyes. "The doctors don't know what to expect. They notified her parents and they're flying in this afternoon from Oregon."

"That's good, right? You'll have somebody here with you."

"They never approved of me and Sandy. I'm afraid, Kimo. I'm afraid Sandy won't wake up. I'm afraid her parents will come and they won't let me see her. That they'll—make decisions—that aren't—what she'd want."

"You don't have a power of attorney, or medical authorizations or anything like that?"

"I have it all. You know how Sandy is—everything's organized. But that doesn't mean they'll pay attention to it. I'm not strong like she is. I can't stand up to her parents, the doctors—it's too hard." She sat in the big chair again, and she was so tiny that she looked like a small child. "It's kind of ironic, isn't it? If we were able to get married then I wouldn't have a lot of these problems."

"I've got an idea." I reached for the phone and called my brother's office. After a couple of minutes on hold, listening to the weather guy's prerecorded voice promising sunshine and breezes, Lui came on. "Hey, brah. I've got a story for you." I ran down Cathy's situation for him. "It's got a hook for you, tied into the bombing last night. You can keep running all that footage. You guys love all those explosions and fires and shit, don't you?"

"Thanks for your high opinion of my job," my brother said. "Let me talk to Cathy."

They spoke for a couple of minutes and then she handed the phone back to me. "How's Dad?" Lui asked.

"I haven't gotten there yet. He's next on my list."

"Jeez, and they say I'm the son that doesn't care. You're in the goddamned hospital and you don't even go to see him."

"I'm getting there, I'm getting there."

"Call me and let me know what you think." He hung up and I turned back to Cathy.

"He's going to send a crew to interview me," she said. "I

hate the thought of having our private lives on television, though."

"Tell me about it." I reached over and took her hand. "It's what Sandra would do, though, isn't it? Fight back?"

She smiled. "Yeah, I guess it is."

I leaned back against the window and told Cathy what I had discovered so far. "Did you see anybody suspicious? Any sweaty-looking guy going into or coming out of the men's room?"

She shook her head. "I was way too busy talking to people. You know how that goes. Sandy and I were trying to chat up the donors, make sure everybody was having a good time."

Cathy smiled, and I looked at my watch. I'd been away from my desk for almost an hour, and I still had to see my father. "I've gotta go, sweetie. You have anybody to come stay with you?"

"Maria Luisa, Sandy's secretary, she's going to come over and sit with me for a while this afternoon, once she gets Sandy's calendar cleared. The doctors are going to come back later for some more tests."

I scribbled the number of my cell phone on a piece of paper. "You need anything, you call me." I handed her the number and then took her hand. "You know Sandra's a fighter. She's not going to let this get her down. You've just got to hold on, OK?"

It was good advice for all of us, I thought.

My father's room was one floor up, and I climbed the stairs figuring I'd pop in, say my hellos, make sure nobody in the family had seen anything, and get back to work. But I couldn't find his room number, and had to ask an orderly. "That's in Intensive Care," he said. "Through those double doors."

As soon as I walked in I saw my mother and Aunt Mei-Mei,

sitting together holding hands behind the glass wall of my father's room. He was in an elevated bed, surrounded by high-tech monitoring equipment. I stopped outside the room and stared.

My father had been kind of a mythical figure to us as kids. At six feet, he seemed like a giant, with broad shoulders and strong hands scarred from years of hanging drywall, laying roofing tiles, digging ditches—whatever he had to do to get his buildings finished. He had a temper as strong as the sea on a blustery day, and yet I remember when I broke my arm surfing when I was eight how gently he'd carried me from the ocean to the car, and then into the hospital emergency room.

Now the tables were turned and I was healthy (well, reasonably) and he was sick. I couldn't get over how frail he looked in the loose hospital gown. When had he lost so much weight? How come my brothers and I hadn't noticed?

My mother saw me in the doorway and got up. I hugged her and hoped she wouldn't notice me wince when her hands touched my back. I smiled over her head at Aunt Mei-Mei. "I'm so glad you're here, Kimo," my mother said. "Haoa was here this morning, but he had to go out and look at a job. Tatiana and Liliha just went for some lunch."

"How is he?"

Her eyes were bright with tears but she made no move to wipe them away. "They're doing tests. All kinds of tests. He was coughing so bad from the smoke when they brought him in, and they put him on this machine, it said his heartbeat was irregular, so they wanted to monitor him." She looked over to him. "At least he's sleeping now. He's not very happy to be here."

As if on cue, Dad woke up and looked around. When my

mother and I walked into the room, he said, "Goddamn it, am I still here? When are they going to let me out?"

"Hey, Dad." I walked over to him. "Howzit?"

"I'd be doing a lot better if they let me out of here. Hospitals are terrible places. People die in them all the time."

"You know why they have fences on cemeteries, don't you, Dad? Because people are dying to get in."

"This is no time for jokes. Maybe now that you're here your mother will listen to reason. Lokelani! Kimo agrees with me. I should go home."

"I don't agree with you at all," I said. "You belong right here in bed, where the doctors can keep an eye on you."

"Useless! You're all useless. I raise three boys and I can't get one of them to stand up for me."

"Well, he certainly doesn't act sick," I said to my mother. She and Aunt Mei-Mei exchanged grins. I sat on the edge of the bed next to my father. "Now Dad, you know we have to figure out what's wrong with you."

"There's nothing wrong with me except an ungrateful family."

"Yeah, and that's what makes those squiggles on the heart monitor. You might as well face facts, pal: you're not getting out of here until the doctors say you can, and until that nice lady over there in the chair agrees to let you back into her house. You got that?"

He stared at me, and I stared back. I won, of course. I mean, I've been to the police academy, after all. If I couldn't outstare one sick old man, even if he was my father, then they ought to take away my badge. "Maybe another day," my father said. "But tomorrow, I want to go home!"

"We'll see. Now, if you don't mind, I've got a job I have to do." I told them all about the progress of the investigation so far, and asked if they had seen anything suspicious.

"I was too busy watching what your father ate," my mother said. "And your father, he was too busy eating."

"Dad?"

"I don't know that woman. I don't know what she's doing here."

I had to laugh, and he didn't appreciate it. "Can you imagine? This is what I do all day. Interview cranky witnesses."

My mother smiled. My father said, "I always wondered what it was you did."

"Dad."

"I didn't see anybody suspicious. Between your mother and your brothers, nobody let me alone for a minute."

I sighed. "So, Aunt Mei-Mei, how's Uncle Chin? Is he as disagreeable as this one here?"

"Uncle Chin a little better," she said. "Jimmy with him. Make him smile."

"That's good." I looked down the hallway and saw my sisters-in-law approaching. "Hey, here come Tatiana and Liliha." I felt this funny pang then, seeing my brothers' wives. Lui and Haoa couldn't be here with my father, but they had wives who could. Partners in the world, who would stand by them and their families, helping out when things got tough. I wondered if I would ever have that. Somebody to be there for me, to hold me when the big storms came.

Chapter 15

FAMILY HAPPINESS

I WALKED OUT into the hallway to intercept them. I knew otherwise it would take forever for the room to settle down so I could ask my questions. Tatiana kissed me on the cheek, her long, ash-blonde hair rustling, and said, "Let me give this magazine to your mother and I'll come right back out."

When she'd gone in the room, Liliha said, "Well, you're finally here."

"Excuse me?"

She was wearing a crisp suit that I was sure was by some famous fashion designer, the kind of solid-color thing with brass buttons and epaulets that Nancy Reagan used to wear. Her black hair was perfectly coiffed and her makeup immaculate. It was hard to remember that when Lui first brought her to meet us she only owned one nice dress and lived with her family in a trailer on Hawai'ian homestead land on the east side of O'ahu.

"It's all your fault that your father is here in the hospital, and you didn't even come to see him last night. And here it is almost 1 o'clock before you're here today. Tatiana and I have been here since early this morning."

I was flabbergasted. "I was investigating. That's what I do, remember? I'm trying to figure out what happened."

"I can tell you what happened. You were indulging yourself

in this perverted homosexual marriage business and you dragged all of us into it. You know what you're doing is wrong but you just won't face up to it. And now see where it's gotten you. Your father is in the hospital because of you."

"How dare you say that, Lily?" Tatiana said, coming out of my father's room. "Al is in the hospital because he's sick, and you know damn well Howie and Lui and Kimo have been trying to get him to the doctor. This is not anybody's fault. Shame on you for saying that!"

"You always defend him!" Liliha said. "You and your silly hairdresser friend. It's sick and perverted, and this is God's punishment on all of us for tolerating it."

I finally found my voice. "Liliha, when you married my brother I took you in like a sister, and I've loved you and put up with your eccentricities and your temper for fifteen years. Because my brother loves you, I love you. I always assumed it was the same for you. That because you loved Lui, you loved me—and Haoa and Tatiana and Mom and Dad, all of us. Isn't that what your religion teaches you, love thy neighbor?"

"Obviously not when your neighbor is gay," Tatiana said.

"I don't have to take this kind of abuse. I'll come back later when things aren't so upset." Liliha turned and walked out of the intensive care unit, leaving the double doors swinging in her wake.

Tatiana looked into my father's room and saw my mother and Aunt Mei-Mei watching Liliha leave, and she led me over to a bench out of earshot. A big-boned woman, she was a cross between a suburban mother and an unreformed hippie, Reeboks and jeans with a tie-dyed blouse and a necklace of big, clunky stones. Her hair, which had been piled up the night before in a fancy 'do created by her hairdresser friend Robertico Robles, now cascaded around her shoulders.

"Lily's just upset," she said. "You know how she is. She feels everything Lui does, and if he feels bad about Dad being in the hospital, he just transfers that to her."

I remembered seeing Lui and Liliha at the Church of Adam and Eve, and I was pretty sure her feelings went deeper than Tatiana wanted to allow. "I never knew she resented me so much."

"Lui keeps her on a pretty tight string. I know she's mad that Howie lets me get away with a lot. She's just jealous. You and I are both a lot freer than she'll ever be."

"I don't feel free most of the time. Sometimes I wish all I had to do in life was get dressed up and talk to the servants once in a while." Lui and Liliha had a maid, a gardener, and a nanny for the kids; sometimes Tatiana and I got together and wondered what Liliha did all day, besides her nails and makeup. I was beginning to get a better idea.

"Makeup can be hell," Tatiana said, deadpan, and we both laughed. I filled her in on my investigation, and asked if she'd seen anything out of the ordinary. "Well, there was nobody there in leather, which I kind of expected," she said. "I mean, everybody was so tame. I wanted to see wild outfits, men kissing each other in fits of passion. I wanted Lily to be outraged. I wanted some guy to come up and pinch Howie's butt."

"Pity the poor guy who does that." I told her about the sweaty guy Gunter and I had seen. "Did you see anybody who looked like that?"

"As a matter of fact, I did. Your friend Gunter and that nice boy Robert were bringing plants in from the lanai, and I was helping them put them in the right places. When they finished, I was waiting for Howie to bring me a drink from the bar, and this guy who was sweating like crazy got in line for the bathroom. He was so polite—this older man got on line behind him, and even though the guy was sweating and obviously in some kind of distress, he insisted that the older man go first. I thought that was so polite, and that maybe he wasn't sick, that he'd just moved here, hadn't gotten accustomed to the climate yet. Believe me, I know what that's like."

Tatiana had grown up in Alaska, and had met my brother while she was bumming around the islands waitressing and sketching portraits on the beach. Theirs was a true love match, and though sometimes awesome fireworks erupted between them, I had often seen the kind of magnetic attraction that kept them near each other at parties, or even just hanging around their house. When Tatiana was anywhere in the vicinity, my grip on my brother's attention was limited.

As long as Tatiana was around, he was OK. And he could be totally with you if she was in a different place, miles away. But if she was in the house or at a party with him, it made him nervous to be out of her sight. He was happiest of all when he was working out in their yard, planting something, weeding, trimming, watering, and she was nearby, reading a book under an umbrella or playing in the pool with the kids. He was grounded by the land and by his love for his wife.

"Would you recognize the sweaty guy if you saw him again?"

"Sure. You know I have a memory for faces. I can sketch him if you want."

"That would be terrific. I sat with the artist this morning, and I'm sending him over to work with Gunter. After he's done I'll have him come up here and compare notes with you."

"I think Aunt Mei-Mei will want to go home soon, so I'll take her and while I'm out I'll stop by the house and get some stuff to draw with."

"How is Uncle Chin, do you think?"

She shrugged. "I think when you get to be that sick you take the small pleasures you can. He seems to like that boy you brought over. Aunt Mei-Mei says his spirits are a lot better."

I looked at my watch. "I'd better say my good-byes. God knows what kind of chaos is going on back at the station."

Tatiana took my hand. "You know we all love you, don't you, Kimo? I don't want you to go thinking that Lily speaks for any of the rest of us."

I kissed her cheek. "You're the best. Like you said, she was just upset." I resolved, though, to move the Church of Adam and Eve up on my list to investigate. If they could make Liliha feel so strongly against gay marriage, what else could they do?

Chapter 16

BETWEEN BROTHERS

BACK AT THE STATION there was a message from Mike Riccardi, which I returned immediately. He'd left three numbers, and I finally reached him on his cell. "Where are you?" I asked. "This connection is terrible."

"I'm on the H3, heading back into town. I wanted to clear my plate so I could go full bore on your fire. I'm thinking it might be connected to three other arsons I've been investigating. The golf ball thing connects them, and the fact that these three places were all gay-owned or serving the gay community. I'll know more when I get the full results back from the lab. Have you got any news?"

"I've gone through all the witness statements the uniforms collected last night, and there's nothing there. But I went over to Queen's today at lunch and talked to some of the people who were hospitalized."

"Lunch? What's that?"

"Don't worry, I didn't eat either." I figured if I concentrated enough on work I'd forget I was hungry. I told him about the artist—my sketch, Gunter's, and Tatiana's.

"These guys are amateurs, I can feel it," he said. "I'm heading in to the lab now, to see if they can connect that golf ball fragment you found to some of the other arsons. I spoke to the ATF guys, and because they think this is an arson, rather than a bombing, they're going to back off and leave things up to us. The FBI's going to hold off, too."

"I'm not sure if that's good or bad. We won't have anybody to blame but ourselves."

"That's the way I like it. I had a couple of guys combing the place this morning, too, and I think we might have a few more clues."

"I want to know what you've got," I said. "Can we meet?"

"I'm not gonna get out of the lab until dinner time, at the earliest. You want to get something to eat around seven? You show me yours, I'll show you mine."

"I can do that."

He suggested an Italian place on Kuhio Avenue and we agreed to meet there. "I'm half Italian, half Korean, you know. It's either pasta or kimchee."

"I'll take the pasta."

Mike swore at a driver who'd gotten in his way, then came back to me. "I'm getting tapes of all the news coverage. You never know who's lurking around in the background of those shots. You got a VCR?"

"Yup."

"Good. I'll bring the tapes. After dinner we can go over to your place and look at them."

I hung up the phone, wondering for a moment or two what Mike Riccardi's story was. I mean, he'd all but asked me out on a date and was already planning to go home with me. That is, if I was right and he was gay, and he was interested in me. Of course there was always the chance that he was busy until dinner, and it was a good use of both our time to eat together as we compared notes. And when we were so close to my apartment, why go back to the fire station or police headquarters to watch the tape?

Right. I gave up speculating and got back to work. I spent the afternoon wading through reports. I arranged for the police artist to go over and meet with Gunter, I sent the paper bag that Robert had given me down to be checked for fingerprints, and I asked the vice mayor's office for a list of the people who had joined his protest outside the building.

His secretary, who sniffled on and off during our conversation, said that because Shira had organized the march himself, the office didn't have any records. I figured that was a code for "Most of the people there were homeless folks hired for the night."

I wrote a memo to all the beat officers and other detectives in all the districts on O'ahu, asking if they'd seen anyone acting suspicious that afternoon or evening, particularly any men in tuxedos sweating heavily.

Lieutenant Sampson said that I could pull one of the beat cops to help with running down leads, and I chose Lidia Portuondo. I had her canvass the neighborhood around the Marriage Project building, hoping someone might report some suspicious activity. I was also looking for witnesses who could tell me more about who'd tossed the manure. I was sure it had to be tied to the bombing.

It might all lead to another heap of useless paperwork, but it had to be done. I also fielded a dozen more calls from the press, including one from my oldest brother.

Usually Lui has his secretary call me, and then he leaves me holding on the phone for a minute or two, reminding me that he is first boy, after all. But that afternoon he called direct. I wondered if he had spoken with Liliha, but even if he had I doubt she would have told him about her outburst. My brother is the most Japanese of the three of us, the most reserved with his feelings. Sometimes I think he was born in a business suit, a little tiny tie hanging around his chubby neck.

"Did you see our coverage of the fire last night?"

"Not yet. I got a guy with the tape; we're watching it later."

"Good story. I made sure they played up the gay marriage side of things. And we're leading with your friend Cathy on the 5 o'clock. We'll see what the reporter does with the story, and if it looks good we'll run it again on the six and the eleven."

"I appreciate it."

"Enough to keep me in the loop when you've got any new leads?"

"You know the drill, Lui. All information is supposed to get funneled through public affairs. That way all the media gets equal access."

"I understand your position. I'm not asking you to shut anybody else out. I'm just saying that if you know something, and you call me first, we'll be able to put together the kind of story you want to see. We're trying to do serious journalism, to give our coverage a little dignity."

I started laughing. "Dignity? Are you sure you're talking about KVOL, Erupting News all the Time? Aren't you the station that shows the clip of those people on the Big Island running away from that lava flow?"

"You want me to say it? You want to make me say it? All right, I will. I deliberately skewed our coverage of the fire to make us sympathetic to the whole gay marriage deal. And you know why? Because I've got this brother that's gay, and I want him to be happy. If he wants to get married to some other guy, I want him to be able to. And I'm going to use the power that I have here at the station to do that. Now are you going to help me or not?"

"Go ahead, make me feel like shit," I said, and I was almost certain I had made him laugh. "Geez, how'd you get so good at making people feel guilty? You must have been listening to Mom all those years."

"I've got three kids. It comes with the territory. So tell me, you in or you out?"

"Seems like the whole island knows I'm out, Lui." I thought about it for a minute. "In the first place, I shouldn't be talking to you at all. Everything you get ought to come from the public information office. And we shouldn't release any information to you that we don't release to the rest of the media. But what I think I can do is give you some direction for your peripheral coverage."

"Like pointing us toward Cathy Selkirk."

"Exactly."

"So where do we look for a lead for tomorrow's news?"

"You know what I think is an interesting angle on this case? The fact that out of all the people at the party, the only one who died was somebody who was on the same side as the bomber. There's irony there."

"A story on Wilson Shira, you mean. What was he doing there, and so on. Maybe there's something in his past that made him so opposed to this idea. You gotta wonder what makes somebody come out and protest a thing like this." He paused, and I could almost hear the wheels whirring in his head.

"Off the record, you might want to talk to some of the people at Homeless Solutions," I said. "A little bird told me that yesterday somebody was going around there, offering to pay homeless people to join the protest."

"I'll get somebody on it. Hey, you ever consider the possibility that Shira was some kind of suicide bomber?" Lui asked. "Maybe he carried the bomb on his body! Maybe he carried it in there himself, planning to plant it, and it blew up before he could get out?"

"The facts don't exactly support that theory, but, hey, you've made KVOL's reputation on that kind of sensationalism, haven't you?"

"Don't get snotty. Remember, you're still the kid brother."

I shook my head as I hung up the phone.

Chapter 17

PASTA PUTTANESCA

IT WAS ALMOST SIX FORTY-FIVE by the time I dragged my sorry, exhausted, and starving butt out of headquarters for the drive to Waikīkī. Not even the prospect of seeing Mike Riccardi could generate much enthusiasm. I'd hoped to get home for a quick nap, a shower, maybe the chance to pretty myself up. No such luck; he'd have to take me battered and disheveled. And to top it off, every time I sat back I felt my shirt rubbing against the raw burn on my back. I was definitely not in a dating mood.

I'd never been to the restaurant he had suggested, a small storefront on Kuhio Avenue a half dozen blocks from my apartment. It was set between the lobby of a cheap hotel for vacationing Japanese and a laundromat, where a bunch of German teenagers hung around their washing like sharks circling an unknowing surfer.

Mike was already there when I arrived, sitting at a table in the back, drinking Chianti and bantering with a waiter. "Man, you look like shit," he said in lieu of a greeting.

"I don't think I know you well enough for such honesty," I said. He looked terrific, of course; he had to have gone home and changed clothes. I didn't know anybody who could keep pressed shirts so crisp after a day in the tropical sun.

"Come on, sit down. Want some wine?"

"Sure." As he poured me a glass, the waiter brought us an antipasto platter, the greens glistening with olive oil, vegetables and cheeses all arranged carefully on a decorated plate.

"I ordered for both of us. I hope you don't mind. They've got a terrific pasta puttanesca here"—he held up his thumb and two forefingers together in a gesture I'd only seen on television, then kissed his fingertips—"you're gonna love it."

This was sounding more and more like a date to me, and frankly I just didn't have the patience for it. I mean, he was a gorgeous, hunky guy, sexy and charming, but all I wanted to do was get his information, watch the video tape, and then go to bed. Alone. I was afraid I might nod off before the pasta arrived.

"Let me tell you what I found out today," I said. Before I left the station I'd printed out all my notes. As I started going through them, I noticed he'd pulled out the battered steno pad I'd seen him with the night before. Every now and then he stopped me for a question or two, making his own record.

When I was finished, he said, "You've been busy."

"It makes the day pass." The waiter cleared away our antipasto plates and refilled our wine glasses. "So, your turn now. What did you do today?"

"Like I told you on the phone, I went up to Central O'ahu to look over an arson—a pair of lesbians with a few acres of pineapple. Somebody torched their storage shed a couple of days ago, and at first I thought it was just kids, because it was so amateur."

He sipped his Chianti. "But when I looked at it again, I saw a lot of connections to the bombing. Looks like the lesbians might have been a trial run for your guy."

I shook my head. "We've got to stop these guys, Mike."

"I know. While I was up there, I had guys go over the site

again, and they found a couple of interesting things. Like a piece of pipe, for instance."

"Pipe like you smoke?"

He shook his head. "Pipe like you put a bomb into. These guys are definitely amateurs. The fragment we found was only about three inches square, pretty standard hardware store issue. But it looks like we're going to get a partial print off it. They were too dumb to use gloves—they must have figured all the evidence was going to blow up."

"There's something I don't get. If they're such amateurs, how do they know how to make a bomb in the first place? I couldn't do it."

"Sure you could. You've got a brain, right? And you know how to work a computer?"

"Pretty much." The waiter brought a big tray of pasta, family style, and two plates. He prepared to dish it out, but Mike waved him away and started the work himself.

"So you get on the Internet," he continued, as he heaped the creamy white pasta onto the plates. "And you do a search for 'bombs.' That brings up hundreds of hits. You start surfing around, you read, you go from link to link, and pretty soon you know almost as much about explosives as the fire department does."

"I'd always heard about that, but I figured it was one of those urban folk tales—you know, some teenaged kid builds an atom bomb for his high school science project, and all he needs is the plutonium to make it work." I paused to drink some more wine. "Can you give me a list of everything you think they might need? I can get some uniforms out canvassing stores, see if we can trace any of the items."

"Everything they used was pretty common, but I'll put a list together. Who knows, you might get lucky."

I was sure that was his leg brushing against mine under the table. We locked eyes and smiled. Mike kept looking at me as he twirled a forkful of pasta, lifted it to his mouth, and tasted. An expression somewhat akin to ecstasy passed over his face. "This is fabulous. Go on, taste it. Tell me what you think."

I tasted. It was pretty terrific. The wine was good, too, and though the place had filled up, our table was partially sheltered by a metal trellis with fake grape leaves twining around it. I was feeling more relaxed. Maybe this could turn out to be a date.

"I'd say this is just like my mother used to make, but my mom's Korean," Mike said. "And my nonna, my Italian grandmother, lives on Long Island, and once we moved here when I was a kid, I only saw her and the rest of the relatives once a year."

"Your folks meet during the Korean War?" I asked.

Mike nodded. "If you believe them, it was love at first sight. My dad had taken some shrapnel, and my mom was a nurse. He came out of the anesthesia, and hers was the first face he saw."

He smiled, and our eyes locked. I remembered the first time I'd seen him, at police headquarters. Would that be our story someday—our eyes meeting over a dead chicken?

"They moved back to New York after the war, and my mom worked as a nurse while my dad went to medical school. My mom hated it out east, though. She didn't fit in, and she wanted to go back to Seoul. So they compromised on Hawai'i, and we moved here when I was eight. They both work out at Tripler."

"So how come you don't have a stethoscope around your neck?"

"Teenaged rebellion? Plus I hated science at the time. Kind

of ironic that so much of what I do now revolves around science."

"You go to school for this stuff?" I asked. "The arson investigation?"

"Took a few courses. Spent a lot of time online."

I was about to respond when he continued. "The Internet is an amazing thing. I'm still exploring a lot of it myself. I mean, it seems like anything you're into, there's something out there. You want to make a bomb, or find out who won the World Series in 1986, or try out some cool new software, all you have to do is point and click." He looked at me appraisingly. "You must have seen how much gay material is out there. Chat rooms and pictures and stories and all."

It was finally on the table, the *g* word. I tried to phrase what I wanted to say carefully. "You do much of that? Hanging out online, I mean."

Our eyes met across the table. I could fall in love with those eyes. Clear, light green, steadily focused on me. "I'm working on it. Finally broke down and bought a laptop, got my own account at home a couple of months ago."

"What's your screen name?" I'd been online with Harry a few times, as he was trying to drag me into the digital generation, and I knew his name was PhysWiz, referring to his Ph.D. in physics from MIT.

Mike blushed.

"Go on, you can tell me."

"Toohot." He paused. "You know, from too hot to handle."

"Oh, baby," I said. We locked eyes again.

Time to get back to business. "So, OK, we've got at least one amateur bomb maker with Internet access," I said. "He may or may not be the sweaty guy who Gunter and my sister-in-law and I all saw around the bathroom. What else do we know?"

We didn't know much more, though we had a seemingly endless supply of questions. Mike believed that the bomb could have been built in anybody's kitchen, without requiring much in the way of special supplies. It wasn't a particularly expensive proposition, either. I laid out for him my plans to research the groups that had opposed the gay marriage lawsuit, and how I had recruited Harry and Lui's station to help. "I managed to catch the five and six o'clock news from the station," I said. "KVOL did a nice piece on Sandra and Cathy. Maybe tomorrow they'll come up with some leads."

By the time we finished off the pasta I was way too stuffed for dessert, but the waiter brought us complimentary little glasses of grappa, a strong Italian brandy. Mike downed his in one shot, so of course I had to do the same.

But I was without the benefit of his Italian ancestry, or his undoubted years of drinking the stuff. Man, did it burn going down! I started coughing and choking, and he laughed. I wondered if this was what dating him would be like, the two of us constantly struggling to get the upper hand.

Somehow that didn't seem too unpleasant.

Chapter 18

SECRETS

MIKE INSISTED ON paying the bill. "The fire department can get this one, and the police department can get the next one, all right?" I doubted he'd actually expense the meal. Though we'd talked about the case, I couldn't see him explaining to his chief that he'd had dinner at a romantic Italian restaurant with the only gay cop on the Honolulu police force—or at least the only openly gay one.

My apartment was a half-dozen blocks away, but we drove over in his truck. "The tapes are right behind the seat," he said, as he began to parallel park in front of my building.

I twisted around to get them and felt waves of pain surging through my back. "Shit." I thought that I whispered, but he heard.

"What's the matter?"

"I've got a little burn on my back. I tried to go surfing this morning and ever since, I get these wicked twinges."

He slotted the truck neatly in place. "I've got some cream you can use. It's one of the necessities of life as a firefighter."

He got the cream from the case in the truck bed, and we climbed the stairs to my apartment. "And you complain about the way my truck looks," he said as we walked in.

I had to admit the place looked pretty bad, even by my standards. It was just one big room, with a kitchenette, though

I had this Japanese-style screen I built from broken-down surfboards that separated the bedroom area from the rest of the room. I usually threw dirty clothes onto it. I hadn't made the bed in the morning, nor had I gone through one of my weekly binges where I put all the sports equipment away neatly. There were piles of books on the floor and a messy stack of newspapers by the front door, waiting for recycling. At least the kitchen was pretty clean; I tried never to go to sleep with dirty dishes in the sink.

He walked over to look at my garbage can. "No fast food wrappers," he said. "That's a good sign."

A good sign of what, I wanted to ask. I was losing my patience again, feeling tired. Oh, I still wanted to get into his pants, and I was getting increasingly confident that he wanted to get into mine as well. But it didn't have to be that night.

I flipped on the TV and the VCR and slotted the first tape into the drive. He sat on my sofa with a proprietorial air and I decided it was time to shift the balance of power a little. "How do you tell when a fireman is dead?" I asked.

He looked at me. "The remote control slips from his hand," he said. "That's the oldest joke in the book."

"Sometimes the old ones are still funny," I said. As the first news credits started to roll, I sat down next to him. Close, so that our thighs were barely touching. He didn't say anything, but he didn't move away either.

We watched all four tapes carefully, pausing and rewinding, but we didn't see anybody who looked too interested. The KVOL tape was the last. "Hey, I know her," I said, as Terri Clark Gonsalves appeared on the screen. "She's a friend of mine."

The reporter interviewed Terri about the party, and the cause. She looked beautiful, and poised, despite having just escaped a major fire. I was sure Lui had approached her to appear on camera. Briefly I gave Mike a quick rundown on Terri, including the recent death of her husband, a cop I'd worked with.

"I guess that's it, then," I said, as the anchor went on to another story. I leaned forward toward the VCR and my back rebelled. I must have winced, and Mike saw it.

"Let me see that burn," Mike said. "Take your shirt off."

"I'll survive. How often should I put that cream on?"

"Let me see the burn."

I unbuttoned my shirt and threw it on top of the surfboard screen. "I can see that comes in handy." Mike looked at my back. "Whoa. You should have gone to the hospital with this."

"I had a fire to investigate, remember?"

"Yeah, Officer Macho, I know." He pointed me toward the surfboard screen, and my bed beyond it. "Lie down so I can put some of this cream on you. You'll never be able to get it on right by yourself."

"Really, I can . . ."

"No arguments." I shrugged and walked over to the bed. It felt terrific to lie down, and I was afraid I'd doze off, leaving Mike Riccardi to have his way with me. Well, that might not be so bad.

There was no chance of that, though. The cream smarted, making me recognize nerve endings in my back I'd never known existed. Mike's hands, though, were sure and strong. "Your muscles are so tense. You ever get massages?"

"Once in a while."

"I get one every week, or else my back tenses up just like this. We've got stressful, physical jobs, you know. Chasing down crooks and dragging heavy equipment around. You've got to take care of your body if you want it to last."

"I take care of my body," I yawned.

"I can see that." He'd given up applying the cream by then, and was gently massaging my shoulders. The ceiling fan above us moved the air around lazily, tickling my bare back and floating scents of aloe, smoke, and saltwater around us.

"That feels really good," I said.

He leaned down and kissed the back of my neck. "You like that?"

"Yeah. I do." I made a half turn so that I was facing up toward him. I hooked an arm around the back of his neck, pulled his face closer to mine, and kissed him. "I like that, too."

"Mmm," he said, licking his lips. "I can still taste the grappa."

I sat up and unbuttoned his shirt. He had well-defined pecs, and small nipples only a little browner than his skin. I began exploring his hairy chest with my tongue and my teeth, and he shivered and groaned lightly. It took us a while to strip totally naked, after an intense exploration of each other's bodies, kissing and licking and rubbing and even biting a little. His cock was average sized, though standing out straight from his body it looked plenty big enough. I leaned down and took him in my mouth, and I felt his whole body go tense.

"Oh, man," he said. I sucked him for just a minute or two, then moved back up to kiss him again. And so we went for at least the next hour or so, learning the intimate geography of armpit and ass, cock and mouth, nipples and knees. I'd had relatively little experience with men by then; you could still count all the men I'd slept with on your fingers and toes and have a few left over. Neither of us were particularly well versed in what to do, but we managed, and we both made up in ardor for what we lacked in technique.

Finally we both brought each other off, him first, then me a moment later, come spurting on our hands and stomachs. I pulled him close to me then, hugging him fiercely, feeling his long, smooth body connecting with mine at a hundred different points. I nestled into his shoulder, smelling the last vestiges of his cologne, my lips nuzzling his neck. He held me gently, careful of my burns, and I fell asleep.

When I woke the next morning it was already light, and I was alone in bed. I had no idea how long Mike had stayed. There was a note on the table that read, AWESOME! I'LL CALL YOU TODAY. MIKE.

I felt alive, sexy, energized. I twisted around to see my back in the mirror and the burns looked less red and angry than they had the night before. I took a quick shower and applied the cream myself, as best I could. I kept smiling, wondering when I would see Mike Riccardi again.

The morning passed in a blur of busy work. I called the hospital and found that Gunter had been discharged, and Robert's condition upgraded. My father had been moved from intensive care to a regular room, and my mother said he was breathing more easily. There were still a lot of tests left to do, though, and the doctors hadn't said when he could go home.

Sandra's parents had arrived late the night before, but after Cathy had appeared on all three of KVOL's newscasts, the doctors were paying attention to her and she and the Guarinos were in a stage of truce. Sandra had shown more activity, moving and blinking her eyes, though she hadn't woken up yet, and everybody was feeling optimistic.

The police artist brought me a composite sketch, based on what Gunter and I had both described, and what Tatiana had drawn herself. I couldn't be completely sure, but I thought it looked remarkably like the guy I'd seen at the party. But was he our bomber? So far the only thing incriminating him was his sweatiness.

A fax came in from Mike Riccardi, listing all the ingredients in the bomb. Depressingly, I recognized almost all of them, and knew that you could find almost everything on the list in any ordinary kitchen or garage. But just seeing his name at the top of the fax gave me a nice little boost.

Lidia came by with a copy of the autopsy report on Wilson Shira I'd asked her to pick up at the medical examiner's office. She seemed excited by the chance to participate in the investigation, or maybe it was just seeing Doc Takayama. Apparently he'd taken the time to go over the report with her. I figured it was seeing him that brought that sparkle to her brown eyes, rather than the details of the charred corpse. I wondered what they'd talk about if they ever went on a date, if they'd share notes about dead bodies over pasta and wine, like Mike and I had.

I was happy to see that she and Doc were taking an interest in each other. "So tell me, officer, did you dig up anything by canvassing the offices around the Marriage Project?"

She pulled out her notepad. "By the time of the party, all the offices in the area were closed, so I couldn't find anyone who had been around who hadn't already spoken to an officer." She looked up. "But I did find something interesting."

"Spill."

"Around three-thirty the receptionist at a computer place across the street was coming back to the office with cappuccino for her boss, and she saw this pickup truck slow down, and a guy in the bed of the truck started throwing paper bags on the sidewalk in front of the Marriage Project. She's pretty sure he broke a window there, too. Then the truck drove away. She said she was so surprised that she didn't think to get a license number."

"We're tying the pieces together, Lidia." I told her about the paper bag Robert had given me. "Good work."

"Anything else I can do to help?"

I handed her the list of ingredients Mike had faxed over. "See what you can do with this," I said. "Most of the stuff is pretty common, but you never know when you'll come up with something." I thought for a minute. "It's a long shot, but my friend Gunter says the tuxedo the sweaty guy was wearing looked rented." I handed her the yellow pages and said, "Want to give it a try? You can use the desk over there."

Within a half hour, Lidia had a list of formal wear rental places, and she left to show around the sketch of the sweaty guy. She agreed to stop downstairs and leave a stack of the sketches for the beat cops on all three shifts; maybe one of them might recognize our guy.

I spent the next hours on the phone. I found out the fingerprint lab had lifted one print, probably a middle finger, from the paper bag that had gone through the window of the Marriage Project's office. They were running it through their computers, but since it was Friday, they didn't expect to get a match before the first of the week. They also had the piece of pipe Mike's investigators had found, but they were still working on it.

I had a couple of reports from beat cops in the district, but only one seemed interesting. Around the time the Marriage Project had been shit-bombed, an officer named Frank Sit had seen a dirty pickup truck with a couple of guys in the back, without a license plate. He'd called it in, but no units had been able to respond. He did remember the back gate had been broken in a distinctive way. That was quite possibly the truck the receptionist had seen outside the Marriage Project's office.

One of the secretaries picked up a plate lunch for me from a vendor outside and I sat at my desk and ate. I was just finishing when Kitty Sampson walked in. She wore a blue UH T-shirt, a pair of cargo shorts, and huarache sandals. On her right arm jangled half a dozen bracelets, some set with gemstones, others carved in intricate patterns.

"If you're looking for your dad, he's not here," I said. "He went to some kind of statewide police conference in Hilo. The secretary out front might know how to reach him, though."

"I know he's not here." She sat next to my desk. "That's why I came in today. I wanted to talk to you, and he'd kill me if he knew."

"That doesn't sound good. What's the problem?"

"I'm a lesbian. Jim and I don't talk about it, but I'm sure he knows."

I was surprised, more by the fact that she called him Jim than by her revelation. Since I came out, gay people have become very open with me. It's like, they know I am, and they want to level the playing field right from the start.

"And you're here because . . ."

"I want to help you investigate the bombing Wednesday night."

"Whoa," I said, holding up my hand. "Let's take this one step at a time. You didn't witness anything, did you?"

She shook her head. "But I've been pumping Jim for everything he knows about the case, and I have an idea. You know that Reverend White and his wife? The ones who are preaching against gay marriage all the time?"

I nodded. "We're looking into them. Investigating everybody who's expressed opposition to the lawsuit."

"They came to preach at UH last week," she said. "A friend and I went to hear them, just to know what they were saying. And I can't say exactly how, but I know they're involved."

"I appreciate the advice. I'll take a good look at them."

"You won't be able to find anything out. They know you're gay."

"The whole island knows I'm gay. Sometimes I think the whole state. But that hasn't stopped my investigation yet."

"You need someone on the inside." She waved her arm and the bracelets clacked against each other. "Nobody knows I'm gay, not really. I want to volunteer to help them, get into their circle. I'm sure I can find out what's going on."

I shook my head. "I just can't let you do that."

"I want to be a cop," she said. "I've been watching Jim since I was a little kid, seeing what it is that he does. And I can be good, too. I can pass every physical test the academy gives already, and I've got my marksmanship certificate. But I know that when people see me they think of me as Jim's daughter. I don't want anybody to think I'm crawling along on his coattails. I've been working on this paper, on the relationship between religious cults and violent activity, and if I can tie the Church of Adam and Eve to the bombing then I can win the essay prize in criminal justice, and nobody can say I did that because of who my stepfather is."

"I can see you're serious. But you've got to recognize that if somebody in that church is responsible, then it's way too dangerous for you to get involved."

"It's too dangerous to sit back and let them keep on killing." She leaned forward. "I can't do that. I'm going to join up with them, whether you help me or not. I have to do it."

"Your father would kill both of us if he knew."

"I'm not going to tell him. You're not either, are you?"

I sighed. "You're putting me in a terrible position."

"They've got a worship session Sunday at that storefront they use for a church. I'm going to go and talk to people."

I thought about it for a minute. Sampson would kill me with his bare hands if I let something happen to Kitty. But she had a point; somebody needed to get into the Church of Adam and Eve and see what was going on.

"I'll go with you," I said. When she started to protest, I held up my hand. "There is no way I'm letting you do this by yourself. These people are *malihinis,* after all. They think all islanders look alike. I'll get myself enough of a disguise to pass. And it'll be easier for you to blend in if you're my wife, than if you're a single girl."

She thought about it. Finally she nodded, and we agreed to meet on Sunday morning before the church service. "But you know," she said, "you don't have to worry about me. I know how to keep a secret. After all, I'm gay, aren't I?"

I had to admit she had a point.

Chapter 19

HERE'S THE AIRPLANE

HARRY CALLED ME late that afternoon to report in. Brandon was better, but Arleen was keeping him at her mother's for the weekend, just to be extra careful. He'd finally caught up on his sleep, and then he'd spent some time surfing the Internet looking for people and groups that were opposed to same-sex marriage.

"Way more than I expected," he said. "I mean, it's amazing. Don't these people have lives? Like those people who were out protesting on Wednesday night. Don't they have anyplace better to be?"

"I don't know, brah." He had printed out a lot of stuff for me, he said, and I told him to fax it over to the station. "I'll read it. Sometime."

"I'll keep looking. I just wanted to get you what I found so far."

The fax spewed out pages for a depressingly long time. I started reading, taking notes, making piles based on how crazy the people seemed to be. Some of the arguments were clear and well reasoned, though they all failed to change my mind. There were a couple of arguments from libertarians, who said that government shouldn't regulate any interchange between private individuals. There was a group of bitter, divorced men who said that nobody should get married because marriage was an institution, and who wants to be confined to an institution?

A few made pseudo-scientific arguments, saying that men had a biological imperative against monogamy. Most of them were ungrammatical rants that strayed into religion and fear of pedophiles. Those writers seemed to believe that once men were allowed to marry each other, the next step was guys marrying their Labradors, or women copulating with donkeys in church. The writers hid behind screen names or pseudonyms, though when I found an actual name I ran it through the computer.

I was surprised, though probably I shouldn't have been, by how many of those who made religious arguments had criminal records. They were my most promising suspects, including a guy in Makiki Heights with a record of felony assault, a woman in Aiea who'd served time for graft, and a guy from Red Hill who had a string of misdemeanors for disturbing the peace, public drunkenness, and indecent exposure. None of them had any record for bombings, arson, or deadly assault.

Lidia called in at the end of her shift. The only item on the list that was unusual was potassium chlorate, and only the Long's on University had sold some within the last month. "I found the clerk who sold it, and he recognized the sketch."

"Lidia, you're a gem."

It was after seven when I finally gave up and left the station. I walked down the street to The Queen's Medical Center, rubbing my arms against a chilly breeze that swept down South Beretania, skittering trash along the deserted sidewalk. The small cafés and convenience stores that serviced the downtown population were closed and the line of parking meters were all available and showing red expired circles in their windows, like a long row of tombstones at an unattended cemetery.

My brothers and their wives had gone home to their families, leaving my mother alone with my father. He was grumpy, refusing to eat his dinner and demanding again to go home. "Maybe you can talk to him," my mother said when I arrived. "He's driving me crazy."

My father sat up in bed when he saw me come in. "Kimo. Do you know where they put my clothes? I want you to find my clothes so that I can go home."

I looked at him sitting there, an IV hooked into his left arm, some kind of wires attaching him to a heart monitor going out the other side, and I started to laugh. "What are you laughing at? I could still kick your ass if I wanted to."

"You couldn't even kick a pebble along the street," I said. "And you aren't going to be able to if you don't eat. What was wrong with dinner?" I pointed to the nearly untouched plate sitting on his bedside table.

"Lousy. They left all the taste out."

"I'm starving." I picked up the fork and tasted the meat loaf. It wasn't terrific, but it wasn't that bad either. "This is OK. You sure you don't want some?" He looked toward the wall.

I moved the table over his legs and sat on the bed next to him. I picked up a forkful of meat loaf and started waving it in front of his face. "Here's the airplane, flying around the sky. It wants to come into the hangar."

"I remember we used to feed you that way," my mother said.

"It didn't work then either," my father said, continuing to face the wall.

I waved the fork around in front of his face some more.

"Come on, open the hangar so the plane can come in." Grudgingly he opened his mouth and I stuck the forkful of food in. He chewed and swallowed, and then looked at me. "How about some mashed potatoes?" I asked. I scooped some up and he took them, a little less grudgingly. "Good."

I fed myself a forkful of the meat loaf, and my father said, "Hey, whose dinner is that, anyway?" I looked at my mother and we exchanged smiles, and my father took the knife and fork from me and started to eat.

It was nice sitting there, the three of us. I remembered what it was like after Haoa had moved into the dorms at UH, when Lui was away at Berkeley. I had my parents all to myself, after years of sharing them. We would sit down for dinner together and I'd tell them about what happened at school, and my father would talk about the job he was working on, and my mother would fill in when conversation lagged.

After my father finished eating, we sat and watched TV together, some dumb comedy I had never seen before. I wanted to call Mike Riccardi, but I was bashful about doing it in front of my parents, because even though I wanted to talk to him about his progress on the case, and about mine, I just wanted to hear his voice, and find out when I could see him again.

So I didn't call. For a while, instead, I forgot I was a grown-up, a homicide detective who was responsible for finding out why a man had died, why my friends and my father had been hospitalized. I hung out with my parents watching TV, like I had done when I was a teenager. It was a pretty nice feeling.

≈

I WOKE UP from a nightmare around two a.m. I couldn't re-member the details, but it had scared the shit out of me. I think I was chasing somebody, and then he pulled a gun. He wasn't aiming at me, though; he was aiming just behind me, and I didn't know who was back there, but I was sure it was somebody I cared about.

I knew I couldn't go back to sleep. I was restless and agitated and worried that the nightmare would come back as soon as I closed my eyes. So I pulled on shorts, a T-shirt, and flip-flops, and went out for a walk.

The air was warm and uncomfortably dry, and the smell of smoke seemed to roll down from the Ko'olau Mountains. I wondered if the case Mike had been investigating up in central O'ahu was related to the bombing, if all those fires at gay- and lesbian-owned businesses had just been warm-ups for the big event. Or worse, if the bombers would continue to terrorize my island. What if the bombing had just been one more step toward a much larger goal?

I walked the couple of blocks down Lili'uokalani to Kalākaua, which was buzzing with activity, mostly of the tourist type. The bars were still open, the street brightly lit, cars cruising slowly. I spotted a couple of prostitutes; it was clear that the vice raids hadn't been completely successful. A couple of the prostitutes were gay men. One of them recognized me and took my arm, trying to entice me off to a motel room with him—or maybe just a dark alley.

I pointedly looked away, and my eye caught a guy in a sedan just across from me. Traffic was stopped at a light, and his window was down.

I recognized the look Gunter had described—that combination of fear and longing. The guy was a john, for sure, and within a block or two some hooker would catch up to him.

But there was something more. Our eyes locked, and then he looked away. Had he been cruising me? He looked familiar.

Had I met him at the Rod and Reel Club late one night? Worse, had I slept with him and then forgotten?

As the light changed and he accelerated away, I realized that he looked like the guy in the sketch—the sweaty guy from the party. I shook off the prostitute's hand and started running, darting between the tourists and the street hawkers, trying to catch the guy. But his car was a nondescript dark sedan, and he was gone before I could get a glimpse of his license plate.

Was it the same guy? Or was I just so tired and sleep deprived that I was imagining things? I yawned, and went back home. I wasn't going to be any use unless I got some rest.

Chapter 20

GUNTER'S OVEN

WHEN I'M INVESTIGATING a case, nothing clears my head like surfing. There's something about getting out there among the waves, surrounded by sea and sky, that helps me focus my concentration, free my subconscious mind to look for patterns, and ask questions I haven't thought of yet.

But my back was still red and scaly, flaking skin all over my sheets that Saturday morning, so I knew surfing was out. I decided to rollerblade instead, and, to make the best of a bad situation, to blade over to Gunter's house and see how he was doing, now that he was home from the hospital. Before I left, though, I tried to get hold of Mike Riccardi but couldn't reach him, and I left him a message.

It was a gorgeous morning, only a few puffy clouds congregating over the tops of the Ko'olau Mountains. The bad news was that meant there wasn't going to be any rain.

The rest of the sky was a luminous light blue. A gentle trade wind ruffled the tops of the palm trees as I bladed toward Diamond Head on Ala Wai Boulevard, shutting out the hotel vans and idle tourists in rental cars, the blaring horns and distant sirens. Instead I concentrated on the serene waters of the canal next to me, on the outrigger canoes full of weekend athletes that pulled past, grunting and shouting. Diamond Head itself loomed ahead of me, its brown-and-green flanks still free of development.

I crossed the triangular intersection where Ala Wai ends at Kapahulu and continued on behind Diamond Head Elementary to Gunter's little house. The windows were open and his car was in the driveway. I skated up to the front door and rang the bell, looking down at the welcome mat as I did. It read, PRIZE PATROL: SORRY WE MISSED YOU. LEAVE THE $1,000,000 CHECK UNDER THE MAT.

Gunter came to the door looking sexy in a tank top that read AMERICA'S MOST WANTED and a pair of tight nylon running shorts slit up the side. He'd gotten a new haircut, shaving the sides down to nothing and leaving only a crown of blond fuzz at the top. I could see rough red patches on one side of his head, and he still had a couple of bandages on his arms.

"Hey, babe, you weren't who I was expecting." He leaned forward to kiss me as I tried to step inside. I caught the edge of my skate on the mat and stumbled into his arms. "If you want to jump my bones there are more subtle ways to tell me," he said, smiling.

I regained my balance and clomped forward into his living room. "When I'm ready to jump your bones you'll know about it." Though I'd been happy in the past to get sweaty with Gunter, I'd experienced something new and different with Mike and I wanted to explore it. "Who were you expecting?" I asked, sitting on the couch.

"The artist you sent by yesterday. We're continuing our artistic collaboration." Gunter posed, as if for a portrait.

"Interesting." I hadn't been kidding when I'd described the guy as fifty and pot-bellied. Not what I'd expect as Gunter's type.

A little disappointment showed on Gunter's face. "Not as interesting as it might be. He's bringing his girlfriend along." A sly smile crept onto his face. "Apparently this is a little fantasy of hers."

"So will you"—I waved my hand a little in the air because I didn't want to actually say the words—"with her, too?"

"I can do it, you know," he said, a little indignantly. "I mean, it's not my favorite thing in the world or anything, but I am capable."

"I didn't mean to imply you weren't."

"Of course, there may be some surprises along the way that they hadn't anticipated." There was that sly smile again. "For both of them. You ever hear of the Eiffel Tower?"

"Big metal thing in Paris? Yeah."

"Not exactly what I meant," Gunter said. "Picture this woman lying flat, her boyfriend at the front, getting a blow job. Me behind her."

"I get the picture. But where does the Eiffel Tower come in? You speak French to each other?"

"The two guys lean forward toward each other," Gunter said. "Straight guys high five."

"Oh."

"And we might do a little ski poling." He made some motions with his hands, which could either be the action of arms on ski poles—or someone jerking two guys off simultaneously. "You can stick around, you know. The more the merrier, I always say."

"I'm sure you do."

"Now, you're not going all closeted on me, are you Kimo?"

"I hardly think that's possible, unless I leave the state."

"Because you know a boy needs sex. I don't want to hear about you going with any prostitutes or anything nasty like that. You know if you need some lovin', just come over to Gunter's oven. It's always hot here."

I must have blushed, because he said, "You are getting some! And you haven't told me about it. You naughty boy!" He sat next to me on the sofa. "OK, dish."

My mind seemed like it was overflowing. I wanted to tell him everything about Mike Riccardi, but at the same time I was scared that talking might jinx things. And there was something else running around in my head, too, something that Gunter had said. I was thinking when he said, "Now, Kimo, you're not going to hold out on me, are you?"

I gave up. I told him about seeing Mike on Monday morning at police headquarters when I was carrying the dead chicken, and then the coincidence of seeing him again Wednesday night. Then about stripping down in front of him, and the look in his eyes.

"Good, your gaydar is improving. So what happened next?"

I must have blushed again, because he dug an elbow in my ribs and said, "You dog. I want to know all the details."

It felt great to talk about him, as if it made what I felt more real by sharing it. "Young love," Gunter sighed. "It's so sweet. I remember my first love."

"How old were you? Thirteen?"

Gunter gave me a look. "Actually I was twelve. I was an early bloomer."

"I'll bet." Then it came to me. "You said something about prostitutes before, didn't you?"

"I did not have sex with a prostitute when I was twelve years old," Gunter said. "I had to wait until I was at least nineteen for that."

"No, what you said about closeted guys going with prostitutes. The guy we saw the night of the bombing, the one you worked on the sketch of. He look closeted?"

"Absolutely."

I remembered catching that glimpse the night before, of the guy in the dark sedan. Maybe it was the same guy, after all. "So maybe I should circulate the sketch among prostitutes, see if any of them recognize him."

"Adult bookstores, too," Gunter said. "And gay bars. You never know who'll show up in one."

"That's true. It's where I met you." I leaned over and kissed him. "Thanks, Gunter. That's a great idea."

I stood up. "I'd better get back on the pavement. I don't want to disrupt your artistic endeavors." This time it was my turn to strike a pose. He jumped up and tried to tickle me but I raced him to the front door.

≈

I BLADED HOME, showered, and changed, then headed to The Queen's Medical Center to see my various charges. Arleen and Harry were there to check Robert out of the hospital, and take him up to Arleen's mother's, where he and Brandon could both be monitored.

Sandra Guarino had improved dramatically. When I got to her room, she was preparing to be discharged. Sandra and Cathy were sitting together on the bed, Sandra in street clothes, and they were holding hands and chatting softly. Sandra's parents were sitting by the window overlooking the highway, not saying anything.

"Kimo! I'm so glad you're here!" Sandra tried to get up, but she was obviously still too weak. Cathy held her arm as she sank back to the bed. I walked over, leaned down, and kissed her cheek. She took my hand and squeezed. "So do I get to call you my hero and bat my eyelashes?"

"I doubt you even know how to bat your eyelashes," I said, smiling.

"Never underestimate the power of a woman," Sandra said.

"Or the power of a gay man who's also a great friend," Cathy said.

"Aw shucks, guys, it was nothing." I sat on a chair on the other side of the bed from Sandra's parents. "So, you're going home?"

"I'm still pretty weak, but the doctor says I can recuperate at home just as well as here." Sandra leaned forward. "Seriously, Kimo, there's no way for me to thank you. For what you did for me, and for Cathy, too."

"Please, you're embarrassing me. I'm just glad you're up and around. Soon, maybe, you can think about what you want to do with the project."

"Charlie Stahl came over earlier this afternoon," Sandra said. "You remember him from the party, don't you? His family owns half of O'ahu. He's donating office space, and start-up funds to buy all new equipment. We're going to be back in business on Monday. I'm taking some sick leave from the firm, so whatever I can manage I'll do just for the project, for now."

"We've been talking to your brother, too," Cathy said. "He's helping us arrange a press conference for Monday, just in time for the evening news. Charlie's buying us an announcement in the *Advertiser*, too, so that we can get a big crowd, rally the troops and so on. It's going to be in Waikīkī Gateway Park, where Kuhio meets Kalākaua. You'll come, won't you?"

I agreed, and then begged off to go see my father. When I got to his room, Lui and Haoa were standing in the hallway outside his room arguing. "How do you think he's doing, Kimo?" Haoa asked.

"He seems to be getting a little better. He isn't so cranky anymore."

"That's just what I mean," Lui said. "You always know Dad is getting better the crankier he gets. He's not acting like Dad now, he's acting like a—like a sick person. I say we need to get him out of here ASAP."

"He has to stay in the hospital until they finish all the tests," Haoa said. "Then we'll know what's wrong with him."

They were faced off against each other in the hallway. Haoa has two inches in height on Lui and about a hundred pounds in weight, but Lui has always been first boy so he retains a big psychological advantage. I hadn't seen the two of them fight since they were teenagers and I wondered who would win. "Is it up to us?" I asked. "What about the doctors? What about Mom?"

Lui waved his hand. "You know Mom will listen to us."

"Mom will listen to the doctors, and the doctors want Dad to stay here," Haoa said.

I said, "Let me go in and see him. Then I'll tell you what I think."

"Good." Haoa crossed his arms in front of him.

"Good." Lui stalked down the hall toward the vending machines.

I went into the room. My father was lying back in the bed, my mother in the chair next to him. They were watching a game show on TV. "Well, at least you ate your lunch today." I kissed him on the forehead, then leaned down and kissed my mother's cheek.

"I'm glad you're here, Kimo. Bring your brothers in. I want to talk to you about my will."

"We're not talking about wills." I was a little scared; there was definitely something wrong with my father's attitude.

"I want to leave the business to Haoa because it matters to him, but I don't want you and Lui to feel like I'm favoring him."

This was very strange behavior. "You're not leaving the business to anybody yet because you're not leaving yet."

I brought my brothers in then, and it took some talking, but we finally convinced him that whatever happened, the three of us would stand together, and there was no need to talk about wills at the present time.

My father's cardiologist showed up, and we talked to him after he'd examined my father. The IV tube was delivering a course of medication, the doctor said, that would finish on Monday. Barring anything unforeseen, it would be safe to take my father home then.

We all agreed that would be fine, and that crisis averted, I said good-bye to my mother and brothers and went to the office. Even though it was Saturday and I wasn't on duty, I wanted to distribute the sketch of our potential bomber to the vice guys, who could show it around to prostitutes and other contacts. But more important, I wanted to feel like I was doing something to solve the case.

Chapter 21

EMOTIONAL INSIGHTS

ON MY WAY TO headquarters I grabbed a sandwich and ate it at my desk as I went back over everything I'd collected so far, looking for anything I'd missed. While I was there, Frank Sit came up to speak with me.

He was the patrolman who'd seen the truck that shit-bombed the Marriage Project offices. I'd known him for a few years, working more closely with him when he was stationed on Waikīkī, too. He was a stocky Chinese guy, in his late forties or early fifties, with a brush cut, a gut, and a swagger.

"I saw that picture Lidia was showing around," he said, coming over to sit at my desk. "I think I saw the guy."

"Really? When?"

"First I gotta tell you how come I didn't do anything about that truck with the missing plates. I was at the corner of Ward and Waimanu when I noticed this Volvo station wagon full of hippies ahead of me had Massachusetts plates with an expired tag. I turned on my flashers and pulled them over."

He took a sip of department coffee, and made a face. "You won't believe this. The driver, this shaggy-haired guy, had an expired Massachusetts driver's license that said his name was Eddie Christ. Turns out the other guys were Christ too, Stan Christ in the front, and Jordan and Fritz Christ in the back. Jordan was black; the other three were *haole*." He went on to tell me that all four of them were in their mid-twenties, wearing jeans and T-shirts. They were on a mission from Jesus, who was their brother, to deliver herbal tea to the islands.

"The back of the wagon was filled with boxes of the tea. I told the guy he had to have a driver's license, even if he was on a mission from Christ, and he launched into this long explanation. That's when I saw the pickup without plates pass by. I had my hands full with the Christ brothers, though, so I radioed in a description."

He put the cup of coffee down on my desk. "But you know how it is. There wasn't anybody else in the vicinity, so the truck got away. And you know what? Each of those Christ guys had different IDs, and outstanding warrants. Took me hours to get them all into the holding cells and squared away."

"What about the guy in the picture, though?" I asked. "Was he one of the Christ brothers?"

Sit shook his head. "That was later, after I was back on the street. I was cruising past the YMCA when I saw this sedan parked on the street, a man and a woman in the front seat. At first I thought it might be a prostitute, so I went up to talk to them."

I looked at him. I still had reams of paper to go through. But I knew if I rushed him he'd get cranky and I might never get the whole story. I straightened a couple of pieces of paper on my desk as I waited for him to continue.

"Woman gave me a story about waiting for a kid to come out of the Y," he said. "At the time, I didn't think anything of it. By the time that bomb went off, I'd forgotten all about them. Then when Lidia was showing the picture around, I thought that might be the guy."

"Was he wearing a tux?"

"Didn't get that clear a look, but definitely a dark jacket and a white shirt."

"You get any information on the car—plate number, make and model?"

He frowned. "If I'd thought it was a john, I'd have done it, but the woman, she looked—you know, young and professional. Not like a working girl."

"Thanks, Frank. This is good info anyway. We know he has a partner, a woman, and both of them were in the area at the time." I knew the Y was just around the corner from the Marriage Project offices; it would have been easy for the woman to pull up there and wait for the bomber to do his business and then return. From the time Frank described, and the timing mechanism Mike had found on the bomb, I figured they were waiting to make sure the bomb went off before leaving.

After Frank left, I was thinking about the fact that the guy's accomplice was a woman, and that Gunter had recognized fear and longing on the guy's face. So maybe he was married to a woman, but not happy, and that was fueling his anger against gay marriage.

It was only amateur psychoanalysis, but it made sense.

When I needed help understanding human emotion, I called Terri Clark Gonsalves. Ever since high school, she'd provided that insight, and when I'd been undercover on the North Shore, her intuition about the behavior of suspects and victims had been very helpful.

I managed to reach her on her cell phone, and found she was just leaving her great-aunt's home in Black Point. Since her parents were taking care of her son Danny for the afternoon, I didn't have to twist her arm too hard to get her to agree to detour into Waikīkī and meet me for a late-afternoon caffeine break.

We met at the Starbucks at the Waikīkī Trade Center on Kuhio Avenue, and as usual, she looked perfect, showing no hint of the trauma she'd been going through since her widow-hood only months before. When I complimented her, she said, "Aunt Emma has high expectations. A Clark always looks just so, you know."

I'd never met her great-aunt, but I'd been hearing about her for years. "A command performance?" I asked.

"Trust business," Terri said. "I asked her about the grant for the Gay Teen Center, and she said absolutely not."

"Oh, well."

"Don't forget, I'm just as much a Clark as she is," Terri said, smiling. "I reminded her that the mission of the Sand-wich Islands Trust is to help the people of the islands, and that if there were young people who were living on the streets, in financial or emotional trouble, it was our obligation as the stewards of the Trust to help them."

"Good for you. Did it work?"

"We agreed to give them some money for a pilot program."

"Have I ever told you I think you're phenomenal?"

"Not often enough." She smiled. "So what's up?"

"Why do you think people are so opposed to gay mar-riage?"

She took a sip of her decaf vanilla latte and considered. "Big question," she said. "I think they fall into a couple of cat-egories. People who accept the Bible as the word of God, for example, and when they see that passage from Leviticus they decide it has to be obeyed."

"But just before that, the priests are telling people that if they mix fabrics they should be killed with stones," I said. "The same for eating shellfish."

"You're trying to apply logic to something very emotional," she said.

"I have a different idea." I took a sip of my raspberry mocha (caffeinated, of course) and said, "Let's say there's a guy who has some kind of same-sex urges. Maybe not strong enough to act on—but enough to make him uncomfortable. Could he feel like those urges are coming from Satan, and need to be resisted?"

"Sure. Remember Lucy Carson?"

That threw me for a loop for a minute, and I had to run through my mental directory to remember Lucy, a girl who'd gone to Punahou, our private high school, with us, and had been arrested for shoplifting. "Yeah?"

"After she was arrested, she started going to church," Terri said. "She decided that it was the devil who was making her steal, and she could pray her way to honesty."

I couldn't remember what had happened to her. "Did it work?"

Terri shrugged. "Don't know exactly. She went to college on the mainland and never came back. I heard a couple of rumors that she'd dropped out of school and gotten into some kind of trouble, but never anything more than that."

"Getting back to my point, do you think the person who bombed the Marriage Project could be some kind of thwarted homosexual, taking out his frustrations on people who are able to be out, when he can't?"

"Why can't he?"

I described the man and woman Frank Sit had seen in the car. "If that's his wife, he could be stuck in a marriage and unable to come out."

"That's a big assumption," Terri said. "I'm sure that there are some guys who are uncomfortable around gay men because they're not sure about their own sexuality. But it's a big jump from making some homophobic cracks or avoiding gay guys in the locker room to building a bomb and detonating it."

"What about the Church of Adam and Eve?" I asked. "Do you know about them?"

Terri frowned. "The trust gives them money," she said. "I don't agree with it, but apparently Aunt Emma went to one of their meetings and she was impressed by the minister and his wife. I think they're nuts, but mostly harmless."

"I'm not so sure. I went to one of their revival meetings last month, and I have to say it made me uncomfortable. I could definitely see somebody getting the wrong idea from what they've been preaching and deciding to do something about it. Vigilante justice." I hesitated, wondering if I should tell her about Kitty Sampson and her ideas about the church. But I knew that would shift the focus back to me and how I shouldn't be doing something like going to church with Kitty behind her stepfather's back, so I skipped it.

"You may be right," Terri said. "Tell you what, I'll look into the funding the Trust provides, see what kind of materials they've given us. If there's anything wrong there, I can convince Aunt Emma to pull the plug."

"Every little bit helps," I said. I finished my coffee and walked Terri to her SUV. "How's Danny doing?"

Terri's son had suffered a lot from his father's death. He hadn't spoken for quite a while afterward, and then only gradually. "He's getting better," Terri said. "It helps that his grandparents spoil him terribly. He always comes home from their house with some new toy, stuffed with treats."

"Give him my love," I said. "I'll try and get out to see him sometime. He's still got a lot to learn before he can call himself a surfer."

"He's only six, Kimo," she said, smiling. "Give him a couple of years."

When I got home, there was a message from Mike. I was

embarrassed, even all by myself, about how eager I was to call him back. "So what did you do today?" he asked.

I told him about rollerblading over to Gunter's, and then going to the office. "I read background material until my eyes crossed," I said. "I talked to my friend Terri about the possible motivation of our bomber, which I can tell you about when I see you. There was a message from Lidia, too. She found the formal wear shop where our guy rented his tux, but he paid cash and gave what appears to be a fake name, so that lead fizzled out. I ran off extra copies of the artist's sketch for the vice detectives to pass around."

"Sounds good."

"Gunter made a good suggestion this morning, to pass the sketch around at some gay bars, see if the guy ever shows up at any of them." I paused. "You interested in helping me?"

Mike didn't say anything, but I waited. "I don't think so, Kimo," he said finally. "I mean, I know this is legitimate, job related and all, but it's just not something I can do."

"You mean be seen in a gay bar with a known homosexual."

"You know the kind of hell you've been through. You must still get some. You want me to go through that same shit?"

"You mean coming out?"

"If that's what you want to call it."

"That's what it's called, Mike. When a gay man accepts who he is and isn't ashamed to let anybody and everybody know about it."

"I can't do that. What I do in my private life is my own business. I don't want it to affect my job, what my family thinks, my friends, the guys I work with."

"So you want to lie to all of them."

"I don't lie. I don't come in on Monday morning with

made-up stories about the babes I scored over the weekend. I just don't tell anybody anything."

"Sounds like a pretty sucky life, to me."

"Kimo, we had a great time Thursday night. At least I had a great time. I want to see you again." He took a deep breath. "I want to kiss you again. I want to suck your dick again. I want to make love to you."

"But you don't want to be seen with me in public."

"Not at a gay bar, for Christ's sake. I mean, everybody knows about you, Kimo."

"Fine, Mike. I'll call Gunter. He's probably done with his threesome by now. He won't be embarrassed to be seen in public with me."

"Can we have dinner? Tomorrow night? I want to see you."

"I want to spend some time at the hospital with my dad tomorrow. I'll call you in the afternoon." I hung up the phone and then sat there for a while. I had been in love once before with a man, very briefly. He was an attorney from Massachusetts who had moved to Hawai'i so that no one back home would ever know he was gay. He was a low-profile kind of guy, and when my life erupted into the press he backed away fast. I wondered if Mike would be the same way. Was it something about me? Was I only able to fall in love with extremely closeted guys? How could I even daydream about a future with Mike Riccardi if I could never go to a bar with him, introduce him to my parents, meet his friends and family?

Maybe I ought to stick with Gunter after all. I picked up the phone and dialed his number. I arranged to pick him up later that night.

Chapter 22

A GUIDE TO THE NIGHT

THOUGH IT WAS BACK downtown and I was already on Waikīkī, I swung past The Queen's Medical Center before going home. My father was still grumpy, but Haoa had smuggled him in a burger from Zippy's so he was slightly more cooperative. He was definitely looking forward to going home when he finished his IV treatment on Monday, and I hoped nothing would happen to set him back. As he'd pointed out himself, hospitals were dangerous places. People died in them all the time.

I got home around five, grilled myself a piece of chicken and some veggies on my tiny hibachi, and then took a power nap. If I was going to be out cruising with Gunter, I needed some more energy.

A few minutes before eleven, I was pulling up in Gunter's driveway. "Any ideas where we can go?" I asked when he got in the truck.

"There's a reason why they have you on homicide, not vice. Let me be your tour guide to the night."

"I'm not exactly naïve."

"Let's start with Ala Moana Park," Gunter said. "After that, we'll hit Waikīkī."

As we drove, I was thinking about Jimmy Ah Wong, hoping he was settling in OK with Uncle Chin and Aunt Mei-Mei. I told Gunter what had happened, and that I was worried that, if Jimmy were put in a foster home, he'd just run away.

"Did you ever run away from home?" he asked.

"Once. I was about fourteen, I think. My brothers were both living at home that summer. Lui was already working at KVOL, some kind of entry-level intern thing, I think. Haoa had just graduated from UH, and he was working on a road crew out near the airport. He had this explicit porno magazine, all kinds of things: men and women, women with dogs, oral sex, anal sex, even a couple of threesomes. The only thing it didn't have was gay sex."

"Let me guess. You stole it."

"Not exactly. He caught me reading it and he and Lui laid into me. You know, snooping in their personal stuff, what a sneaky little weasel I was, that kind of thing. I was mad, so I told them I was going to go away, and they'd never find me, and they'd sure be sorry. They both laughed."

"Brothers. You gotta love 'em. Otherwise you'd kill 'em."

"So I left. I went out into the woods for a while, but then it started to get dark so I came back and hid behind some bushes across the street from my house. I watched my parents go out in their cars to look for me. My mother cruised around St. Louis Heights, and my father went down to Wai'alae Avenue and drove up and down, checking out the bus shelters and the pinball arcade and the drugstore and so on. They made Lui and Haoa go out into the woods with flashlights, looking for me."

"What did you do?"

"As soon as I saw them all leave, I went back into the house. I fixed myself a TV dinner and ate, and then I was watching TV when they all came back. Nobody said a word about it. I found out later that my father had laid into Lui and Haoa—

not about beating me up, but about bringing the magazine into the house in the first place. Of course, by the time I was old enough to get that kind of stuff for myself they didn't care anymore."

"Some comic once said, 'My parents were protective of my older brothers, but by the time they got to me I was playing with knives and they didn't mind.'"

"That's about right." I looked over at him. "How about you? You ever run away?"

He leaned the seat back as far as it would go and pulled his knees up to the dashboard. His legs were so long and skinny it was hard to connect them to the rest of his body. "I remember this once," he said. "I was about sixteen, I think. I was still in high school, for sure. We lived a mile or two from this rest stop on the Jersey turnpike, maybe an hour outside New York. I was hating my life then, and one day, I just couldn't take it anymore, so I walked over to the rest stop and tried to hitch a ride into the city."

I pulled into the park and we started driving real slow along the road, seeing if anyone was out. "I hung around by the men's room for a while, trying to spot somebody who might be gay. I must have been a real piece of work—I was as tall as I am now, but skinny, no muscles at all. I had a ponytail—you believe it? Bell-bottomed pants and a tie-dyed T-shirt. Finally this one guy says to me, 'You waiting for a ride somewhere.' I thought I was real cool, I said, 'Yeah, where you going?'"

He laughed. "He said, 'Come on, little buddy, I know just where you want to go.' He was this big fat guy, beard and a pot belly, drove a big truck. I followed him out to the truck and climbed up in the cab with him. He pointed down at his crotch and said, 'Right there. That's where you want to go.' And you know, it was."

"You ever make it into the city?"

"Nope. Not that time, at least. I blew him, and he gave me twenty bucks. I mean, that was like a month's allowance to me. I couldn't wait to get home and figure out what I wanted to buy." He sat up. "You better pull up and park. We're not going to hand out any of those flyers sitting up here in this truck."

We walked around the park for half an hour or so, threading our way between cabbage palms and kicking up small sprays of sand. The ocean was a constant murmur there, slapping against the shore in the background, fading in and out among the traffic noises on Ala Moana Boulevard and the sound of a car radio somewhere in the parking lot. The fronds of the palms moved mysteriously around us, dancing to an almost hidden breeze, and every so often we found a homeless person camped beneath a banyan or kukui tree, stumbling on signs of humanity in what otherwise was dark and natural.

We handed out copies of the sketches, but either nobody recognized our sweaty bomber, or nobody wanted to rat out a good customer. We were just about to head out when I saw a guy step out of the men's room, and even in the dim glow of the streetlight above the entrance I recognized him as Frankie, the ponytailed kid from the Teen Center.

I motioned silently to Gunter, and we hung back in the shadows for a minute or two, waiting to see who'd follow Frankie out of the men's room. I felt protective of the kid, and I was worried what I'd do if the john turned out to be some closeted old toad who could only handle sex with young boys in public restrooms.

To my surprise, the next guy out was Lolo, the sulky tough guy. I stepped out into the light and said, "Hey, guys, howzit?"

Both of them turned toward me in alarm. "Anybody else in the men's room?" I asked.

They stole furtive glances at each other, and finally Frankie said, "No."

"Hey, it's cool," I said. "I know what it's like to want to play around and not have any place to go."

I turned and introduced Gunter, who was holding the pile of sketches. "You a cop, too?" Lolo asked, surveying his lean build and buzz-cut hair.

Gunter laughed. "Hell, if I was, I'd have to arrest myself every other day for something." He poked me. "Only reason Officer Kimo here doesn't lock me up is 'cause I'd want to fuck every guy in lockup."

"*Detective* Kimo," I said. "Why does everybody get that wrong?"

Everyone laughed. "Either of you guys seen this guy?" I asked, showing them both the sketch.

Lolo nodded. "Just a looker, though," he said. "I see him cruising sometimes on Kalākaua, but he never actually picks anybody up."

"Maybe you're just not his type," Frankie said.

"I'm everybody's type," Lolo said. At the youth center, he'd always worn baggy clothes, oversized sweatshirts, the kind of pants that hang off your hips. But that night he was wearing a form-fitting tank top, and tight jeans that rode low, exposing a band of taut flesh. He was hot, and he knew it.

I gave them both my cards. "Either of you see him, you call me right away," I said. "Day or night, anytime. This is a bad guy. You don't want to mess with him."

"I can take care of myself," Lolo said. He reached out for the other boy's hand and said, "Frankie, too."

"I'm sure you can," I said. "But even so, you call me, all right?"

Both boys nodded. I was about to turn away when Gunter said, "Here, take a couple of these," and he pulled some foil packets from his pocket. "They glow in the dark. Pretty cool."

Frankie and Lolo grinned, and I wondered where they'd go to try them out. On the way back to the truck I said, "You're a sweetheart, you know that, Gunter?"

"Yeah, but don't let it get around," he said. "Bad for my image."

We spent the next couple of hours barhopping on Waikīkī, showing the sketch around, having a few drinks, even dancing a little. Around 3 o'clock Gunter said, "Well, it doesn't look like I'm gonna get lucky tonight. Hanging around with a cop tends to turn away romance."

We were sitting on stools at the Rod and Reel Club, the seedy outdoor bar where we'd first met some months before. A club remix of a Barbra Streisand song was playing in the background, and a few men gyrated athletically on the dance floor. The tables around us were littered with empty glasses and beer bottles and overflowing ashtrays. "So am I gonna get lucky with you?"

I thought then of Mike, and how much I wanted him there with me at that moment. I wanted to be able to kiss him at the bar, hold his butt while we danced, let everyone in the Rod and Reel Club know that he was my boyfriend.

And that meant that I couldn't have sex with Gunter, even though he was hot and sexy and I knew we'd have fun. I had to follow my heart, and my heart had latched onto a closeted firefighter with a dark mustache and dancing eyes.

"You don't have to answer that," Gunter said, smiling. He

finished the last of his Primo, draining the bottle. "You're in love. With that fireman." He turned to look at me. "There's a difference between sex and love, you know. You can have sex without love, but you shouldn't have love without sex." He put his arm around me. "And I love you, man."

I couldn't help it. I burst out laughing, and Gunter looked a little offended. "If you're going to talk like a bad beer commercial you've got to expect me to laugh," I said. "Come on. Let's start walking." I had parked my truck back at my apartment building before we started drinking. My legs were a little rubbery but I managed to keep my balance as we walked down Kuhio Avenue under the stars. Gunter leaned into me a little more than he probably had to, but I didn't mind. It felt good.

We stopped at my building. "You want me to walk on with you for a while?"

"If you're not going to take me upstairs, rip my clothes off, and make passionate love to me, then who needs you?" Gunter asked. "Gimme a kiss, at least."

We leaned up against my truck and kissed, his tongue searching around in my mouth, finding mine, the two of them doing an intricate little dance. Then he started sucking on my upper lip, and reached down to my crotch to grope me. Of course I had a hard-on; I'm only human. But I pulled away. "Hey, you got any more of those glow-in-the-dark condoms?"

"You want to try one out with me?"

"Well, not with you."

"Jesus. What a tease you are." He pulled a couple of the foil packs out of his pocket and handed them to me. "I'm going to be thinking of you," he called, as I started climbing the steps.

"Think of this," I said. I pulled down my pants and mooned him, and he laughed.

"You bet I will," he said, as he staggered off into the night.

Chapter 23

THIEVES AND MONEYLENDERS

WHEN I WOKE UP Sunday morning I was feeling pretty rocky. My head hurt, and the healing burns on my back itched, and I felt profoundly lonely. I wanted to see Mike Riccardi again, even if only to discover that we'd had a great one-night stand that wasn't going anywhere. I just wanted to know. I was also sorry I had been so strong with him the night before—I should have just arranged to meet him after my club-hopping with Gunter was over. If he'd have agreed.

I couldn't concentrate on the morning *Star-Bulletin,* and I couldn't go surfing. I'd gone through all the paperwork at the office the day before, so I had no reason to go there, and it was still too early to go the hospital. I prowled around my little studio apartment killing time until I was to meet Kitty for church, throwing away junk mail, washing the dishes, even making my bed.

I realized, on my way to meet Kitty at the Church of Adam and Eve, that my father owned the strip shopping center on Wai'alae Avenue where it was located, sandwiched among a dry cleaner, video rental store, real estate agency, and a funky beauty salon called Puerto Peinado, its interior walls painted with lavish tropical murals. The salon was owned by Robertico Robles, a gay man who was my sister-in-law Tatiana's best friend, and I knew my father cut him a deal on the rent. I wondered if Liliha had called in the same favor for the church.

I met Kitty outside the storefront chapel. The room was simple: twenty rows of folding chairs facing a pair of lecterns at the far end. Inside, about fifty people milled around talking to each other or sat reading their Bibles. It was a lot less impressive than the mass gathering I'd attended a month before, but I figured this was the core congregation.

I looked nervously around for Liliha and Lui, but didn't see them. I'd worn my clear owl-rimmed glasses, a short-sleeved striped shirt, and chinos. Usually when I dressed for an undercover operation I aimed to look like a *moke,* a Hawai'ian criminal. I had a false gold tooth, torn T-shirts, and tattered shorts. I had always been able to pass; I hoped I could do the same at the church.

Behind the lecterns were a couple of folding screens; I assumed that the ministers used that area to prepare before the service. Both side walls held a collection of posters made by children, with a variety of sayings on them. Some held Bible verses, while others quoted phrases like "The love between a man and a woman is the most sacred thing on earth."

We went inside and slipped into seats next to a mother, father, and two small children. I sat to Kitty's right. The mother sat next to Kitty, with the little girl's head resting on her lap. Kitty smiled at them.

"I'm Fran," the woman said. "I'd shake hands but I'm afraid to wake up Caitlin."

Kitty introduced herself. We'd decided to use our real names; it would be easier, and frankly, every fourth or fifth guy in Hawai'i is named Kimo. Kitty started talking and giggling with Fran in low whispers until the minister and his wife came out from behind the screens and the room hushed. "Welcome, friends," the minister said. We stood so he could lead us in an opening hymn.

That's when I recognized him. The sweaty guy.

But could I be sure? I hadn't gotten that good a look at him at the party. Maybe I had just looked at that flyer too many times. Then I looked at his wife, and she looked familiar, too.

But there hadn't been a woman with the guy at the party. How could I have seen her?

The minister said, "And now a prayer for all our misguided brethren. For the criminals, and thieves, the moneylenders and alcoholics, the homosexuals and their perverted ilk. For all of these, Lord, we pray that you will shine your light to show them the true path. And continue to shine your light upon us, Lord, that we may see your path as well, and follow it to our everlasting reward."

It was a little creepy, the way he linked homosexuals to thieves and moneylenders. I wondered if there were any bankers in the audience, and if they felt as uncomfortable as I did. "Today my wife is going to read to us from Genesis," the minister continued. He turned to his wife, who stepped forward to her own lectern.

"We begin with chapter 19, verse 24: 'Then the Lord caused to rain upon Sodom and upon Gomorrah brimstone and fire from the Lord out of heaven; and He overthrew those cities, and all the Plain, and all the inhabitants of the cities, and that which grew upon the ground.'"

I looked at the paper program we'd found on the seats. The couple at the front were only lay ministers; they were clear about that. Their names were Jeff and Sheila White.

Then it clicked. The Whites lived next door to Jerry Bosk and Vic Ramos, and I'd interviewed them when I canvassed their Makiki neighborhood after the murder of Hiroshi Mura.

I felt a little better. I hadn't recognized the minister from the sketch; I'd recognized him from the canvassing I'd done.

Sheila White closed her Bible and looked out at the audience. "We have had our own Sodom and Gomorrah here in Honolulu. On Wednesday night, the Lord rained down his fire and brimstone upon a group of sinners even here in our own hometown." My mind, which had been wandering, snapped to attention. She went on to describe how those sinners who had challenged God's word on marriage had been punished, how just as in Genesis the flames had devoured the habitation of this terrible group.

I looked at her appraisingly. She was deadly earnest, no trace of irony in her voice as she compared the destruction of biblical cities with the bombing of an innocent office building. She decried the death of Vice Mayor Wilson Shira, a true friend of Christ, who had been martyred in his defense of the sacred institution of marriage.

I knew for a fact that Shira's family were devout Buddhists. I wondered how they would appreciate his Christian martyrdom.

"But friends, the battle is not over yet," Sheila White continued. "There are still people here in our own community who would pervert the sacrament of marriage. They must be stopped, or God will not stop with Sodom and Gomorrah. Genesis, chapter 6, verse 5: 'And the Lord saw that the wickedness of man was great in the earth, and that every imagination of the thoughts of his heart was only evil continually. And it repented the Lord that he had made man on the earth, and it grieved Him at His heart. And the Lord said, "I will blot out man whom I have created from the face of the earth." ' "

She closed the Bible in front of her. "Now we all remember what happened after that. And we live here on an island, so we know how terrible the might of the wind and the ocean can be when the Lord harnesses them in his power. It is a matter of self-preservation, after all. If we do not blot out these sinners, but leave the task to God, who knows what revenge he will take upon us?"

Who knows, indeed, I thought. The service dragged on for a while, and then finally we all stood and bowed our heads for the final benediction. "Christ our Lord, please shine your blessings on these, your children and your soldiers," Jeff White intoned. "Help us struggle in your name for what is right and good and Christian in the world, and fight against evil and perversion with clean hearts and strong bodies."

Everyone joined hands and sang "Onward Christian Soldiers, Marching as to War."

After the service, Kitty and I stood out in the parking lot talking with the couple who'd sat next to us, Fran and Eli Harding, and their two little kids. Traffic was zooming by on Wai'alae Avenue, a couple of customers were going into Robertico Robles' hair salon. I didn't like being exposed out there; suppose Tatiana dropped by to gossip with her buddy Tico and spotted me? What if Liliha stopped by to chat with Sheila White?

The air was heavy with auto exhaust and the faint, lingering smell of smoke, but there was not a cloud in the bright blue sky. There had been another arson the day before, a wildfire up in the Ko'olau Mountains, and I wondered if Mike had been out there to investigate it. I was just thinking of him when Eli said, "It isn't normal. It isn't what God wanted when he created marriage."

I realized that the conversation had turned to gay marriage. "They're jealous of us, you know," Fran said to Kitty, holding on to Caitlin, who was only four, as she struggled to run away and play with her brother and some of the other kids. "What Eli and I have, what you and Kimo have. Marriage. A place in the world. The sense that we're good, God-fearing, normal people."

"We aren't married," Kitty said, holding up her ringless left hand. "But you never know what God's plan is for you until he reveals it."

She smiled at me, and I reached over and squeezed her hand.

"We had to pull Cole and Caitlin out of the public school," Fran said. "They had this teacher there that was a homosexual, and he was teaching them all this terrible stuff about deviants. I went in and complained, and the principal made it seem like I was the crazy one!"

"And don't forget the little girl with the two mommies," Eli said.

Fran nodded. "Cole came home from school one day and said that this one little girl in the class had two mommies. We thought, well, all right, the parents are divorced and she has a mommy and a step-mommy. But no! It turns out there are these two lesbians and she calls them both Mommy! Do you believe that?"

Neither Kitty nor I knew what to say, so we just smiled. "So of course we couldn't keep Cole and Caitlin there," Eli said. "Fran got a home-school course through a church on the mainland, and we use that now."

We chatted for a few more minutes, and then the Hardings

left. Kitty and I walked down along the storefronts, trying to put as much distance as possible between us and any stray members of the church who might be around to overhear. "What did you think?" Kitty asked.

"I don't like the rhetoric," I said. "And the reference to the bombing is pretty suspicious."

"What can you do?" she asked. "Can you get a search warrant for the church? Maybe they've been making bombs out in the back."

"Not so fast," I said. "You need to assemble evidence before you can ask a judge for a warrant." I told her that I thought Jeff White looked a lot like the sweaty guy who'd been seen near the bathroom at the Marriage Project before the bomb went off. "But we don't even know that the sweaty guy is the bomber," I said. "He could have just been some guy who happens to look a lot like Jeff White, who got a bad shrimp from the caterers and got sick."

"It's so frustrating," Kitty said. "I just know there's something wrong about that church. But how do you prove it?"

"Welcome to police work," I said.

I thought about that on the drive back to Waikīkī. Under normal circumstances, I'd grab my board and head out to the water. Surfing freed my subconscious mind to find just those connections that might allow us to pin something on the Whites and the Church of Adam and Eve.

But my back was still red and sore, so I knew I couldn't expose myself to saltwater. I decided to get on my bike and ride instead.

I headed down Kalākaua Avenue, through Kapiolani Park. For a while the street was roofed over by tall trees, like riding through a grotto, almost religious in its way, and I realized how much more spiritual nourishment I got from nature than from organized religion. Then I came out along the base of Diamond Head itself, riding along the ocean, past the lighthouse and the Kuilei Cliffs.

I tried to focus on what I knew for sure. Jeff and Sheila White were the lay ministers in charge of the Church of Adam and Eve. They lived in Makiki, next door to a gay couple. They preached against gay marriage, while their neighbors were strong proponents of the issue. That was an incendiary situation.

A search warrant for their home and church might turn up evidence. But I needed something more than speculation to get such a warrant. I decided to put Harry Ho on their trail, to see what he could dig up on the Whites. They were *malihinis,* newcomers to the islands, and often our newest residents bring with them the baggage of their mainland years. If either Jeff or Sheila White had a criminal record, especially using incendiary devices, I could use that as a toehold.

As I came out to the coastal road, there was a single cloud over Rabbit Island, but no real hope for rain to break our drought and extinguish the wildfires. The hard-core surfers were out beyond Diamond Head, of course, as I probably would have been if my back hadn't prevented it. I rode past the motley assortment of cars parked along the road, waving to a couple of surfers I recognized changing out of rash guards.

I kept going back to my conversation with Terri. What would motivate someone to preach so strongly against an issue like gay marriage? What would motivate someone to protest, to bomb a party? I knew how tough it was to live in the closet—yet despite all my angst I'd never chosen to take out my frustration on anyone else. I'd beaten myself up instead.

I rode out Kahala Avenue for a while, then circled back on the *mauka,* or mountain, side of Diamond Head Road. Heading homeward through Kapahulu I pushed myself hard, as if I could sweat away my worries and fears, and all the guilt I felt over what had happened to people I loved.

Chapter 24

WORKING WITH MIKE

I WAS FEELING SO GOOD on my bike that instead of returning home, I kept going through Waikīkī, all the way to The Queen's Medical Center. By the time I got there, both my brothers and their families were there, standing down in the courtyard waving up at my mom and dad, who were looking out the window at them and waving back. My nieces and nephews were holding up cards with big words printed on them, obviously a group effort. Only Jeffrey and Ashley were feuding, and wouldn't stand next to each other, and nobody had thought to change the cards they were holding. So the message my parents saw was GET SOON TŪTŪ AL WELL.

After a lot of kissing and hugging, my sisters-in-law bundled the kids away to go to McDonald's, and my brothers went upstairs with me. "The doctor was here again. Your father can go home tomorrow," my mother said, when we came in.

"He gets a cut, you know," my father grumbled. "These doctors and these hospitals, they all work together. For every day he keeps me here, the hospital gives him money."

With a straight face, Lui said, "Wow, that's interesting, Dad. I'll have to get a reporter on that story."

I couldn't look at either of my brothers because I was afraid I'd burst out laughing. My father was probably the most upright businessman I'd ever come across; despite the graft that was often rampant in the construction business, he'd always been a hundred percent honest. That didn't stop him from accusing everyone else around him, though.

It was strange, hanging out with my entire nuclear family. Usually when I see my parents, either I'm alone with them, or at least one of my brothers and his family is there. The last time I could remember the five of us together was right after I'd come out, when I'd been hiding at home, and both Haoa and Lui had come home as well, as a result of various problems.

With my father sitting up in bed, my mother in the chair next to him, and the three of us ranged against the wall like suspects at a lineup, we talked, we boys trying to get our father to promise to take better care of his health.

I kept looking at my watch. I wanted to call Mike Riccardi, just to check in with him, but I wasn't going to use the phone by my dad's bedside, and I'd left my cell phone at home when I'd gone out for my bike ride.

"We holding you up?" Haoa asked. "You got some place you need to be?"

"Little brother's busy," Lui said. "Don't you watch the TV news?"

"Little brother's bigger than you are," I said to him.

"Not bigger than I am," Haoa said.

"You know, they've got this thing called Weight Watchers," I said. "If you're at all concerned about being so big."

"Boys!" my mother said. "*Ai ya!* When will you ever grow up?"

The three of us burst out laughing. "Never, as long as you and Dad are around to keep us in line, Ma," Haoa said.

"Speak for yourself," Lui said. His cell phone tweedled, and he flipped it open. "Yes, sweetheart. We're almost done here. Be there soon." He closed the phone and glared at me and Haoa, daring us to say anything. We didn't.

A woman in a blue smock delivered my father's dinner tray, and after another round of kissing, the three of us left. "You want McDonald's?" Lui asked as we waited for the elevator. "Fun time in the play zone with all your nieces and nephews."

Haoa said, "You've been married too long, brah. Can't you tell? Kimo's got a date."

I opened my mouth to protest, but Haoa said, "You can't fool me, brah. I know that look, when you keep looking at your watch that way. It's not some crime scene that's calling to you."

"I don't have a date," I said. We stepped into the elevator, and both my brothers looked at me. "I just want to make a phone call."

"To make a date," Haoa said triumphantly.

"It's not like that," I said, aware that I probably ought to just shut up. "He's a fire investigator. We're working on the bombing case together."

"And you need to check with him on Sunday night?" Lui asked. "Have you got a lead?"

Haoa said, "Lui, you are dumber than dirt. Didn't you ever say you and a girl were 'studying' together?" He waggled his fingers around the word studying, making the quotation marks in the air. "Kimo's 'working' on the case with this guy."

I must have blushed, because both my brothers started laughing as the elevator doors opened on the ground level. "Have fun, brah," Haoa called as he and Lui turned toward the garage, and I walked over to where I'd parked and locked my bike. "Don't do anything I wouldn't do." Lui laughed, and then Haoa said, "Wait, check that."

I laughed for the first couple of blocks back toward

Waikīkī. When I got home, Mike Riccardi's truck was parked in front of my building, and he was sitting in the front seat listening to the UH volleyball game on the radio. "Bump, set, spike!" I heard the announcer exclaim.

"Hey, who's winning?" I asked, coming up to his open window.

"Does love always have to be a game to you?" he asked. "Is one of us always going to be the winner and one the loser?" I had to look closely before I saw the edges of a grin spreading on his face.

"What a goof. So, what're you doing here?"

"You want to go for a ride?"

"I've just been," I said, pointing to my bike. "I need a shower now. Want to come upstairs?"

"Sure." I wanted to hug and kiss him right there in the street, there in front of all my neighbors and the tourists in their rental cars and the birds in the trees, but I didn't. I locked my bike in the rack and led him up to my apartment. I'd barely gotten the lock open when his arms were around me and we were kissing and squeezing each other.

"God, I missed you," he said, breathing into my neck. "You don't know how much I wanted to go out with you last night."

"I know," I said. "Remember, if I could, I'd still have at least one foot in the closet. I may be out to the world, but in my heart I'm still figuring a few things out." I pushed away from him a little. "I'm all scuzzy and sweaty. Let me jump in the shower for a minute."

He lifted an arm to sniff his pit. "I could probably use a little cleanliness myself." There was that grin again, spreading across his face. It must have been contagious, because I could feel it spreading across mine, too. I started unbuttoning his shirt.

We left a trail of clothes on the floor from the front door to the shower, the two of us finally naked as we stepped inside it. I turned the water on high and stood there in the hot, steamy spray, my body pressed against his, kissing him, sucking on his lips, his hard dick pressed against mine. He kneaded my shoulders and I thought I might dissolve there in the water, swirl away down the drain in a flood of lust and ecstasy.

We lathered each other up, rubbing the soap all over our bodies. It was like a scene from some X-rated video except that more of the pleasure seemed to be coming from my heart than my groin. Not to say that part wasn't terrific; considering that neither of us had that much experience at gay sex I think we managed just fine. But I didn't just want to suck him because he had a dick; I wanted to suck him because he was Mike, this guy I really liked, and I wanted to give him the same pleasure I got from just being with him.

By the time we were finished we were both exhausted, and we flopped down together on my bed, letting our body heat dry each other. "I was miserable last night," Mike said. "I wanted to see you. But it scared the shit out of me, thinking about going around to those bars with you, worrying that somebody would see us together."

"We don't have to go out if you don't want to." I held my hand up. "No, I don't mean it like that. I mean we can have dinner, and go to the movies, and go for bike rides or rollerblading or stuff, and as long as we don't hold hands or kiss in public nobody has to know what else goes on between us. Hey, do you surf?"

He shrugged. "I have in the past. I'm not real good."

"I can teach you. And then afterwards we can come back here, or go to your place, and we can have fun in private."

"My place could be a little problem."

I sat bolt upright in the bed. "Shit, you're married, aren't you?"

He laughed. "No, I'm not that fucked up. It's just—well, I kind of live with my parents."

"Jesus! You're over thirty and you still live with your parents? What kind of messed up case are you?"

"I don't actually live with them. We own a duplex together. They live in one half, I live in the other."

"And you never thought that maybe, being gay, you might want to be able to bring a guy home now and then without your mother looking out the window to see who's with you?"

He sat up and brought his legs up to his chest. "Maybe it was a way of keeping myself from doing anything. You know, if I had the freedom, maybe I'd act on it, and that would be scary."

"For a guy who's willing to go into burning buildings you're kind of a chicken."

"And I know how much you like chicken."

"You're never going to let me forget that the first time you saw me I was carrying the stinking remains of a dead chicken."

"It's what first attracted me to you."

"Go on." I pushed at his shoulder. "So how'd you get involved in this duplex anyway?"

"My parents have lived in their half for years. When I came home from college I moved back in with them while I figured out what I wanted to do." He shrugged. "I'm an only child, so I guess my parents spoiled me. You combine that with the whole sexual orientation thing, and I was kind of a fuck up in college. I drank a lot, never studied, just made it through on good looks and native intelligence. There was no way I was going to medical school, not even to nursing school like my mom."

It was a lot like my story. I'd fooled around myself in college, concentrating more on surfing than on English literature, which was my major, and the only way I'd graduated was that I loved to read, and I could write papers in my sleep. Now that I looked back on it, I realized that a lot of my ambivalence about a career had to do with my unwillingness to face my sexuality.

I wondered how many more kids were out there like Mike and me, failing to realize all their potential because of their internal conflicts. It made me see how important my work at the Gay Teen Center was, not just providing a safe haven and a solid role model, but helping those kids come to terms with their lives.

"Earth to Kimo," Mike said.

"Sorry. Guess I drifted off."

"I didn't realize my life story was so boring."

"Go on. You were a fuckup in college, your parents didn't know what to do with you."

He frowned at me. "My dad wanted me to get a government job, you know, so secure and all. I finally decided to become a firefighter, and I kept on living with them while I went through training. Then when I was making money, and I wanted to move out, the people in the other half of the house wanted to sell."

He relaxed and let his long legs stretch to the edge of the bed. I started tickling my hand around his groin and watched his dick react. "You know how expensive it is to buy anyplace these days. We knew everything about the house already, and because we did the deal direct I even saved on the real estate commission."

"What a bargain." I leaned down and took his dick in my mouth. His whole body shook.

We fooled around for an hour or more, mostly just kissing and hugging and rolling around on the bed. Mike got up to go to the bathroom, and while he was in there I called Harry Ho and asked him to see what he could dig up on the Whites and the Church of Adam and Eve.

"Sounds like fun," he said. "I love a good puzzle. Arleen just took Brandon home, so I'll see what I can dig up."

I felt guilty that I wasn't busy figuring out who bombed the Marriage Project, so when Mike came out of the bathroom I said, "Can we talk about the bombing?"

Mike stretched and pulled on his briefs, which I realized were a Ginch Gonch design with fire trucks on them. *Man,* I thought, *was this guy gay or what,* and I laughed.

He looked at me funny and said, "Sure. Got any new ideas?"

I told him about my conversation with Terri Gonsalves the day before, trying to understand the motivation of the bomber. "So you think it's some closeted guy?" he asked. "Maybe even married?"

I nodded. "I know I did some stupid things before I finally gave up hiding," I said. "That pressure can make you crazy."

There was something on Mike's face that I couldn't read. Finally I realized, and I said, "You want to talk about it?"

"It's nothing," he said. "Just thinking about the dumb things I've done."

"Not . . ." I looked over at the bed.

He smiled. "Not you. I'm not regretting anything we've done. Or we're going to do." He was quiet for a minute. "I was at this conference in San Francisco last year," he said. "Arson investigators. Guys I've known for years, from all over the country. I should have just stayed in my room, but it was San Francisco, you know?"

I knew. I'd been to San Francisco just a few months before, doing a favor for a guy who ended up making a big donation to the Gay Teen Center. And I'd been somewhat indiscreet, with an incredible guy I'd met on the street. But I was already out of the closet by then.

"You get arrested?" I asked.

The surprise showed on his face, and then he laughed. "Nope. Probably could have, though. I went to this sex club, and I just went kind of crazy. I mean, I did stuff there I'd never even thought of. I staggered back to the hotel, feeling miserable. My ass hurt and my skin was scraped raw in places. Some guy'd twisted my balls around and it took a day before they stopped aching."

He looked at me. "But the worst part was how I felt inside. Just miserable. Like I'd disappointed myself, like I'd . . . I don't know . . . given something away that I shouldn't have."

"I know," I said. "I've done my share of that kind of stuff, too. The closet's a lousy place. Makes you do that kind of stuff. Maybe even makes you try to hurt other people."

As soon as I'd said it, I wished I could take it back. I didn't mean that about Mike; I didn't think he was the kind of guy who could ever hurt someone, no matter how much pressure you put on him. The kind of guy who'd let it all build up inside him.

Shit, that was just the kind of guy our bomber probably was. I could see the hurt in Mike's eyes, though, so I changed the subject. "I went to the Church of Adam and Eve this morning with my boss's daughter," I said.

"Your boss's daughter?"

I explained about Kitty Sampson. "I gave her 'til Thursday to come clean with her dad, though, or else I will."

I asked Mike about the arsons he'd been investigating, trying to make connections, and we sat at my kitchen table for a couple of hours, going over all the details. We ordered a pizza, drank a couple of Longboard Lagers, and studied every angle, but we couldn't find a connection.

Around 10 o'clock, Mike yawned. "Been a long day, for a weekend," he said. I knew he'd been up at an arson scene most of the day before showing up at my place. "Guess I ought to get to bed."

"You want to stay here?" I asked.

"You're ready for a rematch already?" he asked, and there was a smile in his eyes.

"We could just sleep," I said.

He stood, and in one fluid motion he'd pulled off his T-shirt and shinnied out of the Ginch Gonch briefs. "In your nightmares, pal," he said. "But first, you need some more cream on your back." When I laughed, he said, "Not that kind of cream. The medicated ointment."

While he was rubbing my back, Mike asked, "Wanna hear a joke?"

"Sure."

"Did you hear the one about the policeman and the fire-man who went to heaven?"

"Sounds like us."

"St. Peter gave them both their wings, but he said that if they had even one bad thought their wings would fall off. As soon as they left the wing department, they saw this beautiful girl, and the fireman's wings fell off."

"So this isn't about you and me," I said.

Mike slapped my back. "When the fireman bent over to pick up his wings, that's when the policeman's wings fell off."

I wriggled around trying to grab hold of him, and it felt so damn good just to laugh and have fun with him. We finally did get to sleep later that night. Mike drifted off first, his breathing turning into a regular, almost purring sound. I nestled up against him, inhaling the smell of coconut shampoo, and when I looked up again it was already daylight.

We ran down our days for each other. "I'm hoping Harry dug up some dirt on the Whites and the Church of Adam and Eve," I said. "He's a night owl, so he was probably working while we were playing."

"Gotta love a computer geek," Mike said. He was planning to be around his office all day, going over evidence.

"My dad's going home today," I said. "If I can get away from work early enough I'll go over there."

"I'd like to meet your parents sometime, when your dad is better. And your brothers, too. You think they'd like me?"

I stood up and started to get dressed. "It's hard to say. No, don't give me that look, I'm trying to be serious here. If we weren't gay, and I brought you over as a friend, they'd all love you. I mean, you're a cool guy. You're handsome and smart and funny. What's not to like."

"Aw, you're making me blush."

"If I could make you get dressed, that would probably speed things up around here." He gave me a look, then started picking his clothes up from the floor. "But bringing you home like a boyfriend, that's tougher. I mean, they know that Gunter is just a friend of mine, but at the party they were all looking at him like, 'so, what do you guys do together?' It was a little uncomfortable."

"And you're just friends?"

"Yes, Mr. Jealous. We've fooled in the past, just casually, and Gunter would love to get into my pants again, but so far I've resisted."

He walked over and put his arms around me, kissing me.

"Well, you just keep on resisting."

We kissed for a while. Finally I pushed him away. "Come on, I've got to get going. Anyway, about meeting my parents and my brothers. If you ever do meet them, I want to be proud of introducing you. I want to be able to tell them how I feel about you. And that might take a while—for both of us."

"Will you call me tonight?"

"You bet." I kissed him, and then slapped his butt. "Now let's get going."

Chapter 25

THE WHITE FAMILY

I SPENT THE MORNING doing my own research on the Church of Adam and Eve. They didn't have any kind of official registration, though they'd pulled permits for each of the big events they'd run, which had taken place at the Pupukea Plantation, the place I'd gone the month before. There wasn't much else about them, though I read through a few articles in the *Advertiser* and the *Star-Bulletin,* and I did some background reading on fundamentalist churches and their opposition to gay marriage.

Around noon, the desk called and said Harry Ho was there to see me. "Hey, brah, what's up?" I asked. I brought him back to my desk.

"I got some material on those people you asked about," he said. "I figured I'd better bring it down to you."

"What did you find?"

I sat at my desk, and he sat across from me. He passed a couple of printouts over to me. "Took me a while to dig around, but I finally found them," he said. The printouts were driver's licenses from Texas for Sheila Jane White and Jeffrey Steven White. "That's them, isn't it?"

I nodded. "Yup. They came from Texas?"

"I looked for a marriage license, and I couldn't find one. I thought maybe they'd changed their names, so I pulled up their birth certificates." He passed two more pieces of paper my way.

They'd been born a year apart, in the same hospital. I was almost ready to move on to the next point when I realized what had gotten Harry excited. "Holy shit," I said.

"You see it?"

"The same parents," I said. "So Sheila and Jeff White aren't married. They're brother and sister."

"Kinky, isn't it?"

"We don't know that," I said.

"Kimo, they represent themselves as husband and wife. Don't you think that means they're sleeping together, too?"

I blew out a big breath. "I think I need to talk to Terri."

"I would say that's a good idea," he said. "Call her up."

I pulled out my cell phone, which had her cell number programmed in. "I need to talk to you," I said. "Harry's here in my office. Can we all meet up?"

"I'm at the Foundation office," she said. "You guys want to meet for lunch?"

About a half hour later, we all met up at a little plate lunch place a few blocks from police headquarters. "What's the emergency?" Terri asked, after we'd been seated and ordered our lunches.

I showed her the drivers' licenses and the birth certificates, and waited for her to make the connection. "Kimo, this is creepy," she said.

"That's what we thought," Harry said.

"But what do you think it means?" I asked.

Terri sipped her pineapple soda for a minute while she thought. Finally she said, "There are laws against incest, aren't there?"

"I'd have to check," I said.

"But for sure, you can't marry somebody you're related to," Terri said. "Cousins, siblings, that kind of thing."

"I see where you're going," I said.

"Where?" Harry asked. "Don't go all psychic on me."

The waitress brought our lunches. A plate lunch was an island tradition, developed to serve to plantation workers who needed to keep up their strength through long days. It consisted of a main course, usually fish or chicken, two scoops of rice, a scoop of macaroni salad, and some shredded lettuce. We'd all opted for the chicken, making it easy for the waitress to distribute the food.

"In many states, for years it was illegal for black people and white people to marry each other," Terri said. "And eventually that changed. Now it's possible that the laws against gay marriage will change."

"Yeah," Harry said.

"But I doubt that our society is ever going to change the way we feel about family members getting married," she continued.

"So the Whites probably resent the fact that gay men and lesbians might be able to get married, when they're never going to be able to marry each other, never be able to tell anybody about their relationship," I said.

"So they left Texas, where people knew them, and came here," Harry said. "They said they were married, and nobody ever questioned them. After all, they already had the same last name."

"Would that motivate them to bomb the Marriage Project party?" I asked Terri.

She shrugged. "I guess so, if they were nutty enough. I mean, it's one thing to want to do something that goes against society's rules—and it's another entirely to act against other people."

"Is this enough evidence to get you a search warrant?" Harry asked me.

I frowned. "I don't think so. I mean, yes, it's creepy, and there's probably something illegal about their relationship in some way. But it's hard to make that leap to the bombing."

"But if you got a search warrant you'd find the evidence," Harry said.

"The law doesn't work that way," I said. "The judges call that a fishing expedition."

We ate in silence. Finally, Terri said, "I did some research this morning at the Foundation. We've given the church a couple of small grants. About $10,000 in all. They have to give us an accounting to get any more money, but so far they haven't provided any evidence of what they've used the money for."

"Bombs," Harry said.

"We don't know that, Harry," I said.

"Don't you care about this?" he asked. "These assholes could have killed Brandon, or Arleen, or any of us. Don't you want to stop them?"

"Yes, I do," I said. "But I know that the only way to stop them is through the law. It doesn't always seem right, but if we start trampling on anybody's rights we open the door for all kinds of bad stuff."

Back at the station, I took the evidence I had to Lieutenant Sampson, in case I'd been underestimating what I had. But he agreed with me. "You're right, it smells bad," he said. "But there isn't anything yet that solidly connects these people or this church to the bombing, or any of the other arsons."

He was wearing a navy polo shirt, and that reminded me that when I'd seen Kitty last, she'd worn one, too, at the church service on Sunday morning. "How's Kitty?" I asked.

He looked surprised. "Kitty? She's fine. Working hard at school."

"Good." I guessed she hadn't told him yet about our little investigation, and I knew she still had a couple of days to broach the subject. "Well, I'll keep looking, then."

"Look fast," he said. "I want this case solved soon."

At the end of my shift, I went over to The Queen's Medical Center, and caught up with my parents just as they were packing up. I'd just said hello when my father's bedside phone rang. Since my mother was busy helping my father out of bed, I answered it.

"Oh, Kimo!" The woman on the other end of the line was crying.

I listened to her for a minute, then said, "All right, I'm going to come right over. You stay there, don't do anything, don't call anyone else, all right?"

"Thank you, Kimo. You good boy."

I hung up the phone. My mother had just helped my father into the bathroom, and when she closed the door on him I beckoned her over. "Aunt Mei-Mei just called. Uncle Chin is dead, and Jimmy Ah Wong has disappeared. I've got to go over there."

"Poor Mei-Mei," she said. "I was worried this would happen." She pulled a tissue from the box next to the bed and wiped her eyes, then sat down on the edge of the bed. My parents and the Suks had been best friends for as long as I could remember, and I was sure my mother was seeing the day, some time in the future, when she would lose my father. She looked up at me. "I don't want to tell your father yet. He's still not well, and a shock like this could set him back. You come over tonight. I'll call your brothers, too."

My father didn't want to ride in a wheelchair down to the car—even though it was clear he wasn't up to walking—but I made it clear that he didn't have any choice in the matter. I guess I know where my stubbornness comes from. I pushed the chair downstairs, and waited with him while my mother ransomed her car from the parking garage.

"You know about the old Polynesians and the *māhū?*" my father asked.

I moved around in front of him and sat on a bollard. "Yeah?"

"When a family had only sons, they would raise the youngest as girl. Dress him as a girl, have him help the mother with chores. The *māhū* never married, and always stayed with the family to take care of them."

"I've read about it," I said.

He reached out and took my hand. "You're a good boy, Kimo. But your mother and me, we don't want you to think you have to be that old-style *māhū,* give up your life to take care of us."

I smiled at him. "You have three sons, Dad," I said. "We're all going to be around to help you and Mom with whatever you need. And don't worry, I won't have to give up my life to do it."

I leaned forward and kissed his forehead. Then my mother pulled up in her Lexus and we loaded my dad into the front seat. "Will you be OK with him at home?" I asked my mother.

"He can walk a little," my mother said. "And I have a walker at home he can use."

"I'm right here," my father said.

"Yes, Dad, I know," I said. "You be good to Mom, OK? This hasn't been easy for her."

He snorted. "For me, a big luau," he said.

"Yeah, and who cleans up every time we have a luau?" I asked. "Mom, right?"

I closed the passenger door and watched them drive off. Then I got my truck and followed them to St. Louis Heights, where Uncle Chin's house was not far from theirs. My father and Uncle Chin had been best friends since their days at the University of Hawai'i, when they were young men, before they married and became fathers and successful businessmen. A few weeks after I started at the police academy, I asked my father when he knew that Uncle Chin was a criminal.

"Chin is a very smart man," my father said. He had asked me to take a walk with him, out in the woods of the Wa'ahila Ridge Park, which abutted our property. "You have to understand, back then the *Pākē* kept to themselves, stayed in Chinatown. There was a lot of prejudice against them. But Chin knew he needed to learn about the *haole* world, and he started taking classes at the university, which is where I met him. I think even then he was mixed up in the tongs, probably since China."

"And it didn't bother you?"

My father smiled at me. "When you were a boy, everything was always black or white with you. Very strong opinions, even when your brothers disagreed with you, and they were so much older and bigger. I never felt that way." We wandered down a narrow mossy trail between tall trees, the light shading from clear white to dark green all around us. "I never was like that. I always knew there are many shades of gray in the world."

"Did you ever break the law with him?"

"Ah, now you're starting to sound like a police officer," my father said. "You have to understand what it was like for me, being mixed race back then. It was hard to know where you fit in. I'd go places with my father, who was full-blooded Hawai'ian, and people could look at me and know there was *haole* in me, and of course I didn't speak the language as well as he did. So they would look at me funny, like I didn't quite belong."

We started to walk uphill, toward the stone wall and the gate. "Then other times I would go with my mother into the stores on Fort Street, and they'd see her come in, this proper *haole* lady—you probably don't remember your grandmother very well but she was always beautifully dressed, she wouldn't go out of the house unless she looked like she was ready to pay a social call on somebody—and the clerks would look up, very nice and polite, and then my brothers or sisters or I would come in behind her, sometimes a couple of us, and their attitudes would change dramatically."

"I'm not getting the point."

"The point is that Chin accepted me for who I was, just Al. And I accepted him, too. I was closer to him than I ever was to my brothers. So, anything he did, well, it was all right, because he was all right." We came to a table and bench and he sat down. "I know I avoided your question, but I did for a reason. Do you really want to know the answer?"

I looked at him. I was twenty-four years old, and I had just given up my hopes of being a champion surfer to go to the police academy. I was scared, and angry that I hadn't been able to succeed, and I was wrestling with the knowledge that I was sexually attracted to men, though I didn't want to be. I felt like I'd been knocked off my board, swamped by a huge wave that I couldn't get around, and I still needed some things to hang onto. One of those things, I realized then, was the belief that my father was a good and honorable man who could have passed those traits to me. I said, "You get a nice view from up here, don't you? You can see the whole city."

My dad looked at me and smiled and said, "Yes, you can, can't you?"

I pulled into Uncle Chin's driveway. Aunt Mei-Mei came to the door, crying. It was the kind of thing I'd done hundreds of times before, walked into a house where someone was dead, family members crying around me, and I'd always been able to shut my own feelings off and do my job.

What if Jimmy Ah Wong had been responsible? I'd delivered him to Uncle Chin and Aunt Mei-Mei, asked them to take him in and look after him. How could I live with myself if I had been the instrument that caused Uncle Chin's death?

The only answers I would find were inside.

Chapter 26

PILLS ON THE FLOOR

UNCLE CHIN WAS SLUMPED in his easy chair, out on the lanai where he had spent so many of the last years, surrounded by orchids and African violets with their delicate flowers, bright red anthuriums and the lush succulence of jades and aloes. Small yellow birds in cages twittered nervously as I prowled around. Since their cages were uncovered, I knew that Uncle Chin had been sitting out there with them, not ready to go to bed yet.

The table next to his chair had been knocked over. Without touching anything, I squatted down to look at the items that had fallen: his glasses, and a Charles Dickens book in hardcover he had been reading. In his old age Uncle Chin had taken up nineteenth-century English literature in a big way, working through Jane Austen, George Eliot, Thackeray, and Dickens. I also found a small prescription bottle of nitroglycerin tablets on the floor, the cap a foot away, a couple of tablets spilled out of the mouth of the bottle.

I took a tissue from a box on the other side of the room and used it to pick up the bottle. "Did Uncle Chin take these for his heart?" I asked Aunt Mei-Mei.

She nodded. "Sometimes he have to put one under tongue, when his heart go fast."

I could envision the scene all too well. Uncle Chin feeling

his heart race, reaching out for the bottle of pills, and knocking over the table. But where was Jimmy? He was supposed to be with the old man in case of just this sort of trouble. He should have been there to jump down, pick up the spilled bottle, and hand Uncle Chin a tablet. If he had, then Uncle Chin might have still been alive.

"It looks like he reached for a pill but he didn't get one," I said gently to Aunt Mei-Mei. "He probably had a very severe attack, maybe the pills might not even have helped." I had a thought. "Maybe he even took one, but it just didn't work." I pulled a stool up next to Aunt Mei-Mei, who had dried her eyes. "I have to call the medical examiner now. Whenever someone dies without a doctor present, it's the law."

She sat in the chair next to her husband, and I went back to the lanai to make the call. Then I walked down the hall to the room where Jimmy had been staying. He had made his bed that morning, not quite as expertly as Aunt Mei-Mei might have. I had brought him there with almost nothing, just the clothes on his back, a Walkman, and the money I'd given him. But he had left nothing behind, either. I stood there in the doorway of the room for a while, thinking about Jimmy and wondering where he was.

Then I had a bad idea. I walked back to the kitchen and asked Aunt Mei-Mei, "Did you or Uncle Chin have any money lying around?"

"You think Jimmy stole?"

I shrugged. "I don't know. I think we should look."

She got up and walked over to the counter, where a cookie jar in the shape of a grinning hula girl sat. I remembered that jar from my childhood. Uncle Chin used to empty his pocket change into it, and then when we kids would come over he'd fish around in there for the shiniest quarters to give us.

Aunt Mei-Mei lifted the hula girl's torso. "I not sure how much money here," she said. She tilted the jar enough for me to see there was still a pile of change inside, even a couple of dollar bills wadded up. She put the girl's torso back on her body. "Come, we look jewelry too."

She led me down the hall to their bedroom, and opened the drawers of an elaborate mahogany jewelry chest that sat on the lacquered bureau. Every drawer was filled almost to overflowing with rings, bracelets, and chains. "Look like all here." Aunt Mei-Mei sat on the bed and started to cry.

"I'm sorry, Aunt Mei-Mei," I said. "I had to ask."

"He such nice boy. He so nice Uncle Chin." I sat next to her and took her hand. "What I do now?" she asked. "This morning, I wife. I have boy take care of, too. Not my son, my Robert, but nice boy, need home, somebody take care of him. Now what I have? What I do?"

I squeezed her hand, and put my other arm around her. Aunt Mei-Mei leaned against me, crying softly. After a while, when she felt better, we went back to the kitchen to wait. I remembered stories about Uncle Chin and told them, and we both laughed, and eventually one of Doc Takayama's assistants arrived. He and I did a quick survey of the room and he directed his techs to remove Uncle Chin's body. Aunt Mei-Mei cried again as they carried the stretcher out, the sheet pulled up over his face, and I held onto her and stood by her side and tried to pretend I was just a cop.

My mother had been busy on the phone, and soon after the coroner left, Haoa and Tatiana showed up, followed quickly by Lui and Liliha.

We greeted each other somberly, everyone focusing on Aunt Mei-Mei, and Liliha and I studiously avoided each other.

198 ≈ NEIL S. PLAKCY

After a few minutes, Haoa pulled Lui and me to the kitchen, leaving Liliha, Tatiana, and Aunt Mei-Mei in the living room. "So has anybody told Dad about Uncle Chin yet?" he asked.

"No," Lui said. "I don't think we should."

"I think we ought to tell him, but we ought to wait a couple of days," Haoa said. "See if he starts to get his strength back."

I said, "I disagree. I think we ought to tell him. I'd certainly want to know."

"Not everybody is as strong as you are, Kimo," Lui said.

"He's our father. I think he's plenty strong."

"Lui's right," Haoa said. He opened the refrigerator and pulled out a bottle of water. "You looked at Dad lately? It's like he's fading away. None of us are as strong as you are. Maybe we ought to wait a day or two, see how he feels."

I looked at my big brothers. I'd always felt the weakest of the three of us, the youngest, the one they picked on. Even as adults, sometimes they ganged up against me and I bowed to their will. "You really think I'm stronger than he is, or than either of you?"

They shared a glance. "Of course," Lui said. "Look at everything you've gone through."

I was surprised, but I plowed on. "You guys remember all the stories Dad told? About when he was building his first house, and working nights for other contractors to make money, and then weekends doing jobs he couldn't afford to hire anybody for? I mean, imagine how scary that must be. You've got a wife and three kids, and you've staked everything you have to this one project. Think of the pressure."

"But he's old now," Haoa said. "Weaker. Maybe he can't take as much."

"That's what he's got three big sons for," I said. "I'm going to tell him. You guys want to be there?"

I think it was the first time I'd defied them on something to do with the family. They looked at each other, and then at me. "All right," Lui said. "You tell him. We'll be your backup."

I remembered how they had stood behind me when I came out, when I had to put myself in danger in order to solve the crime that had dragged me out of the closet, and in order to regain some self-respect. I couldn't ask for more from them.

We were just considering how to get over to our parents' house when Tatiana called, "Howie, your folks are here."

When we got to the front door, we saw my mother helping my father walk up the front walk. He'd refused to use the walker, and was moving slowly, my diminutive mother buoying him up. For a minute I doubted my resolve. This wasn't the big, strong father I'd always known and loved. This old man looked weak and tired.

Haoa and I got on each side of him and guided him up into the house, and into a big easy chair in the living room. I looked in his eyes then, and somewhere in there was the old Dad I'd known. I knew then we had to carry through with our plan. "We have some bad news for you, Dad," I said, kneeling down next to him. "Uncle Chin died this afternoon."

"I know." We all looked at our mother, but she shook her head. "Nobody told me. Somehow I just knew." He smiled. "You know Chin and I always had a kind of connection to each other. This afternoon, I felt like the connection was gone. I made your mother bring me over here to see for myself." He reached out and took my hand. "I'm glad you boys told me. I appreciate it."

"We have a lot to do," my mother said. "Mei-Mei will need

our help." Uncle Chin's widow sat across from us on the sofa, and though she was still crying a little, my mother sat next to her holding her hand. She didn't have a family of her own any more, but she had us.

I looked at my father and my brothers. If they thought I was strong, maybe I was. I knew where it came from.

Chapter 27

A SHOT IN THE PARK

I LOOKED AT MY WATCH, and realized that I'd promised to go to the Marriage Project rally at Waikīkī Gateway Park that evening. I huddled with my brothers, and they agreed that I should go, that they'd keep things together between our parents and Aunt Mei-Mei.

By the time I arrived, there were already a hundred or more people milling around, most of them wearing pink triangles or rainbow patches or some other outward sign of gay solidarity. I felt a little uncomfortable moving through them, knowing that many of them knew exactly who I was. People kept slapping me on the back, and I tried not to wince at the aggravation to my healing burns. Guys even came up and kissed me. It was very strange, like I was wearing some big sign that said, HI, I'M THE GAY COP.

It was hot but not humid, and that deep in the heart of Waikīkī there was no ocean breeze to relieve us. I was surrounded by guys in muscle tops and tight shorts, women in bikini bras and compression shorts. A few flat-bottomed cumulous clouds drifted above us, and the sun was beginning to set over the ocean.

As I made my way up toward a makeshift stage that had been set up at one end of the park, I saw Kitty Sampson, who waved at me and came over. I wondered if she'd gotten her taste for polo shirts from her stepfather. This one was white, and she was wearing green sweatpants and her collection of bangle bracelets.

"I'm glad I ran into you, Kimo. That woman we met at church, Fran Harding? She called me this afternoon. They're going on a picnic Thursday afternoon, out in the mountains. Eli's family has a cabin out on Wa'ahila Ridge."

"I grew up near there. It's nice country. What did you tell her?"

"I said you were working, but I didn't have class, so I'd go with them. Is that OK?"

I frowned. "I'd feel a lot better if you told your dad. You haven't told him yet that we went to the church, have you?"

She shook her head. "You know how he is. Too protective."

"Yeah, but he's my boss, Kitty. If he finds out I've been sneaking you out to play detective he's going to kill me."

She smiled. "I have him wrapped around my little finger. After all, I'm his little kitten."

"Is that his nickname for you?"

She shook her head. "When I was born, and the midwife showed me to my mom, I was all curled up like a kitten. That's actually the name on my birth certificate, Kitten. I mean, like, is my mom a hippie or what? My dad's last name is Cardozo, and he's supposedly descended from the Supreme Court justice. But he and my mom didn't stay together for long, so I don't know for sure."

"How many times has your mom been married?"

She started counting, then jumped from one hand to the next. "Six times, I think. There was a guy she met in Vegas and married, but they got divorced when their hangovers wore off, so I don't count him. She says she likes getting married, she just doesn't like having a husband."

"Going back to the picnic," I said. "Maybe you ought to cancel. We don't know anything about these people, and I don't like the idea of them dragging you out into the countryside."

"I have a brown belt in karate and a cell phone," Kitty said. "I can take care of myself."

"I still don't like it." I thought for a minute. I hated to do it, but I felt responsible for Kitty. "If you don't tell your dad, then I will. If he says it's OK, then it's fine by me. But you know what he's going to say."

She shook her fist at me, and the bracelets rattled. "Those are beautiful bracelets," I said, trying to shift the conversation.

"My mom makes them," she said, sliding them along her arm. "That's what she does, she makes jewelry. She has a talent for it."

"Birthday and Christmas gifts?" I said, pointing at her wrist.

She shook her head. "My mom doesn't believe in celebrating bourgeois events like Christmas or, as she puts it, 'the day you came out of my womb.' She sends these to me whenever the spirit moves her. They come out of the blue, usually when I'm feeling down, like I didn't do well on a test or something. It's funny, but even though I hardly see her, and sometimes I don't even know where she is, we have this psychic connection, and whenever I need a boost this little package comes from her."

Kitty saw some friends from UH and waved to them. Then she said, "I'll talk to Jim, OK? Don't say anything yet."

"You have until Thursday morning," I said.

She left me, with a wave of a bangled arm. I looked around. The park was a big open area, some short, twisted wiliwili trees in one corner, but mostly just an expanse of fading green grass. You could tell the impact El Niño was having here, the lack of rain drying everything up. The air smelled of sweat and motor oil, with that slight underlayer of coconut tanning oil that you find anywhere there's a beach in the vicinity.

The crowd was growing. I knew that Sandra and Cathy had chosen a small space to ensure that the turnout would look decent, but it was clear they had underestimated, so I went over to congratulate them, and met Charlie Stahl again. Sandra looked tired and pale, and I wondered if she was really well enough to be up and about. "We're almost ready to start," she said. "You'll come up on the stage with us, won't you, Kimo?"

I shook my head. "I don't like doing that kind of thing."

"You've got to," Cathy said. "You want to show the community that the police are investigating the bombing, don't you? And you can say that anybody who has information should contact you. You know how most gay people feel about the police, Kimo. It's important they see they have a friend in the department."

Here it was again, the debate I'd been having with myself off and on since coming out. I knew I needed to be a role model, that part of my job in life was to show gay and lesbian people that the police were there to protect them, too. And part of me did like the spotlight.

But at the same time, I felt like I had a right to a personal life. I wanted to be able to go on a date with Mike and not hear whispers and see fingers pointed. I wanted to be able to interview witnesses and suspects without having someone say, "Hey, you're the gay cop."

It was a balancing act, but in this case the seesaw tipped down the way Cathy and Sandra wanted it. "You sound like my boss," I said. I knew it was what Lieutenant Sampson would want, for me to stand up there and represent the department. "All right. But I want to go on record as saying I hate it."

"Your objection is duly noted," Sandra said in her lawyer voice. "All right, let's get this show on the road."

From the slight elevation of the stage, I got a great view of the crowd. They were very diverse, from older men in expensive leather jeans to twenty-something party boys in tight tank tops and even tighter shorts. There was a fair sprinkling of women, too, and even a bunch of little kids playing off in one corner.

I saw a few familiar faces. In her pressed uniform, Lidia Portuondo patrolled the area, drawing more than a few admiring glances from the women she passed. Though she normally patrolled downtown, I figured she'd picked up the extra duty for the overtime. Pua, Frankie, and Lolo from the Teen Center were there, standing together in a little group, trying to look older.

Then I saw Mike Riccardi. He was off toward the side, not mingling with anyone, and I wanted to go to him, put my arms around him, draw him into the crowd. Despite how uncomfortable I was with my recognition, what came with it was a sense of community, of belonging. These were my people, I thought, and I wanted them to be Mike's people too. I tried to catch his attention but he seemed to be looking everywhere but at me. A cameraman from KVOL roamed the crowd, taking random shots, and I thought Mike was trying to stay behind him, out of the range of the camera.

Sandra got up to the microphone and welcomed everybody. She started a chant. "What do we want? Equal rights. When do we want them? Now!"

The audience chanted with her. Finally she stopped and

the crowd applauded, then quieted. "Thanks for coming out today," she said. "And I mean that in every sense of the term. It's important for us to be out in all our communities, not just the gay and lesbian community. We have to show our friends, neighbors, relatives, and fellow voters that we are just like them—but with a twist."

"Yeah, we know how to dress," a guy called out from the audience, and everyone laughed.

"So this rally is very important, because it shows that we're going to keep on fighting for what we want, what we deserve," Sandra said. "I'm pleased to announce that a generous grant from Charlie Stahl, one of Honolulu's most prominent citizens, is going to put the Hawai'i Marriage Project back on its feet immediately." The crowd cheered.

Sandra looked back at Cathy, who helped Robert unfurl a big rainbow flag. "You all know those lines from 'The Star-Spangled Banner,' don't you?" Sandra said. Then she sang, a cappella, in a beautiful soprano I never knew lurked within her stocky body. "The bombs bursting in air, gave proof through the night, that our flag was still there."

Her last note was shimmering on the breeze when the series of shots rang out. All was chaos as those of us on the platform dove for cover, and the crowd began to panic. Fortunately the crowd stood paralyzed. The microphone was knocked to the ground and I crawled over to it. "Everybody get down," I said. "There are uniformed police in the area. If you saw where that shooting came from, please let one of them know immediately."

In front of me, the crowd had erupted in a panic, scattering everywhere. To my right, Charlie Stahl was lying on his back, bleeding, while Sandra and Cathy crouched over him. Mothers were scooping up children, and everyone else seemed to be scrambling over each other to get away. I saw Lidia trying vainly to keep order. *Where was Mike,* I worried.

I heard sirens almost immediately, and within moments I saw the flashing lights that heralded the arrival of the police and an ambulance for Charlie Stahl. But leaning over him as the EMTs came through the crowd, I realized they were too late. An unlucky shot had hit him in the neck, right at the aorta, and despite Sandra's attempts to staunch the bleeding, he had bled out.

Sandra was sobbing at the edge of the stage, with Cathy next to her, holding on. I wanted to go over to them but I knew I couldn't. I was afraid I'd break down, too. I'd seen many homicide victims in my career, including one man I cared about, and I'd killed one man myself, but I had never stood next to an innocent man, chatting and laughing with him, only to have him die next to me moments later.

I could feel the pressure building on me, just as it had on Sandra. We'd both narrowly escaped the bombing, and now this. How long could our luck hold out? It was a very scary thought.

The EMTs didn't like the way Sandra looked, so they took her away for tests, with Cathy going along. The park had cleared out in minutes, but there were a half dozen guys at the foot of the stage, calling for me. I got Lidia and a couple of the uniforms to help me and we corralled them into a line, and I sat in a folding chair at ground level and pulled out a notebook. Each guy seemed to have a different piece of information. A tall man, shorter than average, heavyset, no—gym build, no—swimmer's build, dark hair, blond, unshaven, a goatee. No one had actually seen the shot, but they'd all looked around in the vicinity where the shot had come from.

It took about half an hour to get through them all. I took

their names and phone numbers, though one guy said the only way I could contact him was through his post office box. "Sorry," he said, holding up the hand that held his wedding ring.

"It's OK," I said. "It's cool that you were willing to come up here and talk to me." Once the line was clear the uniforms left and the crowd started to disperse. I put my head down in my hands, trying to concentrate. Was there anything else I ought to do?

"How're you doing?"

Mike pulled a chair next to me, sat down, and put his arm around me.

"I'll be OK. Anyway, there's a lot of people around. Somebody might recognize you."

"I don't give a shit about what anybody else thinks." He kissed my forehead and then hugged me tight, and I couldn't hold it in any longer. I let out everything I was feeling about my brushes with death, my father being sick, Uncle Chin's death and Jimmy's disappearance, my frustrations at not catching the bomber, how I felt about all of us unable to live our lives without fear. I cried, and Mike held me.

"I have a small piece of good news for you," Mike said, as I wiped my face with my hand. "I saw your shooter. *Haole* woman in a black T-shirt, black running shorts, white sneakers. Short dark hair."

"You did?"

"I ran after her, but she had an accomplice driving a black Toyota Camry, which slowed as it passed her, and she jumped in. They ran a red light on Kuhio and I lost them."

"Did you get a plate number?"

He shook his head. "Only a partial. The first three digits were HXM."

"It's a start." I stood up, blew my nose. "A woman shooter? You're sure?"

"Yup." He smiled at me. "I do know the difference, you know."

"Come on, show me where you were when you heard the shot."

Chapter 28
PUPUKEA PLANTATION

BY THE TIME MIKE AND I were finished, darkness had fallen over Waikīkī. I spoke to Lieutenant Sampson and filled him in with what I knew, and then Mike and I went back to my apartment.

"Won't your mom and dad worry if they don't see your truck in the driveway?" I asked.

He shrugged. "They've gotten used to me getting called out at strange hours to go investigate fires," he said. "I always call them to let them know I'll be out."

It's funny the things that make us uncomfortable with a lover. Sometimes it's nakedness, physical or emotional. Sometimes it's silly things, like seeing that we don't pick up our underwear or the way we talk to our pets. I had a feeling Mike wanted some privacy to make his call, so I ducked out to the grocery at the corner to get us something for dinner.

When I got back he was lounging on my couch watching baseball on TV, and I sat next to him to watch. My dad played second-string baseball for a few years at UH, and he'd raised my brothers and me with baseball fever. He told us stories of the first baseball game ever in Hawai'i, played July 4, 1866, where the "natives" beat the "*haoles*," 2–1. The great Babe Ruth had come to Honolulu in 1933, and in the 1940s, when my dad was a kid, he used to watch Major League All-Star games in the old wooden Honolulu Stadium, affectionately called "The Termite Palace."

Mike and I were both tired, though he insisted on rubbing more cream on my healing burns. When he'd finished, we started to cuddle in my bed, but we both nodded off before we'd had a chance to get very far. It was so nice to wake the next morning, the sheets tangled around us, Mike snoring softly next to me. I propped my head up on my elbow and looked over at him.

I loved the way his smooth skin flowed over his muscular arms, the way his mouth relaxed into a smile, accentuated by his rich black mustache. There was a puckered scar on his right shoulder that looked like the result of a burn. I wanted to get to know every inch of his beautiful body, tracing my fingers over the fine black hairs on his chest and thighs, connecting the dots of the occasional freckles across his back.

He woke up and saw me watching him. He yawned. "What time?"

"At the sound of the tone it will be 6:05," I said. While I was making my tone noise, he reached down and took hold of my dick.

"Did you say 'tone' or 'bone'?" he asked.

I leaned across and kissed him, and we finished what we'd started the night before. By the time we were done, we had to rush out to avoid being late for work.

My first stop was at the coroner's office on Iwilei Road, where I picked up the bullet that had killed Charlie Stahl. Doc's minions had been busy the night before; Charlie's prominence and wealth had ensured a speedy autopsy. As I'd seen, the cause of death was a bullet wound to the throat. None of the other shots I'd heard fired had connected with a human being, which was something to be grateful for.

From the coroner's, I drove downtown, and took the bullet down to ballistics on the lower level. At the door of the lab someone had hung a big poster of a chicken. Or at least, that's what was on the left side. In case you didn't know what it was, the word "chicken" was written underneath, with BEFORE next to it.

To the right side, someone had drawn what looked like an explosion—jagged little shards flying in all directions. Under that, AFTER was written. Below that was a photo of the bullet that had killed the chicken, blown up so that its distinctive striations were clearly visible.

On the bottom, in big letters, it read, "A case of fowl play. If you have any information about this dastardly deed, report to Detective Kimo Kanapa'aka."

Billy Kim, the ballistics tech, came out as I was reading the poster. "Very funny," I said.

"Hey, you work in ballistics, you take your humor where you find it. No offense?"

"I'll let you make it up to me. Tell me everything you know about this bullet, all right?" I handed it to him in a plastic baggie. "Take good care of it. It's my only clue." *Well, that and a partial license plate,* I thought.

As I was leaving the lab, Billy's phone rang. "Hey, Kimo, hold up," he called. "It's your boss. He wants you upstairs, pronto."

Sampson was in his office watching a small battery-operated TV. Reception was lousy so he kept playing with the rabbit ears, but I could see enough to tell we were watching a press conference with Betty Yamazuki, one of the Honolulu county commissioners, who was demanding to know more about Wilson Shira's death. She stood with her arm around Shira's widow as she fabricated a story that had no relationship to reality. She seemed to be implying that someone within the Marriage Project had deliberately lured Shira into the building, then orchestrated the bombing in order to kill him and shift blame away from themselves. "Is it a coincidence that the only person to die in this blast was one of this group's most formidable opponents?" she said. "I call that a real mystery."

"I call it irony," I said.

Back at the studio, the anchor said, "Citing the confidentiality of their ongoing investigation, Honolulu police officials have declined to comment on Ms. Yamazuki's allegations."

"They're a piece of crap, is what they are," Sampson said. "But until you find something better, they're going to stand. What have you got?"

"You notice how she didn't even mention Charlie Stahl?" I asked. "I'm sure the two cases are related. We've got a bullet and a partial license plate number. I'm going all out on this, Lieutenant. I'll get you the results you want."

"Soon." Sampson looked back down at the paperwork on his desk, and I left his office.

Back at my desk, I worked up a profile on Charlie Stahl, just to eliminate anybody else in his life who might have wanted to kill him. I found out a bunch of things about his personal life I'd just as soon not have known, but I couldn't find anybody who could have killed him. Though he was wealthy, so was the rest of his family, and most of his money was tied up in family trusts. His friends all liked him, and he wasn't involved in any suspicious business deals. He wasn't a drug user or an alcoholic, though his sexual tastes were a little unusual. In short, he was an average citizen.

Just before noon, I got a call from Thanh Nguyen at the fingerprint lab. As soon as I had copied down the information I hung up and did some work at the computer. When I was finished, I phoned Mike Riccardi's cell.

"We finally got a break," I said. "Remember I told you about the rock in the paper bag that went through the window of the Marriage Project a couple of hours before the bomb? We got a make on the prints. I pulled the guy's rap sheet and he's got a half dozen arrests for assault, assault with a deadly weapon, felony assault, malicious mischief, you name it."

"Anything for arson?"

"No, but people change."

Mike laughed. "You got an address on the guy?"

"I've even got a job address. A farm up outside Wahiawa. You want to go for a ride?"

"How could I turn down an invitation like that?"

"Good. Where are you? I'll pick you up."

He gave me an address in Waikīkī, a few blocks from my apartment. I knew the place, a small storefront that rented and sold X-rated videos. I'd stopped there once or twice myself, that is, until someone had poured gasoline behind the back door and set it afire. I thought it was the first of the gay-related arsons.

"You're back there? Got a new lead?"

"Nope. Just tidying up loose ends. They're reopening tomorrow, just wanted to give them some advice."

"Maybe they'll cut us a discount on some video rentals."

"I'll be waiting out front," he said. "I'll be the one wearing the big smile."

"Oh, if only that were all you were wearing." I hung up, smiling to myself. This could be our big break. All we had to do was lean on the rock thrower until he gave up his partners, and we'd be home free.

It was sunny and dry as we cruised up the Kamehameha

Highway toward Wahiawa. "This weather makes me nervous," Mike said.

"Nervous? It's gorgeous."

"Yeah, but you feel how dry it is? We haven't had significant rainfall in a couple of weeks."

We'd passed through the miles of strip malls and light industrial development that marked the outskirts of Honolulu, and we were climbing through the cleft of hills into central O'ahu. I looked out at the fields around us. They were beginning to look parched. "I'm sure it'll rain soon. It always does."

"I hope you're right. In addition to the arsons I've been investigating, we've already started to get some small fires out in the country. We had one near Schofield Barracks the other day—had to evacuate the area until we got it under control."

We drove up the highway beyond the Dole plantation, looking for the street address I had, and then turned off onto a red dirt road that was signed toward Pupukea Plantation.

"I've been here before," I said. "The Church of Adam and Eve had a meeting up here a month or two ago."

I pulled up in front of a low wooden building that looked like it had been a set for some old Western, with an overhanging roof supported by thin posts, sheltering an empty porch. A line of cars and trucks were parked in the dirt in front of the building. "Son of a bitch," I said. I pointed at a green pickup parked at one end. The latch on the gate was broken on the right-hand side, just as Frank Sit had described.

"I've got a good feeling about this," Mike said.

We went through a screen door into the office, showed our badges, and asked to speak with Ed Baines, the guy whose prints we'd matched. The secretary said she'd call him in from the field, and ushered us back to a big room filled with chairs and a speaker's podium. "We use this when we have to get all the workmen in one place," she said, and left us. The walls were lined with safety posters and a complicated anatomical description of the stages of pineapple development. I tried to read one of them but couldn't concentrate. I kept thinking that we were close to solving our whole investigation.

A few minutes later a tall, blond guy with tattoos on both arms stuck his head in the door. "You guys looking for me?"

"Ed Baines?" He nodded. "Come on in." We showed our badges again and introduced ourselves.

His skin was rough and weathered, and he wore jeans and a chambray shirt with ragged short sleeves. A packet of Marlboros threatened to fall out of his torn breast pocket at any moment. "I don't know what you guys want, but I been clean since the last time I got out of the joint. They give me a good chance here, and I'm trying not to fuck it up."

"Then I'm sure you'll be willing to help us," I said. "Like maybe telling us where you were last Wednesday afternoon, for starters."

He looked wary. "I was here on the farm, working. Every day, seven to four."

"You punch a clock?" He nodded. "So I could check your punch out, if I wanted to."

"What's this all about?"

"I'm having a little trouble believing you were here on the farm last Wednesday, is all," I said. "When I've got a paper bag with your fingerprints on it, and that bag had a rock inside it last Wednesday that went through somebody's window."

"I want to call my lawyer."

"Whoa, that's a big turnaround in attitude," I said. "One minute you're gonna help us, the next you've gotta call your lawyer."

"Here's the deal," Mike said, leaning forward. "You want to call a lawyer, that's your right. Under the Constitution. But you know what lawyers are like. I know you do, you've been around the block a few times. Your lawyer steps in, and then we can't do anything to help you. See, we're not so concerned with you, Ed. We've read your rap sheet. Unless you're turning into a firebug in your old age, we're just looking at you as a way to get to who we want."

"What do you mean, firebug?"

I sat back and listened, watching Ed's face for a reaction. "See, this place where the rock went through the window, later that night a bomb went off there, the whole place burned down." Ed started looking pretty scared at that point. I was getting the feeling his involvement had gone only so far, and no further. "We figure the same people responsible for the rock through the window had a hand in the bombing, but that doesn't mean we expect that was you," Mike continued. "Must have been somebody behind you, maybe behind the bombing, too. You turn over that guy, we forget about any charges against you for this rock throwing. Your parole officer doesn't even need to know. But once you've got your lawyer involved, well, it's harder for us to do that."

"I don't know anything about no bombing," Ed said. "No fire either. This guy just said he wanted to do a little mischief. He had us collect a bunch of horse shit, put it into bags, and then splash it on the sidewalk. The rock was just like a calling card, so's the people inside knew what it was about."

"Kind of like a warning," I said. "You know, like get out before we torch your asses."

"There wasn't nothing like that," he said. "I swear it. You can hook me up to a lie detector, whatever you want. I swear I didn't know nothing about any bombs, or fires, or anything."

He looked down at his shoes. "I know I shouldn't a done it. But this guy, he's my minister, and he swore it wouldn't be breaking my parole. Nothing more than malicious mischief, he said." He looked up again. "See, I got this ex lives down by Pearl. What with being in the joint, I'm way behind on my alimony, and she keeps threatening to haul my ass into court. I'd been talking to the reverend about it, and he offered me a thousand bucks to make some trouble for those gay marriage people. That's enough to make myself whole with her."

As soon as Baines said minister, I thought about Jeff White, whose Church of Adam and Eve had met at the plantation. "You got a name and an address on your minister?" I asked.

"Sure."

I pulled out my notebook and a pen, and handed them to him. "Write it down."

"You promise you won't screw me up?"

"You give us the right guy, we forget we ever even talked to you," I said.

"All right." He quickly scribbled a couple of lines on a fresh page in my notebook and handed it back to me.

I took a quick look at it, and saw exactly what I'd expected: Reverend White, the Church of Adam and Eve, and the address on Wai'alae Avenue.

Chapter 29

MAKING APOLOGIES

AS WE WERE DRIVING back down to Honolulu, my cell rang with a call from Terri.

"I know you're probably swamped with the bombing investigation," she said. "But I'm at my wit's end, and I just don't know what to do."

"What's the matter?"

"It's Danny," she said. Her five-year-old son had witnessed his father's murder six months before, and he'd taken it hard. But I thought he'd been coming around. "He's been acting up at kindergarten, and today he hit another boy with a rock. They're threatening to kick him out unless I get him some help. But he's been in therapy, Kimo."

She started to cry. After Eric's death, I'd promised to spend time with Danny, and for a while I had. But it had been a month or more since I had gone to Wailupe just to hang out with her and the boy. "OK, hold on." I put my hand over the receiver. "Can we make a quick detour to Wailupe?" I asked Mike. "My friend's got a crisis."

"Sure."

Back to Terri, I said, "I'm on the Kam now," I said. "I'll get on the H1 and be to you in about forty-five minutes." I paused for a second, to concentrate on a bend in the road. "I'm bringing somebody with me," I said. "I think you'll like him."

Her voice faded out, and then she said, "See you soon."

I hung up and told Mike about my friendships with Terri and Harry, and about Danny. "I had you figured for a Puna-hou boy," he said.

We spent the rest of the ride trading personal information. Where we'd grown up, gone to school, what we'd done, and who we knew. Mike had grown up in Kamehameha Heights, a few blocks from the Bishop Museum. "My parents liked the area because it was convenient to the H1 and the Likelike Highway," he said. "Easy for them to get to their jobs. The neighborhood's gone through some trouble, but it's coming back. Living there, it's easy for me to get down to the new fire department HQ on South and Queen."

He'd gone to Farrington High, a public school not far away. Then he'd gone to college on Long Island, near his dad's family. We knew a couple of people in common, and it was interesting to compare the paths of our lives.

Finally, after battling traffic, we swung into Terri's circular driveway about an hour later. Though the mountains loomed just on the other side of the Kalaniana'ole Highway, Terri's house was on a flat plain that stuck out into the Pacific. A twenty-foot royal palm stood on each side of her ranch-style house, poised like sentinels to protect her and her son.

Danny Gonsalves came running out to meet me, and I picked him up and swung him around. "Hey, sport, how you doing?"

"Are we going surfing, Kimo? I've been going bodysurfing with my friend Chuckie and his dad. I'm getting really good."

"We'll go soon, I promise. What's this I hear about you hitting a kid at school?"

"Who are you?" Danny asked Mike.

"I'm a friend of Kimo's. My name's Mike."

He reached out formally to shake Danny's hand. "Are you a policeman, too?" Danny asked. "My daddy was a policeman. He got killed."

"I'm sorry," Mike said. "I'm not a policeman, I'm a fireman."

"Wow! If I'm not a policeman when I grow up I want to be a fireman. Or maybe an astronaut, or work in a bakery with all kinds of desserts."

"Well, if it's OK with your mom, sometime maybe Kimo can bring you over to the fire station and I'll show you around."

Danny's eyes were as big as coconuts. "Cool! Wait'll I tell Chuckie."

I sat down on the grass and pulled Danny down next to me. "Is Chuckie the kid you hit with the rock?"

He frowned. "I don't want to talk about it."

Mike sat across from us. His body language was open, and Danny moved over next to him. "You know what police officers do, don't you?" I asked Danny.

He looked at me. He'd moved up next to Mike, as if he expected Mike to protect him from me. "Police officers arrest bad people," Danny said.

"This kid you hit, is he bad?" I asked.

Danny nodded eagerly. "Yeah, he's really bad. You should arrest him."

"For what?"

Danny's face darkened, and he was quiet But I'm accustomed to waiting out suspects, so I didn't say anything.

"He said mean things about my dad," Danny said finally.

"Ooh, that's tough," I said. "You loved your dad, didn't you?"

Danny snuggled up against Mike, who put his arm around the boy. "Uh-huh."

"Your dad was a great guy," I said. "I knew him for a long time. He made a couple of mistakes, sure, but we all make mistakes, don't we?"

Danny nodded.

"The thing we do when we make mistakes is we apologize for them," I said. "And then we promise not to do them again."

"That's a good plan, don't you think, Danny?" Mike asked.

Danny looked from Mike to me. "I guess."

"I think you should tell your mom exactly what happened, and then she can talk to this other kid's mom, and maybe, since both of you made a mistake, if you both promise to do better, then things will be OK. I know that would make your mom happy."

"OK," Danny said.

We looked up to see Terri standing in the doorway of the house. She looked worried, but she was slim and tanned, her chestnut hair cut close to her head in an almost boyish look. She wore a vintage aloha shirt with a couple of buttons open and a pair of nylon running shorts. "Danny, honey, why don't you go play Nintendo," she said. "I want to talk to Kimo."

"They're always talking," Danny said to Mike. We all got up, and he asked, "Will you come play Nintendo with me when you're done?"

"Maybe for a few minutes. We'll see. I might have to go back to the station."

He nodded, then turned back to Mike. "Do you get to ride the truck?"

"Sometimes." He smiled at the boy. "Sometimes they even let me run the siren."

"Cool." He turned and ran inside, and I introduced Terri to Mike.

"You look terrific," I said to Terri. "Are you working out?"

"I've been spinning and taking kickboxing. A girl's got to take care of herself."

She led us into the living room. "Sometime you'll have to tell me all about what Kimo was like in high school," Mike said. Terri slid a glance at me out of the corner of her eye. I caught it and I guess I blushed, because she smiled.

"I've got some stories."

"All right, all right. We came here for a reason, remember? And not for everybody to start comparing my faults. I talked to Danny, and I told him that he has to apologize, and tell you why he hit the other boy."

"Why did he?"

"See if he tells you, first," I said. "If the boy keeps giving Danny trouble, let me know, and I'll have a talk with his folks."

"Thank you, Kimo." She leaned over and kissed my cheek. "You guys want anything to drink?"

We all agreed on lemonade, and followed her into the kitchen where she started pouring. "Terri was telling me yesterday that her family trust has been giving some money to the Church of Adam and Eve," I said to Mike. "That may be where Jeff White got the money to pay Ed Baines."

"Tell me about this trust," Mike said. "Is there any proof that's where the money came from?"

"My family used to own Clark's, the department stores, and my great-grandfather was quite wealthy. He fought against statehood because of the taxes, and he created the Sandwich Islands Trust to get around them. When the chain got sold to the Japanese, a lot of money went into the trust, and now it's probably the biggest in the islands."

She paused to move her legs under her on the sofa. "It's separate from our family money, but my Aunt Emma, my father's aunt, has always run it as if it was her own money.

Lately, though, I think she's slipping. She uses a walker now, and she gets tired easily, and I think she's figuring out that she's not running things the way she used to."

"That's why she's asked you to help," I said.

"You want me to talk, or not?"

I held up my hands. "Old friends," I said to Mike. "You can't live with them, and you can't shoot them."

"At least not if you're a police officer," Mike said dryly. "Go on, Terri."

"Thank you. My first order of business is figuring out exactly where the money's going. Most of the board members are old, and they're all part-time anyway, so nobody pays a lot of attention."

She leaned forward, adjusted the position of a couple of books on the coffee table in front of her. Finally she continued. "It seems the trust has been funding the Church of Adam and Eve, as well as some other opposition to gay marriage. I can give you a copy of the cancelled check, if you need it."

"Let me guess, Aunt Emma saw you on TV the night of the bombing and she called you up to complain."

"Actually she did see me, but she wasn't upset I was there, or on TV. Although she would prefer the Clarks kept a slightly lower profile." She smiled. "No, apparently it showed her I had some gumption, and I might be able to do what needs to be done with the trust."

"Let me tell you what we found out today." I told her what Ed Baines had told us, about being hired by Jeff White to throw horse manure at the Marriage Project offices.

"I need to tell Aunt Emma about this," Terri said.

"You can't tell her anything yet. We've still got a lot of investigation to do." I looked at my watch. "You think we can spare ten minutes for Nintendo?"

"If he's got three controllers," Mike said. "You know I've got some pretty nimble fingers."

He wiggled his fingers at me and I laughed. "I know," I said, and Terri looked at me and I blushed again. "Come on, let's go play."

We found Danny playing a fighting game on his Nintendo 64, and he gladly gave us each controllers. We battled together for a while, but in the end he beat us both. "We'll have a rematch," I said, laying down my controller. "Soon. I promise."

Danny jumped into my arms for a good-bye hug. "And you make sure this guy brings you over to the fire house sometime," Mike said.

Danny stuck his hand out to Mike to shake again. "All right!"

Chapter 30

DOING THE RIGHT THING

MIKE AND I WERE DRIVING down Kalākaua on our way back to my apartment when I saw two kids I recognized—Frankie and Lolo from the Gay Teen Center. I pulled over and called out to them from the truck.

They were both dressed suspiciously—form-fitting tank tops that didn't quite reach their waists, and then board shorts that slipped down their hips, exposing both a band of skin and the elastic waistbands of their briefs. Jesus, were they working the street? When I'd seen them at Ala Moana Park on Saturday night, I'd thought they were dating, the way they palled around.

"You guys seen Jimmy lately?" I asked.

Up close, I could see that Frankie was wearing some kind of eye makeup. And either Lolo was very glad to see me, or he'd been padding his crotch. But they were a problem I couldn't address right then.

Frankie and Lolo looked at each other and neither spoke for a moment. "It's important," I said. "I'm worried about him."

Finally Frankie said, "We saw him at Ala Moana Beach Park last night," he said.

"Was he working?" I asked.

Frankie looked down at his feet and shuffled around. Finally Lolo said, "Yeah. He looked like shit."

"If you see him again," I said, "you tell him everything's OK where he was, that they want him back. Tell him to come to me. I'll take care of him."

I opened my wallet and pulled out all the money I had—a few twenties—and handed them to Frankie. "I want to be the only guy you take money from tonight, all right?"

"We can't take your money," Lolo said.

"Why? Because I don't want a blow job in exchange?" I asked. "I've got a lot on my plate right now, Lolo, and I don't have time to fuck around with you. Take the money, go get yourselves some dinner, and stay off the street. Cause if vice picks you up, I will bail you out. And then I will beat the shit out of you. Got that?"

Both boys opened their eyes wide. Lolo reached out and took the money from my hand. "Someday I want a boyfriend like you," he said, and he grabbed Frankie's arm and dragged him away.

"You've got an admirer," Mike said.

"Don't start. Can we go down to Ala Moana Park?"

"Sure. And don't worry, dinner's on me tonight."

While we struggled through the busy streets of Waikīkī, I told him about Jimmy Ah Wong, how I felt responsible for outing him to his dad. "You didn't do it, he did it," Mike finally said.

"Because I told him it was the right thing to do, to testify against those guys. I promised to look out for him."

"And you have."

"Yeah, like I've been looking out for Danny Gonsalves," I said. "Like I'm keeping Frankie and Lolo off the streets. Like I kept Kitty Sampson from interfering in the investigation."

I found I was gripping the steering wheel and consciously tried to relax.

Mike said, "I think you have the kindest, strongest heart of anyone I've ever met."

"Gee, here I thought you only liked me for my looks."

"I've known who you were for a few months now," Mike said. I glanced over and saw that he was looking out the window, not at me. "I did think you were handsome, the first time I saw you on TV. But more than that, I admired you so fucking much for being brave enough to be who you are."

I didn't say anything, but I swallowed, trying to get down the lump in my throat.

"Every time I'd go over to the police station, I'd be keeping my eye out for you. I thought you were this larger-than-life figure, and I kept thinking about you. I knew that the only way I'd get over you was to see you in person."

I felt him turn my way and I looked over at him. "Then when I saw you carrying that dead chicken, I realized that you were a real guy, not just some fantasy figure. I don't know if I'd ever have had the nerve to talk to you, if we hadn't been thrown together because of the bombing."

"Your loss," I said lightly.

We finally passed the Ilikai Hotel and traffic eased up. I said, "You play the hand you've been dealt," I said. "That's all I've been trying to do." I reached my right hand over to him, and he took it and squeezed.

≈

WE PARKED AT THE ALA WAI YACHT CLUB, where Gilligan and his crew had left for their three-hour tour, and we walked the whole park looking for Jimmy Ah Wong, with no success. We ate dinner at the Gordon Biersch at the Aloha Tower, but I couldn't enjoy the sunset, worrying about Jimmy and Kitty and how I'd ever get this case solved.

The beer seemed flat, the food tasteless. The only good thing was that I was with Mike. After we ate, we drove around downtown, checked the park one more time, then cruised Waikīkī for a while. By eleven, we were both exhausted and had to give up.

Wednesday morning I woke up next to Mike. For a couple of minutes I just lay there, resting on one elbow, looking at him. I decided it was a way I wanted to wake up a lot in the future.

A little later, after some fun in the shower, we walked together to a café near my apartment, got *malasadas* and coffee, and then, under the outside stairs to my building, kissed good-bye.

When I reached the main station, there was an urgent message from Billy Kim in ballistics. Rather than call, I went downstairs to his lab. "Kimo, I'm glad you're here," he said. "I found something strange and I want to show it to you."

He pulled out a blown-up photo of a bullet. "This is what you brought us from your shooting victim yesterday."

"Charlie Stahl."

"Right. See the grooves here on the sides? Very distinctive. Comes from a small, lightweight gun, most likely a Chief's Special Airweight."

"Good."

"Wait, there's more." He brought over the poster I'd seen the day before.

"Not the chicken again, Billy."

"You're going to like this, Kimo. Look at the grooves. See? Same pattern."

"So whoever killed the old man and the chicken also used a Chief's Special Airweight."

"More than that. Look at this little notch here. See how it matches in both pictures? That's more than just the same model. It's the same gun."

"You're saying the same gun was used to kill Charlie Stahl as was used in the two shootings in Makiki?"

"I'd swear to it in court."

"Whoa. This is wild." I stood up. "I've got to think about this one. Thanks, Billy—this could be the break I need. If I can just figure out how to use it."

When I got back to my desk my phone was ringing. "Kanapa'aka, Homicide."

"Hey, hey, Special K," Harry said. "How's it hanging, brah?"

"You won't believe what I just found out." I told him about the ballistics match.

"Tell me everything you know about the old man," he said. I did. "Now tell me everything you know about Charlie Stahl's murder."

I did that, too. I could almost hear the wheels clicking in his brain. "Do you think Charlie Stahl knew Hiroshi Mura?"

"I doubt it. I'll check, you never know who knows who in Hawai'i." I thought of something. "You know, they didn't necessarily have to know each other. But they both had some connection to the murderer."

"Yes," Harry said.

"The only thing I've got on Charlie Stahl's killer is a partial license plate. It could take forever to pull up every match and analyze them."

"You ought to be able to automate that a little," Harry said. "Eliminate the vehicle types that don't match. Eliminate cars registered on the other islands."

"Our system isn't that sophisticated. You have to do all that sorting by hand."

"I can write you a program that'll do that. You just get me the data file."

"You can?"

"Sure. The data must have VIN numbers in it, right? And addresses, including zip codes? It's a simple sort. How soon can you get the data?"

"Let me make a call." I hung up from Harry and called our computer tech. I explained what I needed and gave him Harry's phone number. He said he'd take it from there.

I hung up. There was something dancing around the edges of my brain, a connection between Hiroshi Mura and Charlie Stahl. But what was it?

Lieutenant Sampson loomed above my desk. "In my office. Now."

I didn't like that tone. What had I done now?

"Shut the door behind you," he said. He stood next to his desk, and from the way his jaw was clenched and his eyes narrowed, I figured he was plenty mad. I saw his eyes dart across to the picture of Kitty—and then I knew.

"I'm sorry," I said, before he could blow up. "I didn't know what else to do. She was determined to go to the Church of Adam and Eve on Sunday, and I knew that she would, no matter what I said. So I went with her."

"Do I need to remind you that my daughter is not a sworn officer?"

"You know Kitty a lot better than I do," I said. "But she strikes me as the kind of girl who follows through on what she says. Can't convince her to change her mind."

Sampson's shoulders relaxed a little. "I've been trying to convince her not to become a cop since she was twelve," he said. "No matter what I do, she just does what she wants."

"Did she tell you about the picnic on Thursday?" I asked.

His eyes were wary again. "No. Tell me."

"This couple we met at the church." I closed my eyes, searching my brain for their names. I have this trick I use sometimes, connecting a name to something else as a way to remember. I can't use it that often, because of the wild ethnic soup we have in the islands, but I'd connected that couple to a president. Out loud, I started reciting any presidents I could think of. "Carter, Kennedy, Eisenhower, Nixon, Roosevelt, Coolidge, Harding, Taft . . . wait, Harding. That's their name."

I opened my eyes to see Sampson staring at me with something like a grin on his face, which disappeared almost immediately. "Fran and Eli Harding," I said. I shrugged. "They seemed nice enough."

"It's that kind of insight that makes you a great detective," he said dryly. "Tell me about this picnic."

"I don't know much. They called to invite Kitty, and she accepted. I told her that if she didn't tell you by tomorrow, I would."

"So that's why she called me this morning," he said. "If I hadn't spoken to you, she'd probably go on this picnic Thursday, and then Friday she'd say, 'I told you, Jim. You just don't listen to me.'"

"I'll bet you listen to her a lot more than she realizes," I said.

"Obviously, she is NOT going to this picnic," he said. "At least not alone."

I shook my head. "Sorry, lieutenant. I'm taking some personal time Thursday afternoon. My dad's best friend passed away. The wake's a command performance."

His lips set in a grim line. "I'll talk to Kitty," he said. "If necessary, Thursday will be take-your-daughter-to-work day."

I went back to my desk, trying to remember what I'd been thinking about before the confrontation with Sampson, and my phone rang.

"Hey, brah, long time no hear."

"Akoni! Geez, man, this is a surprise. What have you been up to?" Akoni and I had gone through the police academy together, and we'd been detective partners in Waikīkī for three years, before my transfer downtown. "How's Waikīkī?"

"Not there anymore. As of yesterday, I'm in the same building as you."

"No shit? What's up?"

"Yumuri is losing it," he said. I could tell he was lowering his voice in order to speak about the lieutenant who had supervised us in Waikīkī. "Ever since the business with you, he's been acting weird. Rumor has it they're moving him soon, maybe somewhere out in the country where the stress isn't so bad. I heard about this opening in Organized Crime, that they needed a detective for a special project, so I figured I'd come over here for a while, see what happens back in Waikīkī."

"Wow. I had no idea."

"And you know what else sucked? He had me partnered with Greenberg, and the guy's a real asshole. Thinks he knows which way the sun rises and sets. I just couldn't take it anymore." Alvy Greenberg had been Lidia Portuondo's boyfriend, and the one who'd outed me to the rest of the squad. Though he'd been my friend once, I didn't feel bad hearing that he'd turned out to be a jerk. "Listen, reason why I'm calling? A name came up I know you're familiar with. Chin Suk."

"Uncle Chin. You know he died on Monday?"

"Yeah. They sent us the autopsy results, I thought you might want to know."

"Tell me."

"What we all want," he said. "Massive heart attack. Took him right out."

"They think he might have been awake at all?" I explained about the table, the spilled bottle of pills.

"Possible. But there was nothing anybody could have done to save him. This was the big one."

"Thanks, brah." It felt good to know that Jimmy Ah Wong couldn't have been involved. "We'll do lunch sometime, all right? Now you're here in the building."

"Yeah. You gotta tell me the good places to eat. I got heart-burn from yesterday like you wouldn't believe."

"I'd believe it. Nobody told me where to eat the first couple weeks I was here. Listen, brah, I gotta go. I'm in the middle of a big case. But we'll talk."

I stared at the phone after I hung up. It took me a while to get back to work; I kept going back to the idea that Uncle Chin had died peacefully. Then why had Jimmy run away?

Now all I had to do, while finding the bomber, and who-ever shot Charlie Stahl, was find Jimmy Ah Wong and let him know he was off the hook.

Chapter 31

HARMLESS MISCHIEF

I TRIED TO LET my mind relax, to see what kind of connection I was missing, but all I kept coming back to was the name Ed Baines had given us. I raised Mike on his cell, out in the field ruling out arson at a house fire in Mo'ili'ili. "I want to go over and talk to our buddy Jeff White. You want to come with?"

"Wouldn't miss it." I gave him the address and he agreed to meet me there.

A half hour later, I pulled up at the shopping center on Wai'alae Avenue and parked in front of Puerto Peinado, the hair salon owned by Tatiana's friend Tico, where Mike was leaning against the wall in a square of shade. The air was still, not a hint of a breeze to carry the exhaust fumes and traffic noise up to the mountains or out over the ocean. It was incredibly hot and I understood why Mike was waiting in the shade. "You realize this salon is run by a known homosexual," I said.

"You know him?"

"Not in the biblical sense," I said. I explained about his friendship with Tatiana.

"Like your friendship with Terri," he said.

"Gotta have a gal pal," I said. "Every gay man needs one."

We walked up to the door of the church and peered inside. It looked pretty much as I remembered from Sunday, though there was only one person inside, a man in a short-sleeved shirt sitting at a table writing something.

When we opened the door, he looked up. It was the minister himself, Jeff White, though I still wasn't sure if he was also the sweaty guy I'd seen at the party.

"Welcome," White said. "Are you interested in the church?"

We introduced ourselves and showed our credentials, and I could see the man become wary. Mike hung back and let me take the lead. "Mr. White, we're here because your name has come up in an investigation," I said, "and we'd like to give you the opportunity to set the record straight. Tell us your side of the story."

"What is it you want to know?"

"Are you familiar with a farm up in the highlands called Pupukea Plantation?"

"I don't think so."

"Don't you run worship services up there occasionally?"

White looked confused. "Oh, that place," he said. "I get mixed up with these Hawai'ian names. Everything sounds so similar. Yes, we've had services up there several times."

"In your visits out there, have you ever spoken with an individual named Ed Baines?"

"I don't know anyone by that name."

"You're sure, are you?"

White nodded.

"Because, see, the thing is, he says he knows you. He says you hired him to put some horse manure into paper bags and then throw it all over the sidewalk in front of an office building downtown."

I watched as White's shoulders relaxed. "Oh, that. A little harmless mischief. I wouldn't exactly say I hired him. He's a strong supporter of our church and our causes, you know, and we were talking about things that people do now and then. I didn't think he was actually going to do it."

I blew a little air out through my lips in a derogatory way. "Not even when you offered him a thousand dollars? How about when you paid him the money, Mr. White? Did you think he actually did it then? Or do you just spread that kind of money around without thinking?"

"You're a homosexual, aren't you, detective? I wouldn't expect you to understand."

"Did the money you gave him come from the Sandwich Islands Trust?" I asked. "Because if it did you're not getting any more money from them."

Beads of sweat appeared on White's forehead. "I'm not saying anything further," he said. "I want a lawyer present."

"That's your call," I said. I pulled the card out of my wallet and read him his rights. "Do you understand these rights that I have explained to you?"

"I understand them."

"Good." I stood up. "Then we won't take any more of your time right now, but I suggest you engage the services of an attorney, if you so desire. We'll be back, with more questions."

"Why the hell are you investigating this nonsense?" he asked. "The city pays you top dollar, I'm sure, what with all your press exposure. All that just to chase around a little fag-bashing incident?"

"We hardly consider homicide a little fag-bashing incident." I noticed his face went several shades paler. "Especially since to my knowledge the victim was an avowed heterosexual."

"Victim? What victim?"

"Vice Mayor Wilson Shira." I paused to let the name sink in. "Come on, Mr. White, you gotta keep up with the news. A couple hours after Ed Baines threw that horse shit, the building blew up and Wilson Shira turned into a crispy critter."

"You don't think . . ."

"I don't think anything," I said. "The city doesn't pay me to think. They pay me to investigate. And when I find you paid one guy to throw some horse shit at the place, it's not a big leap to consider you might have paid somebody else to plant a bomb there." I looked down at him, still sitting at his desk. "Or planted it yourself," I said.

Mike and I left White to stew over those questions. We walked down the shopping center sidewalk to the newsstand and picked up a copy of the *Advertiser,* then went into the Chinese restaurant at the far end to grab some lunch and check for articles on the case. An editorial columnist had written about public officials who placed themselves in personal danger, and there was an article on Charlie Stahl's life and legacy. He had apparently contributed hundreds of thousands of dollars over the years to liberal causes, and there were quotes from various civic leaders praising him. I wondered if they knew he was, as Gunter had called him, a notorious leather queen. Would that have made a difference in how they treated him? Probably not, as long as he was rich.

"What do you know about this minister?" Mike asked.

I told him what Harry had discovered, that the woman he was representing as his wife was actually his sister. "And they think we're kinky," he said.

"I talked to her when I was canvassing in Makiki," I said. And then it hit me, so much that my mouth dropped open and Mike must have thought I was having a fit or something.

"Kimo? You OK?"

"They live in Makiki," I said.

"Yes. Lots of people do."

"Down the street from the homeless man who was killed the day I first saw you at headquarters."

"Yes, you said you met them when you were canvassing."

"And did I tell you about the ballistics match?"

He shook his head. "The same gun was used on the homeless man, Hiroshi Mura, and the chicken, and Charlie Stahl."

"Whoa."

"Exactly. This is what I can use to tie together the two cases."

"But how can you tie them to the Whites without a smoking gun, to coin a phrase?"

I frowned. I knew I'd need something concrete to get a judge to sign a warrant. I could tie the two murders together, and I could tie Charlie Stahl's death to the bombing at the Marriage Project offices, and I could identify the Whites and their church as opponents of gay marriage.

But the only concrete evidence was Ed Baines's fingerprint on the paper bag, and his statement that Jeff White had hired him to throw the shit bombs. And that didn't tie to anything else, except in a circumstantial way.

"This case is making me crazy," I said. "I know that the pieces fit together but I just need one more to make the puzzle show enough to get the warrant."

We stood up to go, and I saw an elderly man walking by with a cane, a stout younger man, probably a son, helping him. "Shit. I ought to call my house. See how my dad is." I pulled out my cell phone and dialed as Mike and I walked to my truck.

My mother answered. She said everything was fine, and wanted to make sure that I would be at Uncle Chin's wake the next day.

"I will be."

"Did you find anything more about that boy?" she asked. "Aunt Mei-Mei keeps asking about him. The boy who was staying there."

"No. A friend and I went out last night, but we didn't see him. I'll keep looking."

"You think he had anything to do with your uncle's death?" Mike asked when I'd hung up. We stopped next to my truck, and I could see his, the one with the flames painted down the side, a few feet away.

I told him about my call from Akoni. "It should make everybody feel better, except I know Aunt Mei-Mei is just gonna worry more about Jimmy, knowing he's innocent and yet he still felt like he had to run away."

Chapter 32
SEARCH WARRANT

MIKE WENT OFF to write up his conclusions about the home fire in Mo'ili'ili, and I went back to the station. By the end of my shift, I still hadn't come up with that one piece of evidence that would tie the Whites to the bombing or the shootings.

I went into Lieutenant Sampson's office and told him everything I knew. The ATF and FBI hadn't come up with anything more out of their investigation of the bombing wreckage, and Harry was still working on converting the state license plate database into a format that he could sort. After all the research I'd looked through, the only religious group that made me suspicious was the Church of Adam and Eve, but I didn't have anything I could take to a judge.

"You have a partial plate, right?" Sampson asked. "And you think that the Whites are involved. Have you checked their DMV records?"

"The network is down right now," I said. "As soon as it comes up, I'll check."

"How about a lineup?" he asked. "If one of your witnesses can place this White guy at the Marriage Project office, you could get a warrant based on that."

"Funny," I said. "Usually we say '*haole*' when we mean white guy."

Sampson wasn't laughing.

"A lineup is a good idea," I said. "White said he was going to hire an attorney, so it may take a day or two to organize. I'll get things started." I began to wonder where I could round up a group of *haole* guys who looked like Jeff White, and remembered Eli Harding. "Did you talk to Kitty about the picnic?"

"She's not answering her cell phone," he said. "She tell you what time this picnic was?"

I shook my head. "Just that it was in the afternoon."

"If I have to, I'll drive up to her apartment tomorrow morning and pick her up," he said.

Back at my desk, Lui called me looking for a news hook and I had to admit I didn't have anything. "But you can't run that," I said.

"It's not exactly news, is it? The police have no suspects and no new leads. How about the murder on Sunday? You think that's related?"

I debated telling my brother about the ballistics match. I'd trust him with my life, and I had in the past. But he did run a news operation. "It's obvious to me that Stahl's murder is connected to the bombing at the Marriage Project. But I don't have any evidence that links the two crimes other than the fact that Stahl was a supporter. He was at the party the night of the bombing, and he was killed as they were announcing he was funding the project to reopen. That's all I've got."

"We've been hearing stories about some unorthodox sexual activities. You think there's any connection?"

My first reaction was to scoff, but then I reconsidered. "I hate to malign a dead guy, Lui, but I guess it's something we have to consider. The kind of stuff he was into, there's usually a mutual trust between the two parties, safe words and so on."

"Safe words?" he interrupted. "What's that?"

"From what I've heard, and you're my brother so I feel I

have to tell you I don't know any of this from first-hand experience, when you do anything with somebody else that involves pain or bondage or anything, you have these safe words. That way the person getting tied up can say, no, you're hurting me, ouch, and so on, which I guess adds to the fun somehow."

"And the safe words?"

"Well, when things go too far, the person just has to say, pickle, or sandwich, or whatever, and then things are supposed to stop. It's possible that something Stahl was doing got out of hand, and somebody wanted to take revenge on him, but that's a real long shot, considering the circumstances."

"It may be a long shot, but as a tease it'll play on the news. Thanks, brah. I'll get a reporter onto it."

"Let me know if you find anything out." When I hung up I felt like shit. I didn't want to drag Charlie Stahl's personal life through the gutter. He'd seemed like a nice enough guy, and I knew he had that record of good works and charitable donations. But it was possible I was going on the wrong track, linking his shooting to the bombing, and Lui might find something out that could move the case forward.

Thinking about that, I wondered if somebody who lived around Hiroshi Mura might have had sex with Charlie Stahl. Maybe Mura saw them. I had heard he was always snooping around the neighborhood. It was a long shot, but I called Harry and suggested he try to correlate the partial license plate to Makiki. He said he'd try.

I met up with Mike that night for dinner, and a long walk along the beach. We talked about the case, sat next to each other and stared at the gibbous moon, and kissed in the dark behind the gate of the zoo. The air smelled of animal droppings, sea salt, and the sewage pipe that runs out into the

Pacific, but I didn't care. I held onto Mike, heard the palm fronds rustle in the light breeze, and looked out at the crescent of lights along Diamond Head Road. I felt like I had a tenuous grasp on happiness.

We cruised Waikīkī and Ala Moana Beach Park once again, looking for Jimmy Ah Wong, without success, ending up back at the restroom where we'd seen Frankie and Lolo.

"I've got to take a leak," Mike said.

"I'll come with you."

There was something sexy and dangerous about standing there next to Mike at the urinals, seeing the dick that I had sucked that morning poking its way out of his pants. I've never been one for water sports, but I definitely got an erotic charge out of being there next to him in a public place, our dicks out. He was on my left, so I reached my left arm around his shoulders and brought his head to mine so we could kiss.

We finished pissing and I put my right hand on his dick, which was stiffening, as was mine. We kissed and began stroking each other.

"You know this is crazy," I said, between kisses. "Anybody could walk in here and catch us."

"One of those kids you know," Mike said, nuzzling my ear. "Or a cop."

"We could end up in jail."

"You and me in a cell together," Mike said.

My pulse rate was accelerating and I was having trouble breathing. There was a single stall, handicap size, next to us, and I dragged Mike into it. Well, I didn't exactly have to drag him; he was a willing accomplice.

I fumbled in my pocket for one of the glow-in-the-dark condoms Gunter had given me, and handed it to Mike. "Suit up, fireman," I said.

I dropped my pants and boxers and turned, placing my hands flat against the tile wall. "Oh, man, what a sweet ass you have," Mike said. He squatted behind me and began poking his tongue into me.

I pulled my ass cheeks wide and said, "Oh, yeah, that feels good."

He licked and poked, and then I felt his finger dancing around, then penetrating me. My dick was rock hard, and my pulse rate was going through the roof. Every little noise, even if it was just a lizard skittering up the wall, made me think we were about to be discovered. The embarrassment, my fellow officers hearing about the arrest, my family and friends worrying about me, the kids at the teen center snickering behind their hands, Mike outed in the worst possible way. But I didn't tell him to stop fucking my ass with first one finger, then two.

His tongue went back to work on my ass, and I heard the rustle of his pants dropping, the ripping sound of the condom packet opening. Then he stepped behind me and gripped my shoulders.

The pain seared through me as his dick penetrated my ass. I made a strangulated sound and Mike said, "Am I hurting you?"

"Don't stop," I panted. "Fuck me. I don't care if you tear me apart, just fuck me."

He'd done a good job of lubricating me, and once my ass got accustomed to the intrusion, I started to feel waves of pleasure rising through me with each of his strokes. He'd just plunged deeply into me when the door of the restroom opened.

We heard two male voices, giggling in Japanese. Mike stopped moving, his dick slammed up my ass, and we both held our breaths. My mother's father was Japanese, and I had learned a few words to be able to talk to him, but I couldn't understand much of what the guys were saying to each other.

They knew we were there, though, and it didn't seem to bother them. I bucked my ass against Mike to let him know that it was OK, and he started fucking me again, short piston strokes, only his groin moving against my ass.

The guys outside the stall were grooving on us; I could hear them kissing and their bodies rubbing against each other.

Mike reached around and grabbed my dick, stroking me. His hand was rough, but I'd generated so much pre-come that my dick was as wet as a Slip 'n Slide on a hot summer day. As his pace accelerated behind me, he stroked me faster and faster, until I couldn't help but begin to whimper and cry out. Right after I felt his come spurt up my ass, I splattered the wall in front of me.

Mike sagged against me and whispered in my ear, "You are a very bad boy."

"And you are a very good fuck," I whispered back.

He pulled out of my ass and dropped the condom into the toilet. My ass felt stretched sore and uncomfortably liquid, but I pulled my pants up and turned back to him. The two Japanese guys must have finished as we did, and I heard the door to the restroom slam.

We were alone again and kissed once more before we opened the stall door, then walked back out into the cool night.

≈

THE PHONE WOKE US BOTH. I looked at the clock, bleary-eyed. It was only six-thirty. "I did it, brah," Harry crowed. "I came up with a match I think you're gonna find very interesting."

"Harry. You know what time it is?"

"Yeah, it's six-thirty. You're lucky I didn't call you at four, when I figured this out. I thought by now you'd be up and ready to surf."

I yawned. "Oh, well. Tell me what you found."

"There's a black Toyota Camry, license plate HXM 691, registered to a Jeffrey White in Makiki. That's your minister, right? He lives down the street from where you found the old man, and around the corner from the address where the rooster got shot. And your buddy Mike saw the woman who shot Charlie Stahl get into a car that matches this plate."

"Thanks, brah. You're a winner. I'll talk to you later."

I rolled over and looked at Mike. "We've finally got enough to connect the Whites to the bombings and the shootings."

It took us only about twenty minutes to get pulled together. While we drove down to police headquarters, I remembered Frank Sit mentioning the couple in a dark sedan the night of the bombing. I was sure that was the Whites.

Mike helped me write my search warrant. By nine o'clock we were finished, and I drove us over to Judge Yamanaka's office at the Criminal Courts building to get it signed. "Try to get us there in one piece, OK?" Mike asked, as I swerved around slow moving trucks and used the flashing light on my dash.

"Hey, I took the defensive driving course at the academy."

"That's what I'm worried about."

Judge Yamanaka insisted that I tell him everything that had led me to my conclusions. "We tracked the partial license plate that Fire Inspector Riccardi saw on the gunman's escape vehicle to this address," I said. "And we matched the ballistics on both homicides. That gives us probable cause to search the residence and the vehicle, as well as the other vehicle registered at the same address."

"You're also looking for incendiary materials?" the judge asked.

Mike spoke up. "We believe that the homicide of Mr. Stahl is linked to the bombing that killed Vice Mayor Shira, because of Mr. Stahl's connection to the Hawai'i Marriage Project and the context of his murder."

"Somebody really doesn't like the project," I said. "It's our hypothesis that Mr. Stahl was killed in an effort to keep the project from reopening."

"That's a pretty big leap, detective," the judge said. "And how do you connect Mr. Stahl's murder to Mr. Mura's?"

"I can't answer every question without the results of the search," I said. "If this Mr. White was involved in planning or carrying out the bombing, it's possible that Mr. Mura, his neighbor, witnessed something that caused Mr. White to kill him."

Judge Yamanaka looked from me to Mike, and back to me again. He sighed. "All right, I'll grant you the warrant. But I'm warning you, this had better be more than just a fishing expedition."

"It's more than that, judge," I said. "I'm sure of it."

I called Lieutenant Sampson as soon as we left the judge's chambers, and he arranged to meet us a couple of blocks from the address in Makiki with a squad of plainclothesmen. When we pulled up he was standing outside his car looking grim. "I did a pass by," he said. "There's one car in the driveway."

"One of the vehicles we're authorized to search?"

He shook his head. "No. My daughter's. I went to her apartment this morning, but she was already gone. Did she say that she was going out with these people as well as the others?"

"Not to me. I never would have let her go, knowing what we know about the Whites."

"I'm holding you responsible." He pointed an accusing finger at me. "I want my daughter back, safe. Otherwise there's going to be hell to pay."

"I know," I said. Somehow I'd known it all along.

We prepared to move in. Sampson insisted on taking the lead; after all, Kitty was his daughter. Mike and I followed behind him, guns drawn and ready. "Open up, it's the police," he shouted, after knocking loudly. "We have a search warrant."

There was no response. "There's nobody home," a voice said. I turned and saw it was Jerry the cabinetmaker. I'd forgotten he lived next door. He was standing on his front porch looking at us. "They left about an hour ago. Both of them, her in her car and him in his truck. She had another woman with her, the woman who drove over in that car." He pointed to Kitty's car and started walking toward us. "Then he came back, just for a few minutes, and put a bunch of stuff in the back of his truck."

"Was he alone?" I asked.

"No, there was somebody with him, looked like a teenager. Funny hair. Looked like a Chinese kid, but with blond hair pulled up like a Mohawk."

A Chinese kid with a blond Mohawk. That sounded like Jimmy Ah Wong. My mind raced ahead, making connections. I knew that Jimmy had been working the streets, and I'd seen Jeff White cruising Kalākaua as if he was looking to pick somebody up. Did White know Jimmy?

"If I showed you a picture of a kid, do you think you could ID him?" I asked.

Bosk shook his head. "He didn't get out of the truck at all." Jerry came to the low hedge that separated the two properties. He motioned me to come closer. "I think Mr. Whack Job was putting some guns in the back of the truck," he said. "At least, one of the things he brought out looked a lot like a rifle."

Lieutenant Sampson ordered uniforms to check out the perimeter of the property and report back in. "They have a shed in the back, too," Jerry said. "You should check that too."

"You said Mr. White came back," I said. "How long ago was that?"

"Oh, you just missed him. Maybe ten minutes ago?"

"You have any idea where they were all going?" Sampson asked.

"We're not exactly friendly," Jerry said. "But I did see her, Sheila, carrying a picnic basket. And the girl with her had a couple of grocery bags."

The uniforms reported in. They didn't see anyone around the house, and no activity could be seen through the windows. "I don't suppose you have a key to their house?" Sampson asked. When Jerry shook his head, Sampson directed a uniform to break the door down.

Mike and I were surveying the house when one of the uniforms radioed. "I think we found what you were looking for, out here in the shed." We hurried out to where the uniform was standing in front of a small wooden shed, about eight feet on each side. He had cut a padlock off the door and turned on the lights inside.

We could both see that the room had been fitted out as some kind of laboratory. "Bingo," Mike said.

We worked steadily, gathering evidence for several hours. In the meantime, Sampson had APBs broadcast for both of the Whites' cars. He paced back and forth among us like a restless ghost, muttering aloud about terrorist bombers and headstrong kids. I looked at my watch and saw that Uncle Chin's wake had been going on for hours.

I called my father and explained I was running late. "There are lots of people here," he said. "But try and come over for a few minutes. I know Mei-Mei would appreciate it."

"I'll try. Tell her I'm sorry, will you?"

"She knows," he said.

Chapter 33

INCENSE BURNING

BY 2 O'CLOCK THURSDAY we had gathered as much evidence as we could from the house. Mike took all the incendiary materials to the fire department lab and our technicians went back to headquarters to check fingerprint records. We didn't find the small Smith & Wesson we believed had been used to kill Charlie Stahl and Hiroshi Mura, but it was obvious from the empty gun drawers that many weapons of various sizes were missing.

I told Lieutenant Sampson I wanted to stop by Uncle Chin's house for the wake, promising I'd keep my cell phone turned on and handy, and he let me go. The narrow, curving streets of St. Louis Heights were chockablock with cars as I navigated my way there. Fortunately, a neighbor, Mr. Rodriguez, was out in his yard as I passed and he let me park in his driveway. As I walked down the hill toward the house, I saw a familiar face in one of the parked cars.

"Hey, brah," I said, walking up to the passenger side of the car. "You checking out all the dangerous characters going into my uncle's house?"

Akoni turned to me, a sheepish look on his face. "We're just looking at tong members."

"You got a problem with that, Kanapa'aka?" the man behind the wheel said.

I leaned down to look in at him. His name was Tony Lee, and all I knew about him was that he worked in Organized Crime. "Not at all," I said. "You see anybody you don't know, you can just ask me. I've got a couple of great-aunts you might not recognize."

"Blow me," Tony said.

"Hey, be careful what you say. I might just take you up on that someday." I saw Akoni trying to stifle a smile and I stood up.

Uncle Chin's house and yard were full of people and it took me a while to say hello to everyone. There are very prescribed rites that take place when a person of Chinese descent dies, and even though he had a long criminal past, Uncle Chin was very traditional, and he was getting everything he was due.

When I saw the group of old men playing cards in the front courtyard, I realized that Aunt Mei-Mei had gone totally old school, and that Uncle Chin's body had to be in the house, waiting for the funeral. The card players were there because the corpse had to be "guarded" while it was in the house, and gambling helped the "guards" pass the time. It was also said to make the mourners feel better—which I guessed was only true if you were winning.

A white cloth was across the doorway of the house, and a gong had been placed to the left. The wake had been going on since early that morning, and I figured that my family had been busy helping Aunt Mei-Mei prepare everything. A monk stood in the corner, his head shaved, wearing saffron robes and chanting Buddhist scriptures. The Chinese believe that the souls of the dead face many obstacles, torments, and even torture for the sins they have committed in life before they are allowed to take their place in the afterlife. The monk's prayers, chanting, and rituals were aimed to help smooth the passage of Uncle Chin's soul into heaven. From what I knew of his life, he needed all the help he could get.

A trio of musicians played gong, flute, and trumpet in one corner of the living room. Next to them, Uncle Chin's coffin sat about two feet above the ground, with his head facing the inside of the house. The area around the head of the coffin was filled with wreaths, gifts, and a big color photo of Uncle Chin as a young man.

He was quite handsome then, though there was a deadliness about his eyes that was a little creepy, even knowing that he was beyond harming anyone. The coffin was open, with various plates of food placed in front of it, to feed Uncle Chin on his journey.

A comb, broken in half, was placed in the coffin next to him, and I knew that Aunt Mei-Mei would keep the other half. At the foot of the coffin sat an altar, with burning incense and a lit white candle. Joss paper and prayer money (to provide the deceased with sufficient income in the afterlife) are burned continuously throughout the wake. I stepped up to the altar, bowed to Uncle Chin, and lit a stick of sandalwood incense. I folded a twenty-dollar bill and slipped it into the donation box.

Aunt Mei-Mei would not keep the money there, though often families did use that money to help defray funeral expenses. Rather, it would go to some charity in Chinatown, to further honor Uncle Chin's memory.

I looked around. The statues of Kwan Yin and other deities in the house had been covered with red paper, to protect them from the body and the coffin, and the big mirror by the front door was gone, because the Chinese believe that if you see the reflection of a coffin in a mirror you will shortly have a death in your family.

The house was crowded, most people in formal aloha attire. I felt a little out of place, a little disrespectful, in my casual aloha shirt and khakis, but at least I'd made it there. Once I'd paid my respects to Uncle Chin, I sought out my parents, hugging them both. "I'm sorry, Dad," I said. "I know you'll miss Uncle Chin."

He smiled. "I will see him again in the next life," he said. "It's good that you came today."

"Uncle Chin was always good to me," I said.

On the far side of the room, talking to my sister-in-law Liliha, was Aunt Mei-Mei's daughter-in-law, Genevieve Pang, widow of Uncle Chin's illegitimate son and mother of his only grandson, who was unable to attend the funeral due to his incarceration at Halawa Prison.

I made up two big plates of food and recruited Jeffrey and Ashley, my niece and nephew, to take them out to Akoni and Tony Lee. "Make sure you give this one to the thin Chinese guy," I said to Jeffrey. I leaned down and whispered, "That's the one I spit in."

They were both wise to me, though. "Uncle Kimo," he said. Then he and Ashley took off.

I found Aunt Mei-Mei in the kitchen, frying wontons. "You shouldn't be doing this, Aunt," I said, leaning down to kiss her. She wore a flowered apron over her black skirt and white blouse. The matching black jacket was draped over one of the kitchen chairs.

"I need keep busy," she said. "No want think about Uncle Chin."

"He was a good man." I felt the tears I had been fighting for so long start to well up again. "I loved him."

"Oh, Kimo, he love you, too. He love you, your brothers like his own sons." She started to cry. "Now what I do? How I live without him?"

I reached over and got a paper towel, and used it to dry her eyes. "Come on, now, you don't want the wontons to burn, do you?"

I stayed there and helped her for a few minutes. Then my cell phone rang and I walked outside to a quiet corner of the yard to answer it. "We may have a lead," Lieutenant Sampson said. "A sightseeing helicopter going over Wa'ahila State Park saw a small fire, and swooped in for a closer look. He saw a car and a truck there, and though he couldn't see plate numbers on either vehicle, they match the description of the ones registered to the Whites."

"He see anybody around it?"

"Not in the immediate vicinity. But he did see two people who looked like they were running away from the fire. A girl who matches Kitty's description and a skinny boy with yellow hair."

My heart started to race. "Did he describe the hair at all? Was it gelled up to a point?"

"You know who it might be?" I told him what I knew about Jimmy Ah Wong. "What the hell's he doing up there with Kitty?" Sampson asked. He didn't even wait for an answer. "We've got to get some men into that park."

"I'm looking at it now," I said. "My uncle's house butts right up against it. You can set up a command post here."

"Give me the address." I gave it to him, and told him there were already two officers from Organized Crime stationed out in the street. "I'll be there in fifteen minutes. Twenty, if too many asshole drivers get in my way."

Chapter 34

LOGISTICS

I WENT INTO THE HOUSE, found my parents, and explained the situation. "I think the boy who ran away is there, too," I said. "Along with my boss's daughter, and at least a couple of little kids."

"I will talk to Aunt Mei-Mei," my father said. "Uncle Chin's spirit will be happy if we help you find this boy, and these other people." He and my mother started circulating among the guests, sending them home.

Lui and Haoa sent their wives and children away but insisted on staying. "We can help you," Lui said. "You know we know that park pretty well."

On her way out the door, Liliha stopped and turned to me. "I am a very proud woman, Kimo," she said. "But I hope that I am not too proud to admit when I have been wrong. And I was wrong about the church. I hope you will forgive me."

I hugged her and kissed her cheek. "You're my sister, Liliha," I said. "I'll always love you, and nothing will get in the way of that."

For the first time since she'd married my brother, my sister-in-law hugged me back, and I could feel she meant everything she said.

When we pulled apart, I looked up and saw Haoa and Tatiana ahead of us. Tatiana was crying and Haoa was stroking her long, streaked blonde hair. "Be careful," she was saying. "Just be careful."

"I will be. Don't you worry."

Liliha took control of the situation. "All kids in the cars," she said, in a voice that reminded me very much of my mother's. She took Tatiana's arm, gently prying her away from Haoa. "We'll all go to my house, Tati," she said. "I want you to look at this catalogue with me. I'm thinking of changing around the living room."

I watched my sisters-in-law and my nieces and nephews load up and move out. Jeffrey and Ashley complained; they wanted to stay and help, but they were no good in the face of opposition from their parents, no matter how much they complained that they were teenagers and ought to be treated better than the little *keikis*.

When the last of the guests had driven away, I went around to the backyard, where Akoni and Tony Lee where talking with my father and brothers. I could smell a faint odor of smoke on a breeze that came down the mountainside. "Somebody needs to evacuate the park," Akoni said. "Lee and I can do that."

"I'll have backup meet you at the entrance to the park," I said. "Lui, you and Haoa go with them, help them scout the perimeter of the park, then come back here. The fire department should be on their way. You guys will have to coordinate with them, too."

"I've never seen the park so dry," my father said. "You all better be careful."

We all walked around to the front yard. My father looked stronger, more energized than he had the day before, and he was able to walk by himself, only touching my mother's arm occasionally.

Haoa said, "I'll drive," and Lui, Akoni, and Tony Lee jumped into his old panel van to head down to the park entrance.

My parents stopped by my mother's Lexus in the driveway, and I said, "Dad, remember those old maps of the park you used to show us when we were kids? You still have them? We're going to need them."

He nodded, and my mother said, "Mei-Mei, you and Genevieve come with us. It's not safe for you to stay here."

Aunt Mei-Mei shook her head. "No, I stay with Chin. Genevieve, you go."

Genevieve took her mother-in-law's hand. "No, Mother. I will stay with you."

My mother looked at me, and I shrugged. So she and my father got into her car and drove off. Aunt Mei-Mei and Genevieve walked back inside, past the implacable card players, just as Lieutenant Sampson arrived.

"Run down for me what you know so far," he said.

We walked around the house to the backyard, where we could look into the park, and as we did I organized my thoughts. It was about three in the afternoon then, a hot, dry day with variable winds. Perfect weather for a forest fire.

"This case started when somebody shot that chicken in Makiki," I said. "I'm only speculating here, but I think both Jeff and Sheila White are wound pretty tight. They must have gotten tired of the rooster crowing every morning, and one of them went out and shot it to shut it up."

Sampson looked grim. "Go on."

"The homeless man, Hiroshi Mura, was shot because he saw something. Maybe he saw one of the Whites shoot the rooster. Maybe he knew what they were doing in that shed in the backyard. Either way, the same gun was used in both shootings."

I paused to think about what to say next. "Ballistics matched the gun to the one used to shoot Charlie Stahl as well. Until we made that connection, we had no idea that the Makiki shootings could be connected to the bombing at the Marriage Project party."

Sampson's radio crackled. Akoni and Tony Lee had closed the park and gotten the picnic areas evacuated. No one matching the suspects' description had been seen, but I knew there was a lot of wild country beyond the public area.

"Kitty said Eli Harding's family had a cabin somewhere in the park," I said. "My dad's bringing over a bunch of old maps which show the trails and locations of cabins. If we can skirt the fire, we can head up some of those trails."

Akoni said he and Lee were on their way back, and signed off. Sampson turned his attention back to me.

"Mike Riccardi, the fire inspector, was at the rally at Waikīkī Gateway Park, and he saw the woman who shot Charlie Stahl get away in a dark sedan, and he got a partial license plate," I said.

"What was the fire inspector doing at a rally?"

I stopped. When I'd first seen Mike, I'd assumed he was there for the rally itself, that my influence was going to gradually move him out of the closet.

But of course, that wasn't the reason at all. "I think he was worried that there might be another bombing attempt," I said. "After all, the rally was organized by the Marriage Project, and the Marriage Project had just been bombed. You know that some of the arsons over the last few weeks have been at gay and lesbian businesses?"

"I've had my hands full with homicides. I haven't been following the arsons."

"Mike thinks the arsonists are amateurs, that they've been

getting more sophisticated with each attack. At the rally, he was keeping an eye out for suspicious behavior. That's how he spotted our shooter."

I had to stop and regroup. "OK, so we had these shootings that matched up. When I was canvassing in Makiki, I talked to both Sheila and Jeff White. A couple of days later, when I was at the Marriage Project party, I saw a sweaty guy who looked familiar to me, and we identified this unknown guy as a chief suspect. Then we pulled a fingerprint off a paper bag that had been tossed at the Marriage Project office a few hours before the bombing, and we traced it to a guy at Pupukea Plantation, where the Church of Adam and Eve holds some services."

My father and mother returned with the maps, and I set my father to figuring out where the Hardings' cabin might be. My mother went back into the house to stay with Aunt Mei-Mei and Genevieve Pang. Even the increased smell of smoke in the air didn't seem to phase the gamblers, though.

"The guy at Pupukea Plantation, Ed Baines, told us that Jeff White had paid him to throw those shit-filled bags at the Marriage Project office, but White denied it. At that point, you and I were talking about a lineup to try and connect White to the sweaty guy."

"Which we can still do, if we need to."

My cell rang and I could see from the display it was Mike Riccardi. "Yeah, Mike?" I said, answering it.

"I'm on my way over to Wa'ahila State Park, with a couple of engines," he said. "There's a big fire brewing there. I remembered your parents live up there and wanted to tell you they might want to get out."

"Already ahead of you," I said. I told him where we stood.

He whistled. "You think White started this fire?"

"Don't know. But I know he's up there somewhere, with a

bunch of innocent people." I glanced over at Sampson and knew he was thinking of Kitty.

"Listen, I gotta go," Mike said. "Be careful out there."

"You too."

I hung up and turned back to Sampson, telling him what Mike had said. Then I continued explaining the situation. "We got our big break when my friend Harry connected the partial plate Mike saw to a dark sedan that the Whites own. That helped us get the search warrant from Judge Yamanaka. At White's house, we found a bunch of unregistered handguns as well as a makeshift laboratory. Mike is having the materials we found there analyzed at the fire department's lab."

"So we have the Whites connected to two shootings and the bombing."

"That's right. Kitty and I met the Hardings at the Church of Adam and Eve, and it appears that the Whites went with all of them on their picnic."

Lui and Haoa returned from the park then and joined us for the rest of my rundown. I was pretty sure that Sampson didn't want my TV station manager brother to hear every detail of our case, but we were in a crunch situation and as long as we needed Lui's knowledge of the park, he had to hear what we knew.

"The Whites aren't married, as they've been presenting themselves; they're brother and sister. I think that their own incestuous relationship is what's motivating them to protest against gay marriage."

Lui asked, "The minister and his wife aren't married? They're brother and sister?"

I could see the headlines in his eyes. "About an hour ago, a sightseeing helicopter heading up from Diamond Head spotted a fire at a cabin up on Wa'ahila Ridge and flew up to take a closer look."

We all turned to look up at the ridge, and for the first time we could see gray smoke rising above the tree line. A breeze blew past us and the tang of the smoke registered in my nostrils. "He couldn't get too close, but he said he saw a pickup and a dark sedan parked near the cabin. As he was leaving, he spotted two individuals fleeing the area on foot. Based on his description, I think they were the lieutenant's daughter Kitty and a boy named Jimmy Ah Wong."

"Now I start to get lost," Sampson said. "Who's this boy? What do you think he was doing there?"

I explained how Jimmy had been helpful in making the case against Wayne Gallagher and Derek Pang, and that subsequent to his interview with the DA, his father had discovered he was gay and kicked him out of the house. Then I stopped.

"So you don't know where he is now?" Sampson asked.

"Well, not really." I told him I had signed Jimmy out of custody and left him with Uncle Chin and Aunt Mei-Mei, and then Jimmy had disappeared after Uncle Chin died.

"Let me get this straight. You took responsibility for a teenaged prostitute and then left him in the custody of a known gangster?" He looked incredulous, and then something unhappy passed over his face. "You don't have any other interest in this boy, do you?"

My brothers both stiffened, and I could tell from their body language they were ready to jump to my defense. We all knew what Sampson meant. I felt the anger bubbling up inside me but I tried to keep it down. We were both worried about Kitty, up there somewhere on the mountain with a fire raging around her, not knowing where the crazy Whites were or how they fit into the picture.

"Jimmy's a good kid," I said. "He's smart and he's got a sweet nature. He's been coming to the self-defense classes I lead at the Waikīkī Gay Teen Center. But that's my only involvement with him." I took a deep breath. "I know you don't want to ask this but I'll tell you anyway. I am not sexually involved with him in any way, shape, or form. He's just a kid I feel like needs a friend."

"What you did was pretty stupid," Sampson said. "You know how vulnerable you are to any innuendo in the press, don't you?" He took a sidelong look at Lui. "If somebody gets hold of the connection between you and a teenaged boy prostitute, just the speculation could lose you your badge. It would hurt you and it would hurt the department."

"He didn't have anybody else to look out for him." I turned to look at the fire again. "I understand what you're saying, but I'd do it again if it came to that."

"Let's hope it doesn't come to that," he said. "So you don't know how he got up on the mountain with Kitty?"

I shook my head. "I know Jimmy was back on the streets, though I've been looking for him for two days and I couldn't find him. I saw Jeff White out on Kalākaua late one night, and I think he might have been out looking for prostitutes himself. Maybe just to bring them into the church, maybe not. And maybe somebody from the church took Jimmy in. The helicopter also saw another car, a Volvo—looked like it had been abandoned along the trail. We know Kitty was meeting the Hardings and their two children, and there might have been other church members at this picnic."

"So there could be a whole church full of picnickers out there in this fire," Sampson said. "Lovely."

I turned to Lui. "Do you or Liliha know anything about this church that we should know?"

Haoa and Sampson turned toward him as well. "Don't tell me, brah," Haoa said. "You've been going to this dumb church? Your kids, too?"

"We just went to a couple of their meetings," Lui said defensively. "Liliha thought they had a good, family-friendly message."

"Get a pair of balls, brah," Haoa said. "Your wife expects you to choose between her and your brother, who you gonna choose?"

Lui is two years older than Haoa, and since childhood they'd been sparring, each determined to be the best. When Lui threw a luau for his oldest son Jeffrey's eighth-grade graduation, Haoa had to throw a bigger one the next year for the birth of his youngest child. I was lucky that I'd avoided rivalry with them; the only times it seemed that they'd collaborated had been to pick on me, the baby brother.

But there was no time for rehashing old family rivalries. "All right," I said. "Let's table this discussion for later. Nobody's choosing between anybody right now. And besides, Liliha and I kissed and made up before she left."

My brothers were glaring at each other as my father came to the back door and called out, "Come take a look at the maps of the park and the ridge."

We went inside, where he had spread a faded topographical map on Uncle Chin's dining room table. I saw Sampson glance over at Uncle Chin's coffin, at the incense and platters of food, but I guess he knew enough of Hawai'i not to be surprised.

The four of us clustered around the table with my father, who leaned heavily on the table. His hospitalization, and the death of Uncle Chin, wore heavily on his big frame, and though he was clearly healing, I felt very protective of him. I wanted to make him go home, lie down, and rest, but there was too much to do and we needed whatever help he could provide.

"See how the Wa'ahila trail continues up the ridge?" he said. "There are some old homestead cabins up there, just outside the park boundary. No one lives up there full time, but people still use the cabins."

"So somebody set one of those cabins on fire," Sampson said.

"Looks like it. The good news for you is that there's only one road in or out of the area. It leads down into the park."

"My partner from Waikīkī, Akoni Hapa'ele, and another guy from Organized Crime have already gone up there to co-ordinate a blockade and any evacuation."

My father continued. "The bad news is that the road snakes back and forth up the hill. So if your suspects are on foot, they won't bother using it. There are at least two trails that lead down the mountain, but go in different directions."

Akoni came walking into the kitchen then. "We've got a bunch of black-and-whites, and a SWAT team at the park entrance, ready to head in." He'd hitched a ride over with some campers who were leaving. "Tony's over there, but he needs to know what to do."

"Lui, Haoa, and I can each take a team into the park," I said. "We know the trails and the road better than anyone, from all the time we've spent hiking and camping in the park and up on the ridge as kids."

Sampson looked grim. "I don't like to involve civilians, but we're in a crisis situation here," he said. "Let's head out."

We went out front, and I saw the elderly gamblers were still there. Their duty was to protect Uncle Chin's corpse, and nothing short of flames licking at their heels was going to drag them away.

Behind us, my parents, Aunt Mei-Mei, and Genevieve Pang clustered around the front door. My father leaned against the door frame and my mother stood close to him, fiercely protective, clearly torn between her responsibilities to him, to her sons, and to her lifelong best friend.

Lui, Haoa, and Sampson took Haoa's panel truck again, and Akoni climbed in with me for the ride down the hill and around to the park entrance. For a couple of minutes it was like we were partners again. There was so much that I wanted to tell him and no time to do it.

By the time we reached the park entrance, the smell of smoke was overwhelming. The narrow neighborhood roads were crowded with black-and-whites and undercover cars parked in driveways and on grassy verges, as every available unit had been called to the ridge to help search for the fugitives. We could barely snake through in my truck.

The two-lane entry to the park was lined with tall Norfolk pine trees, with wild roosters and hens wandering around below them. We parked next to a stone wall by the tall wooden park gate.

I assembled the cops and my brothers into a semicircle. "We all know what we have to do." I pointed at my brothers. "You guys remember, you're tour guides, not cops. Don't do anything stupid."

"This mountain is dry as a bone," Haoa said. He knelt down to finger some leaves, then held them up to us. "If you see a small fire, you can try to stamp it out, but anything bigger you've got to get the hell away."

I thought of Mike Riccardi then, and hoped he would be all

right. I didn't like the idea of him running into forest fires, but then again, he probably didn't like my going after bad guys with guns either.

I took Akoni, Lidia Portuondo, and Gary Saunders, a uniform I'd known in Waikīkī, on my team. I'd actually punched Saunders in the face after he'd called me a faggot once, but at least I knew him, his strengths and weaknesses. He was a big, strong guy, too, which might help us if we ran into somebody up on the ridge who needed to be restrained.

Haoa took Tony Lee, Frank Sit, Steve Hart, and another uniform, and Lui got Alvy Greenberg and three uniforms.

I was just ready to pull out when Mike Riccardi arrived, loping up the hill from where he'd parked his truck. I was so damn glad to see him—but at the same time, I knew that his presence meant he was about to go into that fire.

Chapter 35

THE HARDINGS

LUI'S TEAM AND Haoa's team went up the mountain in separate directions, so it wasn't long before I lost sight and sound of my brothers. I worried about them, but I knew they both were smart and strong and knew the park well. I turned my attention back to Mike, who was explaining the fire department's plans to Lieutenant Sampson.

"Air–1's in for repairs, so we've got Air-2 on the way," he said. I knew that those were the names of the Honolulu Fire Department's two helicopters. "Air-2 has the Bambi Bucket."

"You're trying to rescue deer?" Sampson asked.

Mike laughed and shook his head. "The Bambi Bucket is a lightweight collapsible container, for water drops on brush fires," he said. "We'll scoop up water from the ocean and ferry it over here. The bucket can pull out of places as shallow as a foot deep. Though this wind might be trouble."

For the first time, I paid attention to the wind around us as something more than a carrier of smoke. "I'd say we've got gusts of up to thirty miles an hour," Mike said. "Might make it tough to get the bucket in. But we'll see."

We looked up to the mountain, and saw rust-red and white clouds of smoke as well as lines of orange flames moving over the hills and into the park's gulches.

Mike's radio crackled and he listened for a minute. "Roger

that," he said. To us, he said, "The state's sending the DNR chopper too," he said. That was good; the park, as protected land, came under the auspices of the state's Department of Natural Resources.

"The chief's worried about the houses in St. Louis Heights," Mike said. "We've got front-end loaders coming up to build firebreaks where we can, but it's tough to get access to a lot of the park. And even if we build them, the wind may just jump the breaks."

I thought of my parents' house, which backed on the park, as well as Uncle Chin's house, where his body still rested, watched over by the gamblers in the front courtyard, Aunt Mei-Mei, and Genevieve Pang. "Will there be evacuations?" I asked.

"Not sure yet. We'll see how the firebreaks go. We're also going to be hosing down the backyards, trying to create a water curtain."

Meanwhile, engines from the 5, 22, and 33 companies were pulling up, disgorging firefighters in yellow suits, their company number on their yellow helmets. Many were already wearing masks, with oxygen tanks on their backs.

The battalion chief got out of his car and Mike leaned over to whisper to me, "You know what CHAOS stands for?"

I shook my head. "The Chief Has Arrived On Scene," he said, and laughing, left to confer with him. It was time to take my team up the mountain, leaving Lieutenant Sampson at the command post.

Lui's team was the first to find anything. After about half an hour of climbing, they came upon the abandoned Volvo that the helicopter had spotted. They radioed the license plate and VIN number in to Sampson, and he called in for an identification. I heard him radio back, "It belongs to an Eli Harding of Palolo," he said. "I'm trying to track down the Hardings. I'll let you know what I find."

Before the report could come back, though, Lui's team ran into Harding himself, along with his wife. My team wasn't far from them, and I met up with Lui to take charge of the Hardings and see what they had to say.

When my team connected with Lui's, I could see that Alvy Greenberg wanted to talk to me, but I didn't have the time—or the interest. Harding was a short, stocky guy in his early thirties, with wiry, sandy blond hair. His wife was about his age and height, a bit slimmer, with blonde hair pulled back in a ponytail. They looked like an ordinary suburban couple, and I could see why Kitty had trusted them enough to go off on a picnic with them and their kids.

They were frantic about their two children, who they said had been taken away by Jeff and Sheila White. Lui was good with them, talking with quiet power about his own kids, and how he understood completely what the Hardings were going through. "My brother knows what he's doing," Lui said, handing the Hardings off to me. "He'll get your kids back."

I wished I felt as sure, but I smiled and said that Lui was absolutely right. He took Greenberg and his two uniforms and went back into the brush, and my team and I started down the hill with the Hardings.

Finally, Eli calmed down enough to tell me his story in something like chronological order. "My grandfather built this cabin—just one big room, about twenty feet on each side, with ten-foot ceilings—in the 1930s, when you could claim a piece of the mountain land by building on it," he said, as we made our way down the narrow, overgrown path. The smoke was heavy around us, and the heat was almost blistering.

"I grew up going there for holidays and summers, and

when my father died I inherited it. I was talking about the place with Jeff White last week and he said he'd like to see it, so we made plans for this picnic." He was wearing shorts and a fake military shirt in a khaki color, the kind with epaulets and lots of pockets, and the sweat was dripping down his forehead.

He started to cough, and Fran grabbed his hand. She continued the story. "The kids were playing outside, and Eli and I were standing by the kitchen counter putting sandwiches out on a platter when Jeff and Sheila walked in." Her arms and legs were scratched, and her white shirt and plaid shorts were smoke stained.

"The bastards were holding a gun on us," Eli said indignantly. "I'm the one took Jeff out shooting at the range, and he had this 9 millimeter aimed at Fran, while Sheila came over to me carrying this rope. I said, 'What's going on, buddy? What are you and your wife doing?'"

He started to cough again, but stopped after a moment. "He said, 'She's not my wife, she's my sister.' I was so surprised I didn't know what to say."

"He made us lie down on the floor," Fran said. "They said that they were going to tie us up so that we couldn't follow them." She reached over and used her shirt sleeve to wipe Eli's brow of sweat.

"We asked them about Cole and Caitlin," Eli said. "At least we wanted them to bring the kids in with us. But Sheila said they were taking the kids for a ride with them. Jeff took the keys to the Volvo from my pocket."

"We started fighting them," Fran said. "I couldn't believe they were taking my babies away from me. Sheila hit me in the head with her gun."

We came to a narrow place on the trail, where there was a steep drop-off to one side, and we all had to stop talking and go single file until the danger had passed. The brush crackled under me, dry as tinder, and tiny pebbles skittered away whenever anyone stepped down. When I took deep breaths I felt a stinging in my throat.

The strap of Fran's left sandal was torn, and it caught beneath her as she walked. She lost her balance and nearly fell down the side of the ravine, but Lidia was right behind her, and she caught Fran and helped her stand up again.

Sweat was pooling under my arms and dripping across my forehead. I couldn't see how Mike could work in this kind of environment. Not just the infernal heat and the sweat, but not knowing where the fire was, and where it might strike next.

After Hurricane Iniki destroyed Kauai in 1992, a lot of people talked about leaving the islands. Cousins of mine moved to Southern California. I figured that at least with a hurricane, you knew what was coming and you had time to prepare. An earthquake could strike anytime, without warning. That's the way I felt about this fire—that at any moment a tongue of flame could spring up, trapping us or turning us into crispy critters. Give me a good old-fashioned tropical storm, wind and rain lashing the palm trees, anytime.

When we'd passed the narrow spot, we stopped for a minute to regroup. I looked at the map my father had given me, and tried to estimate where we were. If I was right, the park entrance was just below us. If I was wrong, we were screwed—lost in the dry scrub with fire raging around us.

"Did the Whites start the fire?" Akoni asked, as we started up again.

"They set the cabin on fire," Eli said. "The bastards. They

stacked charcoal and kindling along one wall, and poured lighter fluid over it. I could hear and smell what they were doing, and we kept calling them and begging them not to kill us."

"Sheila tied lousy knots," Fran said. "It took a few minutes, but we managed to get untied and get out of the cabin before the fire caught." She caught her breath in a little gasp. "But the car was gone, and the kids." She started to cry. "They've got my kids."

I tried to imagine what might have happened if the Hardings hadn't been able to get out of the cabin before it burned to the ground. Chances were we'd have gotten there eventually, and in the ashes we'd have found two bodies, a man and a woman. We'd have discovered the charred wreckage of both the Whites' vehicles, and the easy conclusion would have been that they had died in the fire.

We crested a hill, and below us I saw the bottom of the trail. Lidia took calm charge of the distraught couple, leading them off to get cleaned up.

"What about our kids?" I heard Fran ask.

"We're going to find your kids," Lidia said. "And when they see you, you want to be all cleaned up, don't you? You don't want to frighten them any more than they have been."

Meekly, Fran Harding nodded.

Sampson let all the units know that the suspects were now known to be armed, dangerous, and holding two small children that they might use as hostages. "Be very careful," he said into the radio. "I want no accidents."

I led Akoni and Saunders back up the trail, going off onto a side path we hadn't explored yet. I heard someone crashing through the trees just above us and waved the other cops with me to stop. We took up positions on either side of the trail, our weapons aimed and ready. My throat was dry and the smell of smoke was everywhere around us, though we still had decent visibility.

Just ahead of us, I could see two adults blundering through the underbrush. I pulled my gun and stood in the shooter's stance. "Come out with your hands up!" I called.

The bush parted and the two figures stepped out.

Chapter 36

JIMMY AND KITTY

"DON'T SHOOT," Jimmy Ah Wong called. "Please."

He had his arm around Kitty and she limped down the trail, favoring her right foot. I didn't know if they were armed, but I was sure they had to be scared. Slowly, I stepped into the trail path a hundred feet ahead of them. I whistled, and Kitty looked up.

I hurried up the trail to them. "I'm so glad to see you," she said when I reached them. "The Hardings invited Jeff and Sheila White along on the picnic, and we were right, they're crazy."

I hugged her, so glad to find that she was all right. She was wearing a light blue polo shirt, torn and stained by smoke, and khaki shorts and sneakers. Then I turned and hugged Jimmy. He looked like crap, wearing a torn and stained T-shirt, board shorts, and flip-flops. His face was scratched and there was a trail of blood dripping down one cheek.

We started going slowly back down the trail. Akoni led, me with my arm around Kitty, Jimmy almost dancing around us on an adrenaline rush, Saunders covering our backs. Much as I wanted to find the Whites and the kids who were with them, I had an obligation to get Jimmy and Kitty to safety.

Kitty said she'd be better off walking on her own, holding onto the trees for support, and I let her lead the way, watching

MAHU FIRE ≈ 277

her carefully, Akoni right beside her. The trail was rocky and narrow, and in places we almost lost it. When I was a kid roaming those paths, they were always so cool and green, overgrown with trees and vines, like another world.

Now that world was a frightening one, the smoke blocking our visibility, every tree root and pebble a hazard. It was hard to catch my breath, and I couldn't get my heart rate to slow down.

I radioed down to Sampson and told him that I had the two of them, that we were on our way down the trail. I could hear the stress in his voice when he said, "Be careful. The fire's building all around you."

Lui and Haoa both radioed in, too, telling me their teams were still hunting. I hoped one of them would find the Whites and the Harding kids before it was too late.

As soon as I was finished on the radio, Jimmy started to talk. "I was walking down Kalākaua this morning. This guy was cruising in his truck, and he pulled up next to me, going real slow." He looked over at me. "You know."

I knew.

"He rolled down his window and said hey. We talked for a minute or two and he said he was going to get some beer, and asked if I wanted to come along."

Jimmy lost his footing for a second and I grabbed his arm. He looked over at me, and there was such sadness in his eyes that I wanted to hug him again and promise that it would all be better soon. But we had to get out of the fire before we could think about anything else.

"He said his name was Jeff, and I told him I knew a place we could go." He lowered his voice so that Kitty and Akoni couldn't overhear us. "I started fooling around with him, and he was really into it. I got him to drive to the Ala Moana Mall and park in the back of the garage, behind a pillar. Then we, you know."

I smiled at him, encouragingly. Ahead of us, Kitty was moving slowly, and I could see that every time she touched her right leg to the ground her whole body shook with pain. Behind us, Saunders was swiveling his head left to right and back again, looking for the fire that I was sure was right on our tails.

"I leaned over to, you know, suck him, and this piece of paper fell out of my back pocket," Jimmy said. "It was this flyer I picked up at the rally at Waikīkī Gateway Park on Monday. I didn't even remember it was back there."

I didn't have to ask—I knew it was the sketch of the sweaty guy we'd been handing out. The sketch of Jeff White.

"He looked at the picture and he had this massive orgasm. I mean, the junk was dribbling out of my mouth, it was coming so fast. And then all of a sudden, he went nuts. He was like, waving the picture around in my face and demanding to know where I got it."

A blast of smoke blew past us, bringing singeing heat with it. The fire must have been catching up. Saunders said, "You sure you know where we're going?"

"I've been coming here since I was a kid," I said to Saunders, but really for everyone's benefit. "As long as we keep going downhill, eventually we'll get to the park entrance."

I put my arm around Jimmy's shoulders and hurried him along. Ahead of us, Akoni was doing the same thing with Kitty, letting her lean on him to relieve the pressure on her bad ankle.

"I tried to get away," Jimmy said. "I asked the guy for my money, but he wouldn't give it to me. Then when I tried to jump out of the truck, he grabbed my shirt and wouldn't let go. I twisted and turned, but he got hold of some rope from the back of the truck and he tied me up. I swear, he must be some kind of cowboy or something."

Jimmy started crying. "I promised him that I wouldn't tell anybody, if he'd just let me go. He started up the truck, and I didn't know what he was going to do."

Suddenly, the wind changed, and the fire, which had been at our backs, whipped around in front of us, igniting the dry brush just below us on the trail. We couldn't move any farther downhill without walking right into it.

Behind us, the fire that had been chasing us downhill grew closer. I looked at the map my father had given me, and through the smoke and a stand of ironwood trees I managed to see a glimpse of Diamond Head. That helped me figure out our position. We weren't far from the park entrance, but the easiest route was blocked by the fire.

I radioed down to Sampson to let him know, and as soon as I'd finished Mike Riccardi radioed to me. He must have been listening to my conversation with Sampson.

"You might be getting wet," he said. "I called your location in to the chopper, and we'll see if we can clear a path out for you. In the meantime, you've got to protect yourselves."

I was amazed at how calm he sounded. If I'd been worried about him I doubt I could have kept the fear from my voice. "What should we do?" I asked.

Kitty, Jimmy, Akoni, and Saunders clustered around me, listening to Mike. "Is there any water around you?" he asked.

I looked at the map. "Nope. Just trees and rocks."

"How about a clear, open area?"

Akoni said, "There's a clearing just behind us, off to the right."

Mike's voice crackled over the radio. "You need to get as much space between you and anything that can burn as you can. Get to the middle of the clearing, and try to dig some ditches you can lie in. If you get below the level of the fire, it may blow right past you."

He didn't have to say what would happen if we didn't protect ourselves. "Roger that," I said. Akoni led us a few feet back up the trail and through a stand of guava trees, the nearly ripe fruit smashing around us. In some parts of the park they were considered a pest because they grew so fast; my dad had spent years beating them back from the edge of our yard. But they'd give us some quick kindling to help redirect the fire.

The clearing wasn't that big, only about ten yards in any direction. As soon as we reached it, Saunders headed to the center and started digging. Kitty limped to him, leaning on Jimmy, and they joined him on the ground, using rocks to create ditches.

Akoni and I started tearing off guava limbs and building a firebreak. We hoped that by giving the flames enough to feed on, the fire would circle around us instead of jumping overhead. It was like leaving a trail of bread crumbs, or giving Pele, the goddess of fire, enough to sate her hunger that she wouldn't want to feast on us.

The noise grew louder and louder. Trees falling around us, a roar of fire catching on dry underbrush, the sound of Air-2 or the DNR chopper somewhere nearby. I couldn't hear anything over the radio, and I knew we were on our own. Akoni and I had just finished our firebreak when we saw Saunders frantically signaling to us, and I realized he'd finished shallow trenches for Akoni and me and we had to get into position.

My trough was next to Jimmy's, and I lay down next to him. He was shivering with fear and I reached my arm over his shoulders. He started talking again as soon as my ear was near him. "We pulled up in the driveway of this house,"

Jimmy said. "He told me to stay in the truck. He came back a little while later, with this big leather bag and a couple of rifles. I was so scared. I was sure he was going to kill me."

I heard a boom and a crackle behind us, and knew that the fire had to be close. I squeezed Jimmy's shoulder and he continued his story.

"He drove us up to the park, and he put duct tape on my mouth and made me get in the back of the truck, and covered me up with this thing."

Suddenly, the fire was all around us. I'd thought that the flames at the Marriage Project headquarters were bad, but this was a thousand times worse. The noise was overwhelming, and at any moment I was afraid that a tongue of fire would land on one of us.

I had been in bad situations before, but I'd always felt there was something I could do: talk down a guy holding a gun, use my weapon, run away. But I felt so helpless there on the ground, knowing there was nothing more I could do to protect myself or the people around me.

Thankfully, Pele was watching out for us, and she guided the flames along the firebreak Akoni and I had constructed. As quickly as the fire had descended on us, it had passed us by. I just lay there in my trough for a minute, my whole body shaking, waiting for my heart rate to slow down.

Almost as soon as the flames passed us, Air-2 passed overhead. The Bambi Bucket dropped water on the path below and the cool breeze swept over us. We all sat up, evaluating our condition. "My skin feels hot," Kitty said.

"Mine, too," Jimmy said.

"Anybody burned?" I asked. We all looked at each other. Akoni and Saunders, the biggest of us, hadn't been low enough into the ground, and both their backs had been swept by the flames. Their burns looked superficial, though, just some reddened skin on the parts of their lower arms that hadn't been covered by their shirts.

"I think it's time we get out of here," I said. It only took us a few minutes to descend the path to the park entrance, though we had to be careful of the slippery trail and any smoking embers still around.

Sampson saw Kitty coming and ran up the trail toward us, running surprisingly fast for such a big man. "Don't you ever do that to me again," he said, grabbing her in his arms.

I turned aside to give them a chance to share their tears in private, and was surprised to see my parents, Aunt Mei-Mei, and Genevieve Pang standing below. My father looked pale and tired, leaning against a black-and-white police car, my mother standing next to him. Both their faces were wreathed in smiles when they saw me.

I hurried over to them and hugged them both. Jimmy followed shyly, though Aunt Mei-Mei enveloped him in a big hug, getting smoke smudged on her face and her white blouse.

"We need a quick debriefing, and then you can take Jimmy home," I said to Aunt Mei-Mei. As he and I walked over to Sampson and Kitty, I tried to raise Mike on the radio, to let him know that we were safe, but I couldn't get him. I told both my brothers to get their teams down to the park entrance, that the fire was too strong and we had to let the firefighters take over.

"I thought you said there were kids up there," Haoa said.

"There are," I said. "But we don't know where any of them were when the fire swept through. It's too dangerous, Haoa. Mom and Dad are here. You both need to get down."

Saunders couldn't stop coughing, so he went over to the

paramedics for treatment. Akoni and I sat at a park bench with Sampson and Kitty, and I relayed most of what Jimmy had told me, ending with him wrapped in a tarpaulin in the back of Jeff White's pickup.

"This is where I come in," Kitty said. I saw her squeeze Jimmy's hand. "I went over to the Hardings' this morning for the picnic, and Fran and Eli said that we were going to meet the Whites, too. So we all drove over to their house, and I left my car in the Whites' driveway."

"I saw that," Sampson said. Normally unruffled, I could see he was struggling to keep a lid on his temper.

"Everything was going OK," Kitty said. "Fran and Eli went in the cabin to get the food together, and I took Caitlin and Cole for a walk in the woods."

"Where were the Whites?" I asked.

"I drove up in Sheila's car with her, following the Hardings. Jeff went off to get some beer. When we got up to the cabin, Sheila started unloading stuff. While I was gone with the kids, Jeff came up in his truck, and I saw him go off into the woods with her."

She looked pleadingly at her dad. "Everything was going fine. It was just going to be a picnic."

"I'm just glad you're safe," he said. "But if you ever scare me this way again I'll kill you myself."

I had a feeling my boss might be capable of just such a thing. There was a wildness in him, lying below the surface, the kind of temperament that let him romp around naked in the mud at a rock concert. I'll bet he had worked hard to civilize those impulses.

"I was walking past Jeff's truck when I heard this thumping. I steered the kids over there, and I saw this big bundle under a tarp. I could see a piece of Jimmy's hair at the top, and as

I was looking his foot snaked out from under the tarp, too, and banged on the side of the rail three times."

Kitty looked more sure of herself then, and in that moment I knew that she'd be a damned good police officer some day. "I sent the kids up to the cabin, and once they were out of sight I reached over and pulled back the tarp. That's when I saw Jimmy. His hands and feet were bound with rope and there was a piece of duct tape over his mouth. He looked scared as hell."

"My hero," Jimmy said.

"I didn't know what was going on, but I knew something had to be wrong. I peeled the duct tape off his mouth, and he told me that Jeff was the guy in the picture."

She looked over at her dad. "I know sometimes it takes me a while to listen to you, but everything you've been saying for years finally kicked in. I know I'm not a cop, and that the best thing I could do was call you. But I couldn't get a cell signal up there, so I had to get Jimmy out of there and get down to the bottom of the hill."

"Smart thinking," Sampson said.

"It took me forever to untie the knots around Jimmy's wrists. I kept looking up at the cabin, worrying that at any minute Sheila or Jeff or one of the Hardings would come out and see me there, and know that the game was up. I was so nervous I was sweating, and my fingers and hands were slippery. I finally just made myself stop trembling and eventually I got the knot undone."

She looked over at Jimmy and squeezed his hand again. "We worked together to get his feet loose. Finally he was able to jump out of the truck and we started going down this trail."

"Kitty was awesome," Jimmy said. "She kept us off the road, because she thought Jeff might come after us in his truck. And then we smelled the smoke and I was, like, ready to lose it, and she calmed me down. Then we came to this steep part, and she was so brave. She went first, to make sure it was safe for me."

"I wasn't careful enough," Kitty said. "I was picking my way down, one step at a time, holding onto rocks and trees, when this little tree I was holding gave way. I lost my balance and started sliding. It was awful. I was scared I was going to hit my head on something and die."

She smiled over at Jimmy. "You should have seen Jimmy. He jumped over everything like he was some kind of mountain goat, and he landed right next to me. I hurt my ankle, but he helped me stand up. I wanted him to go on and find help, but he wouldn't leave me."

"We could smell the fire," Jimmy said.

"We hobbled on for a while, but my ankle hurt, so we stopped by this big boulder. And then I heard Caitlin Harding crying. We thought that it was Fran and Eli, and I was so relieved."

"But it wasn't," Jimmy said. "It was creepy Jeff and his wife. With those other people's kids."

Kitty continued. "We hid behind the rock, and we heard the footsteps coming. As soon as I saw Cole I was ready to jump up, but Jimmy was smart and he held me back. That's when we saw it wasn't Fran and Eli with the kids, but Jeff and Sheila. She sent Jeff one way down the trail with the kids, and she started coming toward us."

She looked over at Jimmy and smiled at him. "Sheila got closer and closer. There was no way we could move without attracting her attention, and there was no way she wouldn't see us if she kept coming. I was desperately trying to think of a plan when Jimmy got up. I reached for him, miming madly for him to stay put, but he wasn't paying attention. I was so scared for him when I saw him creeping around through the woods, trying to get around behind Sheila."

Her bangle bracelets jangled a little, and I could see her nerves flaring up again. "I was so scared. I just didn't think Jimmy could do anything." Looking at him, she said, "I'm sorry, Jimmy. I thought you were just the kind of kid who watched too many violent TV shows and movies, that you thought you could take on the bad guys because on TV the good guys always won."

"I surprised myself," Jimmy said. "But I never would have tried anything if it wasn't for Kimo."

I looked at him, but Kitty had resumed her story. "I tried to get up but my leg wouldn't hold me. When Jimmy jumped out in front of Sheila, I was totally surprised. He kicked the gun out of her right hand. He stumbled, regaining his balance, but he made a fist and swung his arm at her stomach like a club."

"That's what I learned from you," Jimmy said. "At the teen center. You taught us that stuff."

Sampson glanced at me, and I'm sure he was wondering exactly what I was teaching those kids. But Akoni looked too, and I felt good knowing that he trusted me no matter what I did.

"I could almost hear her breath come out of her body," Kitty said. "She fell backwards to the ground, and she hit her head on the dirt trail. We'd just left her behind when we ran into you."

"You mean Sheila White's up there on the trail?" I asked. "Why didn't you say that first?"

Chapter 37
OUT OF THE FIRE

BOTH KITTY AND JIMMY looked like they were ready to cry.

"I'm going back up there," I said to Sampson. "We weren't that far up the trail when we found the kids, and the fire's already been past there. If Sheila White's still up there I can bring her down."

"Right behind you, brah," Akoni said. We hurried up the ridge, and it was good to have my partner back again, even if only for a short while.

"Be careful," Sampson called to us. "Keep your radios on."

Akoni and I passed Lui and his team coming down. I wanted to embrace my brother, thank him, and thank Pele, too, for bringing him safely back, but I was worried about the Harding kids and what could be happening to them up on the mountain with Jeff and Sheila White.

The fire had burned to our left, and we were able to take the right-hand trail up to the rise where Kitty and Jimmy had first appeared to us. Because of the shifting wind, it was still unscorched.

From there, the trail turned, and I crept forward, Akoni covering my back. I could see ahead to where a woman lay sprawled on the path. I listened but I couldn't hear anything, and I didn't see her moving. I crept forward, foot by foot, until I reached her.

Apparently, Sheila White had hit her head on a rock when Jimmy knocked her down, and there was blood pooling all around her. Training my weapon on her, I kneeled down and felt for a pulse.

There was a faint one, and she stirred at my touch.

"Jesus, it's you!"

I looked up, and ahead of me on the path stood Jeff White. He had two small, blond children with him, a boy and a girl.

"Freeze," Akoni said, drawing his gun.

I stood up quickly and pointed my gun at White, too. "It's all over now, Jeff," I said. "Throw down your weapons and stay right where you are."

"It's not over." He reached out and pulled the girl in front of him. He held her with his left hand and pointed his gun at her with his right. "What did you do to Sheila?"

"I didn't do anything. I've been out here looking for you, Jeff, and I just found Sheila here."

"I don't believe you. You killed her."

"Your sister's not dead, Jeff. It looks like she fell and hit her head on the ground. But we've got to get her out of here before the fire catches up with us."

"I don't . . . Sheila is the one who always told me what to do." Tears began to run down his face, but he kept the girl and the gun in position.

"Did she know you were gay?"

"What? I'm not queer."

"Sure you are." I started moving toward him, in tiny increments. "You picked up a male prostitute, didn't you? He's just a boy, you know. Sixteen."

"I don't . . . I don't know what you're talking about."

"He told me about you. He told me you picked him up to

have sex this morning. Straight guys don't pick up teenaged boys for sex, Jeff."

"It . . . it . . . it wasn't like that. I was just going to give him a lift and he . . . he came on to me."

"Why did you do it, Jeff? Why did you bomb the Marriage Project and then kill Charlie Stahl? Were you scared about being gay?"

I was only about fifty feet from him by then. "I'm not gay!" he said. "I'm . . . I'm . . . confused. If Sheila knew I'd been thinking about guys, she'd have killed me."

"Why did you kill the old man? Did you try to have sex with him?"

"The old man? You mean the homeless guy?"

"Yeah. His name was Hiroshi Mura."

"I didn't kill him. Sheila did. She's always been the best at everything. She shoots way better than I do. She's the one who learned how to make bombs. I just did whatever she told me."

"Why don't you let the little girl go," I said. "Put the gun down. I'll take you downtown myself. I promise I'll take care of you." He seemed to hesitate.

I'd been wrong about the fire. I thought it had used up all the fuel in that part of the park, that we were safe. But as I stood there across from Jeff White, I could hear the fire had returned, feel the heat, smell the smoke. The kids were so frightened they were paralyzed, but at any moment they could start crying or screaming again, which would make it that much harder to get Jeff White to focus on me. I was also worried that Haoa and his team were going to stumble on us any minute, adding yet another unpredictable element.

Then Pele stepped in once again. Although I can't say I believe in the old Hawai'ian religion, as a surfer I've often seen the power of nature and felt that it's possible there is a divine hand guiding it. Maybe Pele was angry that someone else had started a fire, or maybe one of the other gods or goddesses that protect the islands alerted her and asked her intervention.

First there was a big cracking noise, and some ironwood trees off to the right caught on fire. They lit up the area brightly, distracting all of us for a moment.

I've tried since then to piece together what happened next. I think the little boy, Cole, must have tried to free his sister then, by starting to pummel Jeff White's leg. Jeff lowered his gun hand for a minute to fight the boy off.

That's when Haoa and his team came bursting through the trees from the left. Jeff was clearly scared. He turned and let go of Cole and his sister both, then raised his hand and started to shoot, first at me, then at Haoa and his team. I quickly dropped into a crouch, balanced my arm as best I could, and shot, hoping for the best.

It was all chaos after Jeff White fell to the ground. The fire was raging around us, and I had to take a moment to evaluate. I was feeling a little shaky, but I hadn't been hit in the cross-fire. Neither had Haoa or the two uniforms with him—Frank Sit and another guy I didn't know. Tony Lee, of Organized Crime, and Steve Hart, one of the detectives from my squad, had both gotten what looked like relatively shallow wounds.

Jeff White was sitting on the ground sobbing, holding his upper arm, which was bleeding. He'd dropped his gun and the kids had run to Akoni, who had them both wrapped in his beefy arms. Cole Harding had a bullet wound in his upper chest and he was breathing shallowly, the blood dripping onto Akoni's shirt as my partner talked soothingly to both kids.

Caitlin was sobbing and shaking, but she'd nestled her head against Akoni's bulk.

I inched over to Jeff and picked up his gun. But it was clear that all the fight had gone out of him. I helped him stand, and though I knew he had done terrible things, I couldn't help feeling sorry for him. I'd been stuck in the closet myself, and I knew what that was like.

By then it was incredibly hot and the sweat was pouring down all of us. Haoa took Caitlin Harding from Akoni and said, "We've got to get out of here before the fire comes back."

We started down the path, Haoa leading, with the little girl cradled against him. Akoni went next, carrying Cole Harding. When we'd worked together, he and his wife had been thinking about kids, and I hoped that they would start soon. For a big man, he could be very delicate, and like with Haoa, kids could feel the good spirit flowing out of him.

Steve Hart and Tony Lee went next, holding each other up. Both were bleeding, and I hoped that they were only flesh wounds and that they'd make it down safely to the paramedics.

I picked up Sheila White and slung her over my shoulder, just as I'd done with Sandra Guarino after the Marriage Project bombing. Jeff White stumbled behind me, with Frank Sit keeping his gun trained on him. Within moments the flames were licking at our backs and we had to run, as best we could, down the slippery, twisting mountain path.

It felt like we were souls trying to escape from hell, noise and heat and flames all around us. I wanted to pray but I was too intent on finding the next safe place to put my foot down, holding onto Sheila White and saying, "Stay with me, bitch. I want to see you alive and behind bars." And I didn't want

Jimmy Ah Wong to ever feel he'd been responsible for her death.

A loud noise erupted to our right—and I was sure that there was another set of flames about to hit us—but it was a pair of wild pigs, racing through the underbrush trying to find a safe place away from the fire.

A minute later, we ran right into a line of firefighters, Mike Riccardi among them, and they managed to beat the flames back enough so that we could get clear. I hated leaving Mike behind, fighting the fire, but I knew I had no choice. I had to get the people I was responsible for to safety.

We came around the last curve to see the park entrance below us. Eli and Fran Harding rushed forward to embrace their kids, and soon after, a rescue chopper airlifted Cole Harding to The Queen's Medical Center, his sister and his parents going along. Once the Hardings were gone, Lidia Portuondo took charge of Kitty and Jimmy, making sure their wounds were treated and they got some fluids in them.

Sheila White woke up while the paramedics were giving her oxygen, though she refused to say anything. Jeff White stayed with Frank Sit behind a fire engine until an ambulance had taken Sheila away to check on her concussion and a couple of second-degree burns. Gary Saunders had stopped coughing, so he went along to make sure she remained in custody.

I was drenched in sweat and the healing burns on my back itched like crazy, but I had to talk to Jeff White before he was taken away for booking. Sampson got a digital tape recorder from his car, and Frank Sit brought White over to the picnic table, standing alertly a few feet back in case White decided to bolt.

I read White his rights again. He shrugged when I asked if he understood them.

"You have to say something for the tape," I said.

"I understand," he said.

Sampson sat next to me. "Why don't you tell us what's been going on, Jeff," I said gently.

"Ever since we were kids, Sheila's been the boss," he said. "When we were teenagers, we started, you know, fooling around."

He looked up at me, and I could see that tears stained his face. "I love her," he said. "Just not the way she wants."

"Must have been tough for you in Texas," I said. "Hiding."

He nodded. "That's why Sheila said we had to leave. When our parents died we inherited a little money, and we decided to take a vacation together. We came here and Sheila decided that we should move here, start over in a place where nobody knew us."

"How'd you come to start your church?" Sampson asked.

"We were looking for a business to start," Jeff said. "I wanted us to buy a copy shop, but Sheila and I had been lay ministers in our church in Texas, and she thought we should start a church instead."

I looked over at Sampson. Just a business decision, I guessed.

"Sheila was really upset over the whole gay marriage thing," Jeff said. He looked down at the rough wood of the picnic table. "I think she knew—about me. And maybe she was worried that I would leave her if I found some guy. She got crazier and crazier, especially with those gay guys next door, and with the rooster down the street. The damned rooster used to wake us up every morning, and Sheila hated that."

He looked up at me. "She had her routines, you know. She liked everything to be quiet in the morning—I wasn't even supposed to talk to her. She'd put on her headphones and go for her run, and by the time she got back she liked me to be up and have breakfast on the table."

I was starting to get a picture of life in the White house, and it only made me pity Jeff even more. "One day she came home from her run and she told me that she'd shot the rooster, and then the homeless man. I didn't know anything about it until she told me. I mean, I knew the old guy, he was kind of creepy, always spying on what people were doing. He told her he knew about what we were doing in the backyard, and so she didn't have any choice. She had to shoot him."

"What made you want to bomb the Marriage Project party?" I asked.

"Sheila saw this show on TV about the bombings in Oklahoma. She got really interested in that sort of thing, started investigating how to make bombs, how to set fires. We practiced on a couple of places—all places she said deserved it."

"Yeah, small business owners trying to make a living," I said.

"I couldn't do anything," he said. "It was like, Sheila said we would do something, and we did it."

"So you rented a tux and went to the party. You left the bomb in the bathroom?"

"I was so scared," he said. "I was sweating like crazy. I was afraid Sheila might not have gotten the fuse right, and it would have blown up on me."

"Why'd you come to the rally at Waikīkī Gateway Park?"

"Sheila was so pissed that it looked like those people were going to get their offices back. She said we had to do something. She was always a great shot with a gun. We used to go out and shoot prairie dogs."

I just didn't want to listen to him anymore. There would be plenty of time to go over his story in endless detail, but right then, despite the pity I felt for him, I was afraid I might punch him in the gut. His failure to confront his sister, and his sexuality, had led to untold damage and the deaths of three men: Hiroshi Mura, Wilson Shira, and Charlie Stahl. They'd had nothing in common other than being in the way of Sheila White's murderous lunacy, and her brother had done nothing to stop her.

I looked at Sampson and I could see he felt the same way. "Let's wrap this up," I said. We finished the formalities for the tape, and then Frank Sit took Jeff White downtown for booking. I know I'd promised him I'd go with him—but that was one promise I didn't mind breaking.

The fire raged on for another hour or so, until the wind shifted and a band of rain showers blessedly swept down from the tops of the mountains and put out most of the flames.

Lieutenant Sampson, Kitty, Jimmy, my family, and I regrouped at Uncle Chin's house. The gamblers were still there, as if a forest fire hadn't been raging next to them, as if nothing had gone on all day other than the game.

The paramedics had wanted to take my dad in again for smoke inhalation, especially after his experience at the Marriage Project bombing, but he'd refused, and he did seem to be breathing better, sitting with my mother, Aunt Mei-Mei, and Genevieve Pang on picnic benches in the backyard.

An ocean breeze had come up, blowing the smoke from the park fire back up into the Ko'olaus, and the sun had come out. A rainbow stretched high above us.

I kept worrying about Mike, even as we walked through a quick postmortem on what had happened, making sure no one else was trapped on the mountain.

"So what are we going to do with you, now, son?" Sampson said to Jimmy when we were finished.

"Can he stay here with Mrs. Suk?" I asked, motioning toward where Aunt Mei-Mei sat, Genevieve Pang holding her hand like a dutiful daughter-in-law, even though her own husband was dead, her son in jail.

"She does have custody of him," Kitty said. "Temporarily, at least."

Sampson shook his head. "That was invalidated when he ran away."

"Who says he ran away?" Kitty asked. "He went out for a walk, and Jeff White kidnapped him. That's not running away."

"Kitty," Sampson said, but she stood her ground. He looked from her to Jimmy, who was standing silent. "Why did you run away from the Suks' house in the first place?" he asked.

Jimmy looked down at the ground and scuffed his feet. "I had to go to the bathroom," he said finally.

We all looked at him. That didn't sound like a reason to run away from a good home.

He looked up. "When I got back to the lanai, Mr. Suk was lying there in his chair. He was dead. And I was so scared that it was my fault. I could see he'd been reaching for his pills, and if I'd been there . . ."

"You couldn't have done anything," I said. "I heard it from the medical examiner. Uncle Chin's heart attack was too much for him, even if he'd gotten a pill."

The relief was evident on Jimmy's face. "You're not going to run away anymore, are you?" Sampson asked him.

"No, sir. Kitty and I talked a lot when we were up there. She says the only way I'm going to make my life better is to start trusting some people, and go back to school, and work hard, and become responsible for myself." He paused. "So can I start with you? Trusting you, I mean?"

Sampson looked at me and I looked back at him. "All right," he said, after a moment. Jimmy got up and hugged him, and then shyly went over to Aunt Mei-Mei, who rose and began to fuss over him.

A paramedic had taped up Kitty's ankle, and after she and Sampson had said good-bye to everyone, she hobbled away with her dad, leaning on him. I was happy she had him in her life—and equally happy that I had my own father, and mother, my brothers and their families.

My father asked if I wanted to spend the night at their house, and there was a hopefulness in his eyes that I wanted to respond to. I knew that I would have to make more time for him and my mother in the future, to make sure that they knew how much I loved them before something else bad happened. But I had one more thing I had to do that night. My family was expanding beyond the one I had been born into.

I shook my head and said my good-byes. But instead of heading for home, I drove my truck up St. Louis Drive to Ruth Place, the entrance to Wa'ahila State Park. Along the way I passed a black pickup with red and orange flames painted along the side, parked by the side of the road.

There was one fire truck from the 22 company left up there, and a couple of cops cleaning up the roadblock. They left as I went over to the truck.

A single fireman was there, and I asked him if he knew Mike Riccardi's whereabouts. "I'm Detective Kanapa'aka," I said. "I've been working with him on this case."

"Oh, I know who you are," he said. "Let me see if I can raise Mike on the radio."

I stood there in the damp, smoky air waiting for a response from Mike. "Yeah, he's just up the road," the fireman said, pointing uphill. "He's on his way down."

I took a deep breath. I didn't realize until then how scared I had been. Scared for the safety of the innocent people on the mountain, Eli and Fran Harding and their kids, Kitty Sampson and Jimmy Ah Wong; for the houses in St. Louis Heights, homes of my parents and their friends and neighbors. For my brothers, out on the trails of the mountain with fire on one side and two crazy killers on the other. For myself. And for Mike.

I was on the other side of what my family must have felt about me, what the husbands, wives, boyfriends, girlfriends, and family had to feel about my fellow officers every day. I wondered if this was what it was going to be like for both of us, each knowing that the other could be in danger any time. Just the pain of being separated, of not having him close, was tough enough. I wondered how people dealt with it.

And then he was there, coming out of a stand of trees in his yellow fire suit, the helmet pushed back from his face, his curly black hair slicked down with perspiration, a smudge of soot on his right cheek. I remembered how I had seen him the night of the bombing, how I'd wanted to clean his cheek that night but had restrained myself.

I wasn't holding back anymore.

Chapter 38
AFTER

I COULDN'T KEEP SITTING and waiting there. I left my mother, Lui and Liliha, and Haoa and Tatiana in the waiting room down the hall from the operating room and walked outside. The doctors said this operation to reopen some blocked valves in my father's heart was routine, but it was still pretty tense there with nothing to do except imagine complications and loss.

Besides, I needed to think about what had happened over the last couple of weeks. I had spent a lot of time at The Queen's Medical Center in the recent past, too much. First there had been the visits to those injured in the bombing at the Hawai'i Marriage Project, including my father.

Then Mike and I had spent some tense hours in the waiting room with Fran and Eli Harding as doctors operated to remove the bullet that had lodged in Cole's chest. He had come through the surgery all right, and quickly bounced back. I had nearly held my breath for days, waiting for ballistics, hoping that in the crossfire none of my shots had gone astray. We found, in the end, that the bullet had come from the same Chief's Special Airweight that had been used to kill Hiroshi Mura and Charlie Stahl. Fortunately, Jeff White wasn't the crack shot his sister was, or there might have been greater casualties.

The Hardings came out of the fire pretty well, considering the challenges they had endured to their family and their faith. Cole's birthday party was coming up, and Eli had called me to ask if I'd be the guest of honor. I said I didn't know how great a guest I'd be, but I knew a fireman who loved kids, and Eli said I was welcome to bring him along.

KVOL had covered the whole story, giving Hiroshi Mura his moment, and pointing out that the department had solved the murder of his daughter as well. Wilson Shira's family even issued a public acknowledgement of the role that the department had played in catching his killers.

I was pleased that Sandra, Cathy, and Robert had reopened the Hawai'i Marriage Project, in new offices with better security. Popular sentiment seemed to have changed, too. With the death of Wilson Shira his community group fell apart, and the Church of Adam and Eve closed down after Jeff and Sheila White were arrested. Both of them were in custody, awaiting psychological evaluations and eventual trial for the deaths of Hiroshi Mura, Wilson Shira, and Charlie Stahl. It looked like both would be behind bars for a long time.

The news fallout affected the Sandwich Islands Trust, and Miss Emma Clark retired, putting Terri in charge as chair of the board. She immediately began reviewing all the programs the trust supported. The new job revitalized her and gave her a focus beyond Danny and just getting through the days.

Jimmy was pretty traumatized by his kidnapping and fiery escape. He stayed with Aunt Mei-Mei, studying for his GED with a tutor and seeing a psychologist. I was hoping that seeing him a hero on the news might have convinced Melvin to change his mind, but that hadn't happened, and Jimmy didn't think it ever would.

The day after the forest fire I was catching homicide cases again. Mike went back to work at the fire department. A couple of weeks later I invited him to meet my parents, and they liked him. I hadn't met his folks yet, though once when I was at his house I saw them through the front window. That was all right with me, for now. We'd see what the future held.

I was standing out on the sidewalk catching the sun when Mike pulled up in his truck, the one with the flames painted along the side. I looked around. "No fires here."

"You're always on fire." He motioned me over to the open window of the truck and we kissed. I didn't care who was watching. Then he opened the door and got out.

"What's up?" I asked.

"I came to sit with you. You told me your sisters-in-law were here with your brothers. I guess I ought to be too."

I felt like a sap, standing out there on South Beretania Street with my eyes welling up. Mike said, "If there's H2O on the inside of a fire hydrant, what's on the outside?"

I smiled. "Don't know, but I'll bet you're going to tell me."

"K 9 P," he said. Then he put his arm around my shoulder and said, "Come on, let's go in."

And laughing together, we did.

ACKNOWLEDGMENTS

A big *mahalo nui loa* to Cindy Chow and Deborah Turrell Atkinson, for their help with Hawai'ian life and customs. All the mistakes are mine, though.

Thanks to Joe Pittman, Dale Cunningham, Anthony LaSasso, and all the nice folks at Alyson, without whom this book would be a mass of bits and bytes on my hard drive.

Every successful writer is supported by family, friends, and the generosity of other writers, and I'm no different. Lots of gratitude goes to my mother, Shirley Globus Plakcy, and to friends Andrew Schulz, Eileen Matluck, Lois Whitman and Eliot Hess, Neil Crabtree, Pam Reinhardt, Sharon Sakson and Steve Greenberg.

Special thanks to the members of the Bluewater Writers' Group: Ware Cornell, Natasha Salnikova, Christine Kling, Mike Jastrzebski, and Marie Etzler.

Kudos to John Spero, Leigh Rosenthal, Gerry Kennedy, Steve Wahl, and the other members of the Ft. Lauderdale GLBT book group.

Thanks once again to my colleagues in the English department at Broward Community College, to my Florida International University classmates and friends, my fellow members of the Florida chapter of Mystery Writers of America, and everyone who's emailed me or stopped me at a conference to say they've enjoyed meeting Kimo and learning about his life.